Parade of Streetlights

by Itua Uduebo

Published by

Read (v): The act of interpreting and understanding the written word.

Furiously (adv): To engage in an activity with passion and excitement.

**Read Often. Read Well.
Read Furiously**

A Window

"Well obviously that guy was a prick, because if he wasn't a prick, that would make me the bad guy. He had it coming."

"'Had it coming?' Really? He had an elbow to the ribs coming?"

"There are rules of etiquette when it comes to ordering shots at the bar, and one of them is you don't get so drunk that you spill all four of them on a stranger's new shoes."

"Physical violence is not a response to social miscues."

"Says the guy who almost murdered his freshman year roommate for eating his burrito."

"OK, first of all, still wasn't physical violence, and second of all, that guy was a klepto, it was more of a boiling point than a random outburst."

"Whatever, you hypocrite, the point is—"

I won't lie and say that I wasn't entertained, but that was the point where I had to check out. As they sat on the couch, in front of the TV but ignoring its content, I couldn't help but look out the window to see what the light was touching. I love looking out the window, but I love looking out the window for the opposite reason that I love looking at the world when I'm outside, counterintuitive as that may seem. The thing about windows is, they're permanent. Each time you pass by, every time you think to peek out, the view rarely offers anything new to experience. Buildings. Rooftops. Wires.

Windows. Sky. People. People in buildings, looking through their windows, maybe up in the sky or down, probably hoping to see a change in the scenery, then leaving, unamused by the show. I guess you can say that the people changed each time, but really, they all seemed the same to me; faces with no context or ideas to define them in my head, distinguishable only by color and shape. Eight million people in New York City and aside from the relative handful of faces I'd interacted with, the rest were essentially meaningless. I like to imagine that at least occasionally, when I find myself peering past the planed glass, someone else out there appreciates the same thing I'm seeing, the stillness and stability where others may see only stagnation, the beauty of something that never moves or changes, forever there for the eye to behold. I just think there's too much happening sometimes, that's all.

You don't always have to pay attention to the scene in front of you to understand what's going to happen next. Curtis wasn't the type to let something this egregious go unchecked, and once he felt that it was his responsibility—nay, his duty—to right a wrong so foul, he wouldn't cease. And by "wouldn't cease" I really mean he wouldn't shut the fuck up, not even if you paid him. Not even if you offered to pay him fifty dollars, or if you offered to clear his bar tab. He was as admired for his conviction as he was avoided for it, which, I suppose, is about the highest praise a man of conviction can receive.

"Huh?" I blurted out, reflexively responding to the mention of my name and the promise of a bothersome interaction.

"I said, do you think that asshole who spilled his shots on me deserved a quick one to the ribs, or do I have, as Ravi puts it, 'anger issues?'"

"Well, I'll say this much," I began, adoringly annoyed, "ordering four tequila shots while being too shitfaced to operate two legs is a terrible choice, and choices have consequences. Definitely would have at least gave him a shove if they were my new shoes. That being said, you are a violent motherfucker, that's a fact."

"So what I just heard was that I'm right and that he can blow me, is that more or less accurate?"

He's gonna make a great congressman one day.

"If that's how you choose to interpret reality, who am I to stop you."

"HA! Kola's on my side, dickhead."

"There can't be a winner or loser if I was never actually fighting back, but OK. Now can we please go and get dinner already, before we die of malnutrition? Your ego may be robust but it won't do much for sustenance."

"Yeah, yeah, I'm starving anyway. Mr. Rahmani's?"

"Let's roll."

I was hungry, that much was undeniable, but I wasn't so hungry that I was willing to brave the humidity. I decided to take my chances and play every millennial's favorite game, "Did My Dumb Ass Forget to Get Groceries Again?" I prepared myself, mind racing, trying to go through all the meals that I'd taken to work, what I'd gotten the last time I went grocery shopping, how much money I had spent on food that week and what exactly I even wanted to make. By the time I had gotten to the fridge I was in a state of panic; as I gripped the handle on the fridge door, my hand beginning to feel the sensations of trembling as the door followed

Newton's Third law at first but gave way to my pull, and as I finally saw the light appear, I felt a calming sensation. The answer to my question and this crossroads moment of my evening were about to come to a natural conclusion; I took a deep breath and faced my fate.

Eggs. Milk. Two egg rolls. Strawberries. A piece of cake from Stacy's birthday party the week before. Bacon. Tomatoes. Just enough to make an edible meal but not enough to make the effort feel worth it. And, just to taunt me, half a cauliflower, which I personally consider to be one of God's biggest mistakes in all of creation, right behind AIDS and The Learning Channel, in no particular order.

Fuck. I sighed and grabbed my shoes, ready to brave the heat for my supper. The long march from starvation.

A Walk Down
A Quick Stroll

New York moves to hard beats and the flows of great MCs. Rock and roll had its day, and the Top 100 certainly had its place, but for me, hip-hop is the only soundtrack to life in the concrete-contained madness. That night was no different as we walked along our path.

I remember the first time - at fourteen and having only lived in the US of A for a few months - that I repeated a few choice lyrics of modern-day wordsmith 50 Cent's love ballad "Candy Shop" in the vicinity of my father's bat-like hearing. It'a about as dirty as a Willy Wonka porn parody set to 808s can be, and definitely not safe for singing in a Christian home. I'd picked up a few words of the song at school before deciding to listen to it on my own, and after the first hundred or so plays on my Walkman, I pretty much had it down pat. One Saturday afternoon while playing with my toy robots, I happened to find myself singing the song aloud, bobbing my head to the iconic beat and even feigning some classic rapper hand motions.

For context, my dad hated rap music, and not just in the "I can't believe you like this filth" way. He hated it in the "If I hear this shit in my home you're dead" way. So, just imagine (or if you're an experienced parent, reminisce) if you can, being my loving father, trying to raise three good, respectable

children in a new country, walking by your eldest son's door-
-the child that you brought with you all the way from Nigeria
to give him a better life--as he gleefully sings the phrase: "I'm
a seasoned vet when it come to this shit

After you work up a sweat, you could play with the stick

I'm trying to explain, baby, the best way I can

I melt in your mouth, girl, not in your hand

If you're a child of immigrants, know any children of
immigrants, or are even just a minority, you already know
damn well what happened next. If you're one of my more fair-
skinned brothers and sisters of the human race, then all I'll say
is that my father loved me and my siblings very much and that
I didn't even understand the concept of Child Services until I
was fourteen, nor would I have cared either way.

Despite all the yelling and stress this would cause between
my dad and I in the years to come, rap music became an
integral part of my world, the soundtrack to my formative
years. Walking and the sound of music became so deeply
intertwined that on those rare occasions where my device
was dead, or I had forgotten my earbuds, I would find myself
annoyed by the silence of the simplest action imaginable.
I learned to move to the beats in my head even when I was
motionless, head bobbing millimeters in each direction and
fingers providing the percussion.

As the years passed, as my mind expanded and absorbed
more of the world around me, the subtle instrumental plays
between the incessantly hard beats continued to bump in the
background. Biggie and Tupac filled me with nostalgia for a
time I had no reason to care about, while a young and angry
Slim Shady filled me with a rage over times in my life I hoped

would never come. Kanye West (then) thrilled me with an artistry leagues above his colleagues while Lil Wayne hit me with the nastiest ghetto rhymes on the radio. None of them though, not a single one could hold a candle to the man I considered my personal icon and only three steps behind the Big Guy upstairs on my adoration list: Jay-Z, HOV himself. If rap music was the soundtrack to my life, then Mr. Carter and his unapologetically Brooklyn soul was the soundtrack to the city I had come to claim.

"Heart of the City" was an anthem for the hard-knock-life soul of the town, and if you claim that you can listen to "Izzo" without busting into dance, the younger Kolawole would have advised you to check your pulse. In my eyes he stood as a metropolitan icon, and the more I found myself connected to the music, the more I fell in love with my adoptive city. To avoid sounding like a tourism ad, I'll leave the words of praise to the incomparable Alicia Keys:

> *These streets will make you feel brand new*
> *Big lights will inspire you*
> *Let's hear it for New York, New York, New York!*
> *New York.*
> *New York.*
> *New Yor-*

"You get paid to be the DJ for the whole fucking street or do you just do it out of the goodness of your heart?" Sometimes I really do wonder what Curtis thinks would happen if someone actually got out of the car any of the times he'd been so bold as to scream at a total stranger.

"Why do you always bother people who aren't doing anything to you? I thought you liked that song anyway." Ravi appeared bemused but he asked out of genuine curiosity: the thought of doing something so needlessly bothersome wouldn't even occur to him. This was a guy who'd once let someone offer him an amateur—and wholly inaccurate— explanation of a topic that he'd done a thesis on, just because the other person had started talking first. He just never felt the need to express any thought that could lead to a detour in the conversation, anything that would distract. He was that interesting kind of quiet where you can sometimes forget he's there until he says something that either stuns or bewilders you at the drop of a hat. "I'm just waiting for the day some MMA fighter gets out of the car and decks you."

"Three years of Brazilian jiu jitsu, man, I got that covered," he replied, somehow under the impression that five lessons in three years equaled a title belt, "Besides it's not about the song—Jay Z's alright, but whatever—it's evening-time on a Saturday, some people might be trying to enjoy a nice night in or some shit, and this guy decides that it's absolutely crucial that everyone be made aware of how well his speakers work."

As you can imagine, I was fuming over his dismissal of ROC Nation as simply "all right," but I felt that I would eventually forgive my friend of ten years for the slight. I also didn't want to spoil my mood; despite his reasons for mentioning it, the blowhard was right, it was a nice evening out. The sun was still kissing the horizon and leaving those last few streaks of purple and orange in the sky, a vision that God gave us to make up for the fact that late June in Northeast America is a terrible thing that should not exist. The soul of the summer was at its peak and it was hitting us with the full force of its powers. Fortunately for me, I only had to suffer this Hell minimally due to another great gift--the monstrous AC units that were the sole thing separating the amiable comfort of our apartment from a standard Viet Cong prison cell, psychological torture and all. I'm sure that if you listened closely to the still air you'd be able to hear the damn things humming in symphony, a mosaic of white and grey rectangles poking their way out of red and brown buildings, singing the night away with the wind.

"Yo Kola," Ravi said, ruining the opera that was being composed for myself and myself alone, "what's been going on with that girl Stacy? You still talking to her?"

"Huh? Nah man, it's not like that. We hooked up a few times last month and we saw a movie that one time, but I pretty much knew it was over last week at the party. She invited me to the damn thing and then barely spoke to me. It was just weird, I don't know."

"Sounds like one of your usual affairs then," Ravi tacked on, "three lays and a date. At least the party was fun, I even met a few people there myself."

"I thought you were still with that Asian chick, Jenny Zhang or whatever."

"Zhou, Curtis, it was Zhou and no we only went out that one time, I tried texting her again but you know my policy: 'Two Then Through,' so I just left it alone. Easier that way, less trouble in my life. And I assume you're still just prowling on Tinder."

"If by 'prowling' you mean 'laying down primo game' then yes, yes I am."

As Ravi and I performed a simultaneous eye roll, we turned the corner on the way to our meal. The neighborhood had a particularly enchanting glow that night, a mix of store-sign neon red and streetlight yellow. We'd always considered our place a stroke of absolute fortune, a nice three-bedroom space in Kips Bay, one of those multi-ethnic Manhattan neighborhoods that you only see in the movies and TV whenever someone wants to make their bland white lead character seem "down-to-earth." Smack in-between the East Village and Midtown, between the loud lights of waning youth on the weekends and the sleek shine of an adulthood that called our names every weekday morning. All without having to deal with NYU kids or corporate drones fresh out of Ohio.

There was a strong mix of cultural flavors in the neighhborhood but the main attraction was Curry Hill, a stretch of Lexington Ave between 29th and 27th populated with the best Indian food this side of the Ganges River. With all the words I didn't know how to read and all the foods I couldn't resist, every day became a new chance at discovery. Between an African childhood and a Harlem adolescence my palate was blacker than a Richard Pryor set, so I never really did too much cultural exploration, unless Chinese take-out counts.

The second week after we moved in I decided to try some Indian food for the first time in my life, unsure yet fascinated, and fully prepared to hit up the pizza guy if things didn't work out. Delhi Delight is your classic local Indian-American eating establishment; from the smell of fresh naan bread, to the linoleum floor, to the cricket match on the television that you have to assume is a different match from the last one but you're never quite sure. I grabbed a seat and looked around at the other patrons, trying to get a visual read on what meals looked good. There was a family there that day, mom and dad, three kids, all right on the edge of growing from rambunctious balls of energy to annoying punks eager to push their parents' limits. The two brothers were having an argument about a recent WWE bout they'd seen, with one of them laying out a sophisticated defense of steel chair usage on your opponent while the referee wasn't looking. "If you don't get caught, then who cares? Besides it's just cheating, not murder or anything." It's nice to know our future is in such good hands. The girl, meanwhile, seemed to be incessantly bothering the father about buying a new hijab, "just like Basmah got," which I took as a reminder on the universal nature of blind materialism and social pressure.

I didn't actually get much of a chance to look at their plates before I was compelled by my stomach to just get up and order something. *Chicken,* I thought, *there's gonna be some sort of chicken. Just pick a curry that sounds good and hope for the best.* It was a simple enough plan in my head, until I realized that the first four items all looked exactly the goddamn same, forcing me to read through the descriptions and pick the most tolerable-sounding combination of words. I ended up going with the mutton curry, figuring my twenty years of consuming goat meat regularly would come in handy for the first time ever. I braced myself for disappointment, took my first bite, and opened my eyes to a new, wonderful, moderately spicy world of flavors. The rest, as they say, was history, served with a piece of naan and typically followed up by several visits to the restroom.

The restaurants and eateries provided a never-ending feast for the body while the stores provided one for the eyes.

My personal favorite was Lost Palace, this sari shop a few minutes away from Mr. Rahmani's. Rainbows were always one of my favorite things as a child, so when I found a little slice of one on the street near my apartment that first day a few years ago it was like a never-known dream had been fulfilled. The window gave a taste, an assortment of colors and shapes, golden lacings as far as the eye could see. I had to enter, had to see if the outside was an illusion or an introduction. Stepping inside, I couldn't help but stare at what looked to be a limitless amount of fabric, stitched into garments that would one day dance with the wind off the hips of some beautiful women. I asked the lady at the desk what these clothes were for, and she told me that saris are for those all-too-rare days when the sun smiles down with love, eager for a celebration. If that isn't the most goddamn beautiful way to say "formal attire" that you've ever heard, then I don't know what is.

I took a little look into the Palace as we passed, close enough to our destination that we could see see the sign's outline. Curtis and Ravi were still going at it, completely unaware of my lack of engagement. It had always been that way with the three of us, ever since that first day of college. I had known Curtis since our days at an all-boys prep school, a fabulous institution where a combination of expertise and sheer willpower allows teachers to transform hormone-fueled, idiotic degenerates into young men ready to become decent members of society. We'd met on the first day of freshmen football tryouts. I was going out for defensive line (being 6'2" and 250lb demanded it), while a yet-unknown-to-me Curtis was trying out for running back, an appropriate position for someone just begging to get popped in the mouth. After that first day we ended up being the last two to finish changing, and while exiting the locker room and engaging in standard fare small talk, he asked me the question that would lead to a lifelong friendship: "You think this is the kind of school where the lady teachers are trying to fuck or no?"

Oh, to be young.

Four years later, on the third day of college, two young roommates would enter the dorm common room and see a tall brown guy reading a book of poems. They would make their casual introductions and try to start up a conversation. He would nonchalantly yet kindly tell them that he would love to talk but that he promised himself he would finish this book today, so maybe some other time. They would leave, confused yet not offended. Two weeks later, those same two roommates would see that same brown guy at a party. Having made a few friends by now, they would feel less inclined to go over, especially with all the lovely women in their view. This wouldn't present an issue, however, as he would take it upon himself to approach them. How would he choose to start the conversation, given the last time's events?

"Neruda, that's who I was reading, Pablo Neruda. And my name is Ravi Gupta, nice to meet you again."

There's always that little moment when someone does something totally fucking bizarre where you don't know if they're the strangest person you ever met or if you're weird for not knowing that what just happened is really common.

"Kolawole Idowu, but people call me Kola, and this is Curtis Branson, nice to meet you again too. So, you're into poetry?"

"Not really, but I found the book in my room, must've

been left over the summer. I always finish every book I start, so I figured I could just knock it out in a day. Sorry if I seemed rude about it."

"…the fuck is wrong with you?" This was the start of an argument between him and Curtis that would last for the next seven years, and the three of us were inseparable from that point on. So inseparable, in fact, that the same conversations had lasted the entire time, all the way up to our walk that day.

"I don't understand what's so hard to understand, if you open a book and start it you should finish it. Why leave a piece of literature unfinished? What if there's a page or passage in a book that you've never finished that contains something that you'll never forget for the rest of your life, something that you'll be telling your kids when they ask you for advice. Remember that part of *Master of None?*"

"Which part?"

"The part where Dev reads the book in Strand, the Sylvia Plath book, the quote about the fig trees and choosing one fig before they all turn black just like your path in life. You said that that was one of the best things you've ever heard in your life, but you could've seen that quote literally anytime since the day you learned to read, since *The Bell Jar* was published in 1963. What if you'd started *The Bell Jar* and then not finished it, maybe you wouldn't have gotten to that part and missed it by *just* that much. You see what I mean? Point is, read more, and read completely."

"All right, all right, whatever, but I still think it's weird th–"

"We're here, dumbasses," I snapped, "quit walking." It was like having two dogs that barked in full sentences.

A Meal

Samir Rahmani, age 75, married fifty-one years with eight children and thirteen grandchildren (so far, as he loved to say with a grin). He was a man who believed that a day without laughter was a day wasted, and refused to allow anyone who came to him to leave with anything less than a smile on their face. As far as he was concerned, there was no problem in life that couldn't be solved by a good meal, a good drink, and a good conversation, and at Mr. Rahmani's, you could find all three in abundance. As we entered the door, the enchanting aroma of fresh rice and last night's hookah greeted us, capturing our attention, and putting us in the proper state of mind for a meal at our second home. The table by the window, perpendicular to the counter, a home of many memories.

He kept the place open until 2 AM, not for business reasons, but because he hated going to bed before 3:00. He felt that the nighttime was the home of the interesting and curious, and that those who slept early were missing out on a world of possibilities. is experience had proven him correct; one time a group of Wiccans came in at 12:20 AM, starved from having gone to a party/sacrificial ritual a little while away and looking to try some Pakistani food that night. There he was, a man who could recite the Qur'an forwards and backwards and wasn't as entirely opposed to blasphemy laws as you might hope, hanging out and drinking with a bunch of honest-to-God witches. He would later describe the experience as something that could only happen in America, and that he hoped could never happen back home.

I could tell you more about the curious individuals who'd ever had the pleasure of Rahmani's chicken combo platter, but all the stories just seem to end with someone leaving the place a little better for their time. I honestly think he would be the kind of guy to give a stick-up robber all the money in the register and still offer him a meal after, maybe trying to get his money back, but more focused on finding out what led him to crime.

He was a truly special guy, and once you got to know him, that same special quality could be felt in every inch of the place. It served as a strangely accurate reflection of the man; aged but not withered, classic music from his homeland as the default but never opposed to the latest hot track on the radio, and filled to the brim with charm. On that particular occasion, Earth, Wind & Fire's magnum opus "September" was jamming in the background, and for a few moments the funky fresh joy lifted me out of my funk.

"Yo! Mr. Rahmani! Where you at, my man?"

"Back here, back here, calm yourself," came that familiar, charmingly accented voice, cheerfully exasperated and ready to see some of his favorite regulars, "the usual orders I'm assuming?"

"You already know, brother."

He came out of the back room, pipe in hand and reaching for his matchbook in the front pocket of his red shalwar. He had the kind of white hair covering his head that makes aging seem almost attractive, and a beard that made me think of all those old men in my illustrated childhood Bible. His wrinkles were defined and featured prominently across his brow, a series of lines and crevices across his face that couldn't even attempt to mask the youthfulness of his bright smile. He would always say that the heart of a child never grows up, it just learns how to adapt to the times when it isn't strong enough for the job.

"And how are you today my boys? Hungry, I hope!" He had started calling us his boys the third time we came in as a group, and since then we had basically refused to let him use our real names or any other title.

"As always Mr. Rahmani, ready for a feast." I knew what that response would get me, like a trained dog.

"Ha ha ha, very good, I'll make sure you get some extra rice then. Any fun plans for the night? Wasting the weekend is a sin you know, very bad for the soul."

"Yeah, we got some fun plans, that is if this pussy over here decides to change his mind and come out with us. C'mon Kola, you know this club is gonna be lit, we have to check it out tonight, my cousin got us on the list. I got freakin' Ravi to say yes, and he hates them even more than you do."

"I never said that I hated clubs, I said that the last time you took us to one it was like being stuck in an Axe Body Spray-scented gas chamber but without the sweet release of death. If you can promise me that this new club isn't full of college kids who all drank more than they could handle at their pre-games, then I'm not opposed."

"Look even I'll admit that the last place was awful, but this time it'll be different, this is one of the hottest spots in town. C'mon Kola, you have to come tonight!"

"OK, first of all I ain't no pussy all right? Calm down

before I throw your ass into that wonderful-smelling kitchen. I'm not feeling in the clubbing mood this last week, I've just been in bit of a funk. Right now, all I want is some quality weed and about three or four episodes of *Breaking Bad*."

"What is this *Breaking Bad* you speak of about?" Mr. Rahmani wasn't really big on TV, preferring much more the company of his books and old films, but he always liked hearing us talk about our generation's preferred medium. Our biggest accomplishment had been convincing him to use his son's HBO account to check out *Game of Thrones*, which he went on to cheerfully describe as "crazy violent, smart writing, but a bit too haram for me personally." Everyone's a critic.

"It's a show about a guy who gets cancer and starts making drugs to pay for his treatment and leave money for his family, but things get more and more out of control until he becomes a super-rich drug kingpin."

"Ah I see… wait, this man has very bad cancer, yes?"

"Lung cancer, yeah, just about the worst I think."

"But he lives long enough to become that rich?"

"He goes into remission, so for a while he's better."

"So, he stops making the drugs once he's better, right?"

"Um, well, no he doesn't really stop, but there are a lot of factors that keep him fr--"

"Does he try as often as possible to get out of the drugs so he can spend more time with his family?"

"Well, yes, but he never seems to have much luck."

"Hmph, well it just sounds to me like a man making excuses for his love for drug making and crime, I feel bad for his wife and children, I hope she remarries." It's amazing how accurate some people can be given only the most bare-bone information. "You Americans and your drugs, crazy people the whole lot."

"You know what's even crazier than that though," Curtis leaned forward, smirk half-cocked ready to resume his cherished pastime of goading me, "this club that Kola's coming with us to tonight."

"Your optimism honestly inspires me sometimes." If the remark is somewhat true then I don't think it really counts as an insult, even though that was definitely the intent. "OK Mr. Rahmani, what do you think I should do? You just said yourself that wasting the weekend is a sin."

"It is a sin, my boy, but not taking care of your mind is the greater sin still. Why are you so down anyway?"

It was a perfectly valid question, nothing more than a fatherly expression of concern, and yet I couldn't help but take some offense. Does there always need to be some reason? I didn't have anything particularly terrible happen to me that week, nothing more dramatic than usual. I'd had a few lackluster conversations with Stacy, awkwardly stumbling back and forth between small talk and probably-less-than-subtle attempts at figuring out our latest status update. The text message tango came to an anticlimactic end after about the fourth time she replied to me with "OK cool," at which point I figured we both could plainly see that nothing was going to be resolved on a screen-to-screen basis.

Work was pretty good, no immediate career advancements on the horizon but my boss was happy with my performance. At the time, I was a senior associate at my consulting firm, Midas PLC. There were a few less-than-exciting projects on the horizon, probably some travel involved, but nothing worth being upset over... well, besides the general anxiety that goes along with actively burying your dreams, but that doesn't count. There were, obviously, other things I imagined myself doing with my life at the time, most unrealistic—the NFL doesn't tend to give tryouts to out-of-shape consultants—but others only unattainable due to my own inertia.

As for family, thankfully there was nothing to report: my weekly phone call to the parents had come and gone, my little brother was still in college and my little sister hadn't broken any house rules or gotten pregnant, so overall just another standard week for the Idowu family.

Nothing was wrong, exactly, yet the funk persisted. In hindsight, it probably had a lot more to with Stacy than I care to admit, but even now I find it hard to understand why. I'd never pictured her as my girlfriend or anything, and I sure as hell didn't think she was the girl of my dreams; she was a cute girl that I had met at the park, gotten drinks with a few days later and had then proceeded to take to bed.

The sex was good, flexible—gymnastics, you know—but nothing mind-blowing enough to capture the heart. I liked her, I liked her long red hair and frantically freckled face, I liked her pretty sundresses and her cute shoes, and we had some fun hanging out, but I guess that you can't just rely on having fun after six weeks. I knew it wasn't going anywhere, but I also knew that I wouldn't mind if it never ended, so there I was, trapped between a longing for inertia and a resignation to movement.

Where was I stuck at? What is that place between satisfaction and fulfillment? How did I end up there, after all the work and effort to get somewhere so different?

It hadn't occurred to me before that moment but I'd been living under a fog of complete disinterest for the better part of a year at that point. There was work, and there was going out for drinks, and there was ten hours of chasing girls for every twenty minutes of actual fucking. Weed and nice restaurants and failed workout plans, rooftop parties and pop-up shops and keeping up with my podcasts. All the trappings of the made-it New Yorker covering an empty shell. It hadn't occurred to me before that moment, but I wasn't actually feeling down. That would imply I could remember what "up" was.

There's no up or down when you're floating on concrete.

I still didn't have a proper answer to Mr. Rahmani's question, so I just reverted to some adolescent vagueness: "I don't know man, I'm just not feeling it, it's no big deal."

"Hmm…," Having raised eight of his own, I'm sure he could tell when a child was being less than forthcoming, but he didn't seem to want to press the issue, "Well in that case, I say yes. If you don't know what's troubling you, then how can you say for sure that staying in will be the cure? It's better to take the chance at enjoyment than to submit to malaise."

Damn. The old man had me stumped once again.

"All right, all right, if you say so then it can't be that bad an idea. You win this round, Curtis."

"HA, yes! Thank you, Mr. Rahmani, once again your wisdom has made this poor fool over here see the light of reason," Curtis gloated, thankful for the assist, "and I hate to be that asshole right now, but where's that food at anyway?"

"Ah! Of course, of course, I have no idea what's taking my boy so long. Let me go check."

"Wait, no don't go! I didn't mean that you had to get up man, I'm just starving."

"Nonsense, child! You boys may be dear friends but this is still a place of business, there are standards that must be maintained. I will be back momentarily."

He rose out of his chair, proceeding to finally light that mahogany pipe of his, and parted the curtain door separating the eating area from the back. We then heard some angry words being spoken in Urdu, a language that I still couldn't make heads or tail of even after all of Mr. Rahmani's impromptu lessons. Instinctively I turned to Ravi, my mind associating brown skin with a brown language, but he already had his "Dude, we've been over this a thousand times, Urdu is not Hindi" glare locked on me, so I caught myself mid-turn. Thankfully my white-bearded savior returned, his youngest son Saad not far behind, food in tow.

"Dig in boys!"

We all rushed at the invitation, and as we continued to chat with mouths full of rice and meat, I could feel that melancholy haze start to fade. Nothing clears you up quite like a family meal, especially with the family you choose.

Even if they happen to be two dickheads and an old man.

A Drink or Two
or Seven

"Is it even physically possible for you to look like more of a douchebag right now?" I did mean the sentence rhetorically, but honestly, I wouldn't have minded getting a peer-reviewed answer.

"Why do you always gotta hate man, you know I look damn good in this shirt. What do you think, Ravi?"

"Hmm… what exactly are the benefits of wearing a shirt that shiny?"

"Because the last three times I've worn it clubbing I've gotten laid, and I have the screenshots and naughty texts to prove it."

"Well, you may be an asshole but you're certainly a rational one. I'm afraid he has a point, Kola."

I didn't press the issue any further. After all, despite our constant ribbing, he was by far the most adept with the ladies. Ravi and I always did OK - we cycled between one-night stands, short-lived flings, and bouts of solitude. Curtis, on the other hand, was something else entirely, a walking tornado of libido and rough-around-the-edges charm. He was the kind of guy who'd watched men like Barney Stinson or Don Draper on TV and had learned all the wrong lessons, the kind who knew Tyler Durden was supposed to be the villain in *Fight Club* but didn't care because he's the one fucking Marla.

He had forged himself from a regular schmuck into a lady killer through sheer force of will, and in the process, he had mastered the elusive skill of being able to switch from hyper-masculine bravado to witty, self-deprecating charm at the drop of a hat, depending on what the situation called for.

Ravi was the intellectual of the group, always stuck in a book or ruminating on some piece of Far Eastern philosophy, and it certainly showed in his love life. He could barely stand to be around people who didn't match up with him on his brain power wavelength, let alone actually make it through a date. It wasn't that he was some pretentious snob who looked down on people who couldn't recite a passage of Dante or accurately discuss the implications of post-9/11 era media culture, it was more that you couldn't convince him to enjoy an interaction if he didn't already feel it. If someone didn't pique his interest after the first few attempts at an intellectual discussion, he would simply move on to the next one in hopes of meeting someone more compatible. It was a harsh method, but I honestly can't say that it wasn't fair.

I guess you could say that Ravi and I were similar in that we couldn't enjoy ourselves around girls that didn't pique our interest for too long, albeit I was a lot more charming in my interactions and a lot more willing to stomach my disinterest in the pursuit of casual sex. The main difference between us, however, was that where Ravi craved stimulating intellectual discussion and a partner who'd prefer a lecture date to a lunch, my desires were a bit simpler: humor. The key to my heart always has been and always will be through my ready-to-burst lungs and eyes teary from painfully long laughter. There's just something about a woman who can spin together a joke just offensive enough to warrant an angry blog post but more than clever enough to bring joy to my day that really gets me going. I knew I was in love with my first serious girlfriend Marcela when, in the middle of a romantic lunch picnic date at the park, she happened to spy a dog happily rolling around with his child owner in an unfortunately suggestive manner, to which, without a second thought, she noted, "Here I am, can't even get my dog to respond to 'sit' or 'stay,' and they've gotten theirs to do 'Catholic Priest' - unbelievable."

Curtis was finally back from the bathroom after having applied the last few gallons of hair product to his blondish curls, shiny silver shirt neatly pressed and paired with jet-black slacks and black dress shoes. After making sure everything he had on was as visually offensive as possible, he proceeded to prepare our pre-club libations, laying out three shot glasses, three cups for mixers, a six-pack of premium Belgian beer and some of our more choice liquors. We had hosted a party about a month before and we were still working our way through the leftovers.

Personally, I've always been a rum man, but Ravi had an affinity (the polite way to say addiction) for wine and Curtis was never more than a pinch of salt away from a tequila shot at any given social function. We always tried to keep the liquor cabinet as stocked as possible in the case of any unexpected causes for celebration, such as the time Ravi had gotten a promotion at his asset management firm or when Curtis landed his first solo design project for a new high-rise on the West Side. In the three years that we'd been living together in the city there'd been a lot of good days, a lot of reasons to celebrate, and just as many days that just simply demanded a stiff drink to make it through the last few hours. That cabinet was just as much a drop off point to desolation as it was a ticket to party-town, but we kept it full all the same, never knowing for what - just in case.

Ravi had decided to go with a plain black cardigan over a classic white and black horizontal tee, with black jeans and his favorite pair of Converse sneakers. He was particularly fond of this outfit, often saying that it made him feel like he was in one of those classic French films that I'd introduced him to, only needing a lit cigarette, a pale moonlit night, and a deep existential crisis to complete the image. As he began to deliberate between contact lenses and his horn-rimmed glasses for the evening, Curtis turned on the speakers and put on what I'm going to say was probably a Chainsmokers song, judging by the complete lack of impression that it left in my ears. Ravi gently reminded the aspiring DJ that there really wasn't much of a point dressing like adult men if we were going to be subjected to music for eighteen-year-old white girls. Curtis responded with profanity laced exasperation, but changed the music to "The Way You Move" by Outkast.

As for me, I had chosen one of my go-to ensembles: crisp white shirt, grey blazer, navy pants, brown belt, and complementing shades to be hung from the buttons.

"All right boys, let's get this show on the road. This place we're going to is crazy expensive so we should load up here, enough to keep us drunk until we get there but hopefully not so much that we all die on the subway." Curtis always loved to play the ringleader of our little circus, particularly when he was explaining simple concepts as if he'd invented them.

"Do you have an exact amount to hit that equilibrium or

do you just recommend eyeballing it?" Ravi asked.

"I recommend you shutting the fuck up, and I also recommend that you start with one of these beers and take it from there. My buddy at work told me about them, said they're delicious."

"Hmm," Ravi murmured, looking one of the bottles up and down, "yeah you're right, I think I had one of these at this place in the city, The Sunrise Inn. You should check it out sometime."

"I think Stacy talked to me about that place once too, said her cousin had told her about it. Maybe we should all check it out next Friday," I asked, reaching for the bottle of Captain Morgan, "and we also have to see that new movie too, the one where Nic Cage plays that crazy person."

"Nah, I can't do anything next Friday, I'm seeing the Yankees game that day with my cousin. They're playing the Red Sox so there's no way I'm missing that shit. You and Ravi should go, though."

"What row seats?"

"Right behind the plate, baby. He's dating one of the player's half-sisters nowadays so as long as he doesn't fuck things up with her I'm pretty much going to any game I want."

"Lucky bastard. All right, what do you say, Ravi?"

"I might be able to but I also wanted to go see this gallery exhibit."

"I'm down for a gallery visit man, where is it?"

"That place near Houston Street, Blank Space." Ravi's eyes always got a spark in them whenever he started talking about his new favorite thing in the art world, "I've wanted to go for months but never had the time. They're running this exhibit for the summer, this Dutch artist Nemo Jantzen. Disintegrated mixed media photography, interesting stuff."

"Damn, sounds like a spectacle. I think I'm free that day, let me check," I said, opening my phone to check out my list of upcoming events, "…I'll have to get back you on that, there's a showing of *2001: A Space Odyssey* in 70 mm that I want to see, which I just now realized I have to find someone to go with, so I probably can't go to your thing and that too."

"No problem, man, some other time."

We continued our conversation, discussing upcoming yet-to-be-abandoned plans and more-or-less important people involved in them. As the drink tally started to get higher and higher and anticipation for the night to come began to build, we started slurring our words and I felt my gestures becoming exaggerated, intertwining with the bellowing laughs. I've never been too much of a drinker but I had a decent tolerance backed up by size and general enthusiasm for rum. Curtis was a bit smaller but a good deal more muscular to make up for it, and like every other aspect of his "cool guy" persona, his ability to put back shots was a culmination of years and years of practice.

Ravi, in contrast, was an absolute lightweight, tall and lanky with the "giggly drunk" condition to wrap it all together. Every time we went out, we would inevitably have to spend the last five to ten minutes of our evening prying an almost empty wine bottle from his clutching hands, and that night was looking to be no different.

"All right dickheads," Curtis announced, sounding like the world's least-motivational life coach, "it's time to roll. It's around 11 so we should be able to catch a train in about ten minutes. Anyone need a condom or anything?"

"I can't tell what I love more," I replied "the fact that you just casually offered extra condoms or the fact that you added 'or anything' to the end of the sentence."

"What, man? I may be a pig but I'm a clean pig, gotta keep the sausage FDA-approved if you know what I mean." Curtis would one day go on to develop an animated TV pilot about a vulgar, hypersexual pig living on a farm full of degenerate animals, in what one network executive would later call "a *Charlotte's Web* remake from the mind of a disturbed child," but that's a story for another time. "Ravi, you ready man? Don't make us have to drag you out."

"This is my last glass."

A Cover Charge

You start with a room, large and empty, with a few exits to keep traffic flowing. Add a stage, a bar, a mezzanine level, and a shit ton of electrical outlets. Next, you need the lights-- big, fat, obscenely bright monstrosities designed to weed out the weak and the epileptic alike. After you're done with the visual component of the show, the next thing--and some might say the most obvious--is the speakers. You need to make sure that they're just loud enough to make someone deaf but not loud enough that it happens too often and you end up with a class action.

Now that you've got the specs and tech all figured out, let's talk about the drinks. Like most parts of business, what you have to figure out here is the math: how little alcohol can you put inside the drink while still being able to charge triple what it would cost at somewhere where people respect themselves, how many minutes can your bartenders ignore customers on average before they realize they're better off going home (assuming they don't have a kink for that kind of thing, I don't judge), and lastly, what percentage of your procurement budget do you need to spend on cheap shit versus actual quality liquor. (These are normally rhetorical questions but thankfully I've blacked out at enough of these places to have an answer: one shot worth, thirteen, and totally depends on how many finance bros roll through.)

You've built a suitable location, and you've stocked up on the necessary supplies, but now you need to tie it all together, so what you're going to need to figure out is the name of your establishment. It has to be something so simple that it looks like you barely put any effort into thinking about it, yet also as carefully selected as possible in order to be distinguishable and easy to put in a promotional hashtag.

Follow these steps and you'll end with a hot, new nightclub, the next happening spot in town full of the young and beautiful, just like this one place that you might have heard of…

"Welcome to Delirious!"

"Curtis, I have to admit, you were right about this place, it's stunning," Ravi remarked, truly taken aback by the club's subtle mixture of art-deco and cubism, all wrapped in a futuristic ambience, "it's like a retro Kubrick set."

"I told you I would deliver, my man. What do ya think, Kola?"

"This shit is wild, man, I'm honestly pretty damn excited." That might have been the alcohol talking for me, or maybe it was the part of me trying to force some enjoyment, but I genuinely felt excited about the night to come. I'd had a slog of a week, never quite understanding the reason but suffering all the same, so a chance to become deliriously (ohhh, that's why) drunk and let the world go was exactly what I felt I needed.

"All right you two, time to start the hunt. Kola you scout around the bar, I'll hit up the dance floor, and Ravi you start scoping near those lounging couches, and we'll meet up in 15. Ready? Break!"

"Who died and made you commander?"

"Have either of you ever fucked a Japanese supermodel?"

"There's no way that you- ," Ravi turned and saw me giving him the deflated nod of begrudging acknowledgement. "OK fine, whatever, see you in fifteen."

I approached the bar area, but decided to take a gander at the bottles first. The variety was staggering, in both design and contents, as if Willy Wonka had transitioned from candy to alcohol as the way to cope with his life's problems. I decided to ask the bartender for a White Russian, a request that he replied to with a look of extreme judgment that I somehow mistook as appreciation of fine taste. A White Russian is essentially an Irish Starbucks concoction, and no one knows that better than someone who spends a significant portion of their life dealing with all varieties of alcoholics.

Remembering my mission, I began to check out some of the women near me, and immediately became discouraged. It's not that they weren't all attractive, but they all seemed to be in groups of two, four and, from what I could make it, a gaggle of thirteen obnoxiously loud sorority sisters yelling the only three Greek letters they probably ever bothered to learn. All of them worth pursuing, but none matching the proper three-on-three dynamics required for a team effort or the one-on-one required for me to fly solo.

"What kind of vodka do you want with that?"

"Surprise me."

I'm pretty sure he rolled his eyes at that point, but I wasn't looking.

Oh well, I thought, I'll just grab this drink and look for the guys. I was still in a good mood, but I was starting to remember that it takes more than just effort. You can get all dressed up and hope for some music video-caliber extravaganza, but you're likely to be left with little more than a hangover, an abused wallet, a used condom and a pretty face in the morning, and those last two are only if you're lucky. Oh well, I thought again, drink's here, bottoms up.

I took my first sip, then another, trying my best to lose track of time. Then I ordered two beers to follow up before going back to the creamy goodness of Russia's strangest export.

Just then, just as I was about to take that first sweet, creamy sip, that's when it happened.

That's when it all changed.

That's when I heard the words that I would remember for the rest of my life.

A Girl

"Hey, sorry, I know you're getting your drink on right now, but would you mind getting your friend the fuck away from my roommate?"

"Umm… I'm sorry, what?"

"Your friend, over there," the woman said, pointing out Curtis and some Latina girl on the edge of the dance floor, "the one in the light-up shirt and the bad 90's boy band haircut. He's been talking to my friend all night and she's not interested anymore."

I looked over to assess the situation, but it didn't seem that concerning, "Well, I don't mean to mansplain to you or anything, but she seems like she's all smiles over there. You sure they're not having a good time?"

"Am I sure that my friend who just texted me," she said, shoving the phone in my face "'Get me away from this idiot,' isn't having a good time? Yes-- yes I am."

"Huh. Well, maybe she meant it as a term of endearment."

"You think 'idiot' is a term of endearment?"

"Well if it isn't, then I'm kind of a dick for making that my brother's nickname for ten years."

"As fascinating as childhood trauma usually is for me, I'm gonna need you to get up and help."

"Can I quote you on that in my next therapy session?"

"Of course," she replied with faux sincerity, "I'm happy

to know there's at least one person interested in your schtick."

"Eh, I wouldn't call it 'interested'— 'concerned' and 'curious' might be more accurate. Maybe 'confused' if we're being totally honest."

She gave me a curt but cute look that signified the joking was over. "Are you coming or not?"

Groaning but grateful for the bit of fun conversation, I picked up my still-full White Russian and proceeded to make my way over to my Casanova companion while the girl strutted in front of me. She was a short one, looked about five-foot three or four, but the heels probably bumped her up to about five-seven that night. She had on a short red dress that looked like it was born to hug her curves, ample on both the top and the bottom with a potbelly in the middle that matched her dark-chocolate complexion. I hate to think about how I might have looked admiring her so intently, up and down like that, but it wasn't me who dressed her up like that and made her lead me across a club--my male gaze just couldn't help itself. Her long dreads flowed down her back, swinging in rhythm with the rest of her sashay, like her body danced on its own to some song playing her head. She was quite a view.

"Abi, by the way, with one 'b' and an 'i.'" She turned her head around and raised her voice to make sure I heard her, keeping her words from drowning in the sea of bass.

"Abi?"

"Abiodun, so I use Abi for short. I could tell you're African too."

"Kolawole, but everyone calls me Kola."

"Nice to meet ya, Kola. Oh, there they are, right there."

"I got this. Yo Curtis!"

He looked and caught sight of me, flashing a boastful grin. Smug bastard had no idea this was a rescue mission.

"Heyyyy man, wassup? Oh, María, this is my friend Kola."

I could immediately tell that he was much drunker than he was when we had first arrived. We'd been in the club for less than an hour so I honestly couldn't figure out how he'd manage to get so inebriated, until I remembered something: on the train, while Ravi and I were debating the merits of online activism, that clown had been taking hits out of his flask, probably straight tequila too. It was at that moment I knew I was in for a very long night.

María and Abi went off to the side to hold a war council.

"You good, María?"

"Yeah chica, he's just drunk, not crazy or anything, a lot less cute now though so let's evac. Who's that guy?"

"His friend, I saw them walk in together with a third dude, so I just grabbed him."

"The friend ain't too bad-looking. What do you think?"

"Um...."

"Bitch, you are awful at subtlety, ain't no point being dark as all hell if I can tell when you blushing like that. You want to talk to him?"

"Hmm... I don't know, he's all right. Kinda funny."

"Sounds like love at first sight to me."

"Shut the hell up," she shot back, pouting, "and yeah he seems cool enough, but whatever, I only got him so we could get you away. Hell I should've moved the white boy myself at this rate, so let's go already."

"Uh-uh, no way, it's been like five months since you broke up with what's-his-face and this is the first time you haven't chased a guy away in the first five minutes."

"María, what the hell are you th- "

"Hey boyyyys! Let's go chill over in the lounge, I see an open table."

Abi's face froze in an awkward rage as her friend gleefully beckoned all of us to follow her lead. I'd been just able to overhear them as Curtis mumbled something about how great he was doing, speaking in a language I assume he must have thought was English. Seeing the opportunity to get him in a chair and force some water into his system, I accepted. At that point, I wasn't even thinking about the fact that we were about to talk to two beautiful girls (María was a good deal taller than her companion and had the thinness to match, like a stretched-out Shakira), I was more concerned with what I'd be stuck with once he lost a few more brain cells and started speaking in tongues. By the time we'd gotten to the table, I could see that process starting already, with his attempt to sit down and slide into the middle of the semi-circle table resulting in something resembling a bad slapstick scene. I managed to nudge him in, mostly to get off my feet but also as a subconscious act of wingman-ship.

"You guys want to get anything?" María asked as she and Abi made their way in.

"No thanks, I have mine, and this one is cut off."

"The fuck I am," Curtis responded with indignity. "I'm getting me some whiskey and that's that. What about you mamacita, what can I buy for ya?"

"Oh, you'll be paying for me this evening?"

"Watching while a beautiful lady pays for her own drinks? I would never be able to forgive myself, it's part of the gentleman's code." If I didn't know any better I would swear alcohol gave him split personalities, having no other explanation for those two statements coming one after the other from the same person. "You wouldn't expect the priests at Aphrodite's temple to watch her prepare her own offerings, would you?"

I rolled my eyes hard and glanced over at Abi, only to see that she was rolling her eyes even harder. We caught sight of each other and shared a little laugh. It was different from how she'd faintly chuckled before; this time her whole face lit up, matching the white diamonds. María smirked at his overly-researched remark, the kind of telling nonreaction a girl gives you when you're leaving an impression. Considering how this all had started, I was starting to get the feeling that María wasn't able to decide whether the chico guapo in front of her was a decent guy douching it up for her attention or a douchebag with a talent for acting like a decent guy. I already knew that she would end up falling for it like the hundreds (he claims) before her, but I held out hope, putting about as much faith in her as I do in the Knicks.

"OK, Mr. Priest, get me a margarita then."

"You got it," he said, laying down the bait for his clever trap, "but, you know, us gringos don't really know jack about tequila, except maybe what we learned in Cancún on spring break. Maybe you can come along with, make sure I don't end up getting you some white boy shit. Besides, with you on my arm the bartender won't take more than three seconds to get our order, so these two won't be lonely for long."

She gave Abi a look. Abi gave her one back.

Oh my God, yes.

Bitch, no.

But he-.

No.

But he's ju-.

Do you see that shirt?

Yeah but do you see those arms?

Yeah, and it's fucking working.

If you get up from this table I swear to Beyoncé that I will wring your skinny little ne-

"OK, Blondie, let's go. I'll show what some real tequila looks like."

She got up from the edge and Curtis basically climbed over me, not wanting to take the risk of his charm wearing off at any given moment, and just like that, there we were, marooned on Small Talk Island, left to either fend for ourselves or float away in the Awkward Silence Ocean.

"You want some of this?" I asked, passing the glass over, "it's like alcohol and Starbucks had a mixed-race baby."

"Does that mean it tastes better than both its parents?"

"Ha ha, exactly. I honestly never understood how that one worked. Like literally, I have seen some of the ugliest interracial parents walking around with little Abercrombie & Fitch models, I don't get it."

"Maybe it's just God's way of saying racism is bullshit."

"Yeah, maybe. Well, they might be more attractive but I can do without the identity issues, being full Black works fine for me. You're Nigerian too, right? I'm guessing Abiodun is Yoruba."

"Ah, so you know about the tribes. You'd be surprised

how many of us born here can't tell."

"I moved here when I was thirteen, straight out of the wild lands of Lagos. More of a concrete jungle than this place I'll tell you that much."

"Ooh foreign man, nice; I don't know a lot of real immigrants our age, now that I think about it. How often do you go back?"

"Never, unfortunately. Back when I was a kid and really wanted to, we didn't have the money for a family vacation; now that I have the money to go by myself, I don't really feel like it. Funny how that works, huh? Besides, it wouldn't feel right going without the parents I guess, so I'll just have to wait."

"Well that sucks. Do you miss it?"

More than you could possibly know, for reasons that I can't even begin to understand.

Well, one reason.

Him.

"Yeah, a little bit, but I'd have to say this is my home now. You from the city too?"

"South Jamaica, Queens, born and raised. Live in the Village now, somehow. What about you?"

"Harlem, but I went to high school in the Bronx, Ignatius Prep."

"I thought that was an oyinbo school?"

"Trust me it was, twenty-four niggas in the whole building, not including the janitors and definitely including the teachers. We had about a thousand kids, to put that in perspective."

"Sounds like hell on earth. I went to public school, only white people around were the teachers, the ones that stuck around anyway. A lot of my classmates weren't the nicest bunch. You ever seen *Freedom Writers?*"

"My third favorite white savior movie of all time, right behind *Blood Diamond* and *The Power of One,* a true classic. So, you were one of the good ones I'm guessing."

"What makes you think I wasn't a troublemaker?"

"No one with little chipmunk cheeks like those could be dangerous."

She cracked a smile through her show of offense.

"Humph, well you're a big guy, how do I know you're not dangerous?"

"You've seen one of the two clowns I walked in here with, I don't exactly roll with a tough crowd. I played football way back in the day, did a bit of rugby in college, but now I mostly use my size as a deterrent on the subway and to inconvenience people in cramped elevators."

"Gotta use the gifts God gave you."

"Amen, sister."

Her phone buzzed and as she began to read her screen, a sudden thought crossed my mind: Where the hell is Ravi? I pulled out my phone as well, hoping that he'd sent me a text or something, but, my inbox was empty. I scanned the bar and spotted him, off in the corner with his tongue shoved down some guy's throat. It'd been a while since he'd brought any guys around so I'd almost forgotten that he played both sides of the field, but I guess that's one benefit of having more varied tastes, the lack of need for consistency. The guy looked like a classic finance guy, complete with the Patagonia fleece vest and slicked hair. Guess he and María have similar tastes in douchery. It was then that I remembered why Abi and I were alone in the first place, and she must have picked up on my sudden realization because she put her phone down and announced: "Looks like your friend is better than I thought."

"Huh? Oh, ohhh, wait, you're not serious."

"YUP. Like, five minutes ago, just hopped in a cab back to our place."

"The man does it again," I giggled, "unbelievable."

"Don't tell me that guy actually gets with a lot of women?"

"Huh, how do I put this…Imagine that the really hot guy from high school had the ability to sync up his personality traits with the desired attributes of any woman he wanted. That's basically Curtis. He's like a chameleon."

"You know there was a movie about that, right? *What Women Want*, Mel Gibson starred in it."

"Well that explains that, I'm not a fan of Mel Gibson. And no, not because of the sexism and anti-Semitism, even though that should play a factor; I genuinely do not like the *Lethal Weapon* franchise and no amount of *Braveheart* is going to make up for that. You big on movies?"

"Well," she said, feeling more comfortable by the second with this still-a-bit-of-a-stranger, "it's kind of important in my line of work, so yeah, you could say that."

"You work for a studio or something?"

"No, I'm… I'm an actress."

"An actress?!" I exclaimed, in a mixture of impressed amusement and genuine shock, "Really? Sorry, I didn't mean any offense, it's just… well, I was raised under a very strict African perspective of the arts, and I imagine you were as well, so I'm a bit taken aback."

She quickly transitioned from the hurt frown at my

incredulous response to a forgiving smile and shake of the head. "No, it's okay, I get it. And trust me, we were the same way on that front. I've been doing it since I was a kid, but I never thought it would really go anywhere. I went to college for four years and was getting ready to look for work when I just decided to take a bit of time to explore acting seriously under the strict condition that if I failed, I would stop, on my word. It was a harsh ultimatum, but it was fair enough. I tried for a really long time, had a few auditions, but they weren't going anywhere. I was honestly completely ready to just pack it up and tell my parents they won, but lo and behold, I got a commercial spot, and that turned into another commercial, and that turned into an episode of *Law & Order: SVU*, and, eventually, a stage gig. All the while, I was paying the rent with a combination of babysitting and dog-walking for rich people up on Park Avenue."

"Damn, paying NYC rent off babysitting and dog-walking, that's more impressive than making it with acting by a mile. How'd you manage that?"

"If you're asking if I ever gave any 'extra service'- "

"I definitely wasn't, but I also definitely wouldn't be opposed to any regaling stories on the topic, if that's the case." I got another chuckle from her out of that one.

"Sorry to disappoint, but no I wasn't selling myself off— at least not like that. A lot of them were the super-liberal, save-the-world hashtag activism type, the ones who send money over to help the refugees but still get a little scared when the guy with the turban gets on the plane. I always use to put on the thickest accent I could muster and beguile them with 'stories from the village' about my mom and thirteen siblings and the twenty civil wars that happened a year. They'd eat that shit up and feel the rain of white guilt pour down upon them, so not only did a bunch of them give me a little extra on the side, but they would also give me leftovers, some cosmetics here and there, hell, I even got this fashion lady to give me whole bags full of 'last season's' clothes, which would then find their way to the bootleggers down in my old neighborhood, all for a fee, of course."

"Bravo, bravo. Exploiting first world sympathy for profit and giving back to the neighborhood at the same time, good job."

"A hustler and a humanitarian, I'm the full package."

"You're certainly something."

She flipped her hair in a faux-vain fashion, posing for the fictional paparazzi.

"So, what about you? Did you follow your African parents' wishes?"

"Eh, depends on how far up I can go at my consulting firm. I'm probably still going for that MBA at some point but I honestly don't care much about it, as long I don't start lagging behind the pack it doesn't make a difference. Most likely I'll just get a few more promotions, with the raises to match, and then end up in a senior management position where I'll stay until the kids are off in college. We'll see what happens."

Oh no, we're heading into the cliché topic territory. Five more minutes and we'll be talking about our favorite happy hour spots. I couldn't quite put a finger on it at that moment, but I already knew that there was something I liked about this girl. I don't know if it started when she didn't storm off at my first joke, or when we shared a laugh over Curtis' heroics, but

I really felt something hit. I knew that I couldn't let this night end on an awkward wait for a cab coupled with a customary number exchange and half-hearted plans to meet up for drinks. I decided to go for it, my mind racing to think of my next move.

"You wanna go see a movie?"

You. Dumb. Bastard.

"Um…"

Oh God, please kill me now. I deserve it. I want it.

"Yeah, sure. Why not?" She'd been taken aback by the suddenness, that much was obvious, but she wasn't alarmed. It was probably my well-honed ability to mask internal panic with a stone-cold serenity that made the difference. "When were you thinking?"

"Like, now. Now, as in let's get out of here and go see something. If you're down, that is." If I was going to go down in flames, I was going to go all the way. "There's this theater I love down on Ludlow, I went and saw a Groucho Marx flick there one time and I've always wanted to go back. They always have shows at this hour."

"Late night show with a stranger? Why does this sound like I'm about to be the victim in a *Law & Order* episode?"

"Look, trust me, if I was a serial killer I sure as hell wouldn't use classic cinema to lure in my victims, I'd be doing too much damage to the arts community. I'd probably just use chloroform or stalk the parks, something simple."

"So was that supposed to make me feel better or…"

"I hope I get points for effort at least," I replied, "So, is that a yes? Now, I do understand the hesitation, I really do, but I can promise you ten-thousand percent, that a night out with me is far more enjoyable than sitting in your apartment pretending not to hear my roommate grunting for a few hours, and it will be the best night of your life compared to having to wade your way through this pool of unchecked masculinity and pricey booze. Speaking of which," I said before proceeding to down the rest of my drink, letting the vodka and cream wash out my mouth before I gulped it, "Ah!"

"Aww, I kinda wanted to try your mixed-baby drink."

"Oh, don't worry, I'm pretty sure they sell alcohol at the theater, and I'm pretty sure they sell babies in the alley behind it, so either way I think you're good."

"OK, OK, you've convinced me. Yes, let's go watch this movie."

Not bad, dumbass, not bad at all. But the night ain't over yet.

A Conversationalist

"OK, I get all that, but I still can't really understand Quinlan's motivations for planting the evidence in literally all of his cases. I mean, he didn't even try to find out who actually planted the bomb, he just found the first Mexican guy related to the victims and then framed him. Even if he's just a shitty cop, if you're a captain you can at least try to have a real investigation every once in a while."

We ended up seeing *Touch of Evil*, an Orson Welles picture from '58. Corrupt cops, the evils of marijuana, the danger of the Mexican border; it's like a cinematic conservative campaign ad, which I guess you could say about a lot of movies from the 1950s, but still. The place we went to was pure arthouse, resembling Patrick Bateman's apartment more than anything, the blaring whites drowning out the artistically crafted signs and the reds and blacks of the lounge furniture. The concessions area was off in a well-lit corner, packed with all the foreign candies and artisanal popcorns a person could ask for. We got jalapeño-goat cheese popcorn, Japanese sour gummies and the most pretentiously-named craft beers we could find.

"Yeah," I concurred, "I'll agree with you there; they didn't do a great job establishing his motivation outside of his own ego, and that made him pretty one-dimensional. I still think Orson Welles did a good enough job to make up for the less-than-stellar writing, not to mention Charlton Heston playing Vargas. Overall, I'd give it a seven."

"So, the movie was only about as good as your joke earlier, then?"

"Oof, right in the heart." I clutched my chest and pretended to stagger as we kept walking down the moonlit street. "So what would you rate it?"

"Hmm… I'm thinking a solid six. Maybe I need to watch more really old stuff, I've only ever really seen the true-blue classics."

"OK, favorite 50's movie then."

"*The King and I* or *Sunset Boulevard*, easy. Et toi?"

"Ah, tu parles français aussi ?"

"Oui oui, un peu. I wanted to minor in French but I bailed junior year, little too much effort just to be able to be the most annoying person at a French restaurant. You?"

"Je l'ai etudié pour six ans, and that's about as much as I'm able to do on a drop, so there might have been better uses of my time." I mentally added another check to her column, delighted by the fact that she knew enough French for us to add lingual spice to a conversation, but not so much so that I would have to worry about barrages of well-accented babble being thrown at me constantly. "Well, I'm going to go with *12 Angry Men*, one of my all-time favorites. There's just something very relatable to me about having to convince male counterparts to shut the fuck up for a few seconds and think. Do you watch any French films?"

"No but I really should watch more of them, the ones I have seen I loved to death. *Joyeux Noel* is magnificent beyond words."

"That's the one about one Christmas during World War I, when all the enemy soldiers declare a ceasefire and celebrate the holiday together, right? That one was a beauty man, cried my damn eyes out."

"What's the most you've ever cried over a movie?"

"You know anything about Bollywood?"

"Not even a little bit, no; my roommate Samaira tried to get me to watch one though. I guess I'll work on that too."

"Well you should start with one called *3 Idiots*. You start out thinking it's a simple college comedy about three numbskull friends, then all of a sudden it turns into a scathingly graphic critique on Indian university culture and suicide, then it turns into a tragic love story, then a mystery, and they keep going back and forth on the timeline. All the while there's a song just about every ten minutes. It was the definition of an emotional roller coaster, but what got me fucked up was that they spend, like, ten minutes in this one scene convincing you that a baby is going to die, then they deliver the baby, but then the baby is stillborn, which is when I cried, but lo and behold, they resurrect the dead baby with the power of poorly-harmonized singing, which is when the tears of pain transitioned to joy. It was… it was a lot."

"Yikes. I'm gonna have to prepare myself for that one. OK, what about favorite 60's films?"

"The 60's, huh? Hmm, that's a tough one…"

We kept walking under a motionless parade of streetlights and stop signs, aided by a full moon as we navigated empty streets. After the movie, we'd gotten on a train since I had volunteered to walk her back to her place and then catch a cab. I knew fully well what the walk back home implied, and believe me, I was absolutely game for that, but I also genuinely felt my duty to get her back safely. Call me old-fashioned, but when people constantly confuse you for a football player and you've gotten out of trouble simply by dropping an ice-cold stare on more than one occasion, you don't let an objectively tiny woman walk home by herself after a night out in the middle of the damn city. Like Curtis said, "Gentleman's Code."

We kept talking, and talking, and talking; we talked about movies both seen and to-be-viewed, and did the same for our favorite TV shows; we talked about our mutual hatred for the club scene and everything wrong with the place where we'd just met a few hours before; we exchanged snide remarks about the handful of late-night strangers as we people-watched them, keeping the words to a whisper but letting the laughs howl into the wind. We could have walked until the sun came up, but alas, that's not how those kinds of nights end; eventually she had to say the words we'd both been forgetting about.

"Well, this is my stop." I couldn't really read her mind in that moment, her standing next to the steps and me a few steps in front, having already started my next bit of dialogue.

"Oh... well, I guess I'll have to hear that crazy babysitting story some other time." I knew I only had a few phrases left before the end of my time, so I had to make the most of it. "So, listen, I know that the first night is supposed to end with me trying to finesse you into giving me a number and a little chit-chat about getting drinks soon, but seeing as how we just had an amazing first date/not-first-date/definitely a first date," I proposed, gauging her amused reaction by the second, "how about I skip that part, I just ask you when you want to meet up next weekend, and then you give me your number because it's far more personal than me adding you on Facebook later."

Nailed it.

"Wowww, you really just went on some Cassanova shit huh, some rom-com repertoire? Ok then, Romeo, I'll throw you a bone," she said, chuckling while taking the phone from my outstretched hand and proceeding to type, "but I have to be somewhere next weekend, so Saturday, in two weeks, works better. And… done! Here ya go."

My phone was back in my hand, and I'd moved my way closer while she was typing. She hadn't put a foot on the steps yet, clearly anticipating that there would be one more act in tonight's main feature. The moment had finally arrived, and while I remained calm and cool, my mind was still racing: *Do I kiss her, or should I wait for her to move a little closer? Should I grab her by the waist? No, no, that's too much; I should lean in, real subtle, all cool-like, and then go in slow…No, no you idiot, this isn't some cheesy 80s movie, that'll just be too slow. All right, all right, I'm just gonna do it now, I'll just do it, I'll just take two more steps forward and put one right on her, right on the l-*

Before I knew what to say, she'd hopped one step up the stairs, putting herself right at my height level, and given me a sweet, soft smooch right on the cheek. I must've looked like one of those cartoons, a big red set of lips plastered to the side of my face.

"See ya later, Funny Man." And just like that, she skipped up the steps, opened the door, and disappeared into the comfort of her home.

Damn.

So, there I was, left to find my way to a long night's

sleep with nothing to do but reflect on a beautifully unusual evening. As I started to walk, I checked my phone and read all the updates that I'd ignored while I was with Abi. Ravi had apparently ended up at a rave somewhere in Brooklyn, or at least that's what it looked like with all the shirtless people and neon in the photo. I couldn't see the hipster from the club, but I was sure that they'd come together, and that my friend was definitely going to be gone till tomorrow morning. Curtis was already back home, fresh from a sexual encounter I was sure I'd be hearing about in great detail the next day. By that count it seemed I was the unlucky one that night, if only in one sense.

The empty nighttime always feels different depending on whether you're alone or with people; when you're with people, it's something open to be explored and observed, fresh marble ready to be sculpted into some sort of shared memory. When you're by yourself, walking in the vast rigidly structured expanse, it's something else entirely; it's like you're swimming on two feet, with every step conscious and every twist and turn premeditated. The night becomes something physical, surrounding your body. As I walked that night, I saw the things that I always saw; the bright rectangles poking their way out of blacked-out constructs, the rats running around their temporary territories, the strange people walking around as well, some on their way home, some on their way to no good, but everyone going somewhere, trying to find their way out of the thick black water. All the while, the frozen light parade marched on over me, keeping me from drowning completely.

The visual desolation was starting to get to me, so I decided to retreat to sonic isolation instead with my go-to walking playlist. Realizing that my headphones weren't in their assigned pocket position, I figured that I would take advantage of the empty space and play out loud. I hit shuffle and let my sounds fill the void.

"In A Sentimental Mood," Duke Ellington. All too appropriate.

The more I walked, the more I reflected; I kept going over the night that I'd just had, the turns of events that had brought me to this last step of my adventure. Abi had really made an impression on me; our conversation had flowed like music, but it wasn't so much a composition as it was freeform jazz. Every lead-in got a punchline, every stray observation got an accompanying musing, every random statement was followed by an even more random rebuttal. We must've sounded like we were practicing for one of her shows, one where all the couples insult each other poetically and show their affection through their joy. I really didn't have the best way to describe it.

"I don't know, I really don't know; I mean, I know she's something special, but it was only one night, y'know? I mean, what if next time we hang out it's not as good, y'know? Am I just imagining some magical night that didn't even happen that way? Am I just blocking out any awkwardness that happened? Am I crazy?"

The stray cat didn't respond. It had ran off somewhere. The silence was deafening.

"What about you, huh?" I asked, nodding to the one on the corner, "What do you think of all of this? Am I just repeating the usual mistake, thinking something's real when it's nonexistent?

It remained as silent as the others. I began to lose hope.

"None of you feel like talking tonight I take it. C'mon guys, a little help would be nice here. I'm losing my shit over here over a girl I just met like four hours ago. I need some goddamn perspective, please, anybody?"

They didn't respond. The silence was deafening.

I groaned, checked the time on my phone, and turned the corner, five minutes' walk away from the apartment. The stray cats scurried back into the alley, somehow the least confused party to emerge from that conversation.

Never a great sign when you're the loneliest one among a pack of homeless animals.

A Record

"See you later, big head."

Abi turned with a deliberate swish to her hips and walked up the stairs gingerly. The heels that she'd been convinced to wear had taken a year off her ankles' lifespans but evidently they'd worked their charm. Right outside the door behind her was a man, a tall, somewhat talkative man who had just walked her home and was surely pining for more than a peck on the lips. Right on those steps was a still-buzzed, newly-infatuated victim of her divine feminine charm and she felt the thrill of that power through her whole body.

To her joy, the building elevator was an empty space for her to take a long moment. Once the door closed and the box started moving, she let out the wildest, most gleeful laugh of her night. Smiling, dancing a slight dance, even doing a spin for no one watching. For twenty whole seconds her elation, in all its corny glory, was on maximum display.

Practically skipping, she entered the loft in an unusually quiet manner. Like the rest of her living mates, Abi normally announced her presence with a loud greeting to anyone within hearing range. There were never any phone calls of serious importance being made, the kind of importance that involved work anyway, so the noise was hardly an issue. Their announcements would reverberate off the red pipes scattered across the ceiling, bounce off the massive windows that always faced the best part of the sun at exactly the right time on exactly the worst hungover mornings, and arrive in the kitchen/bar area/smoking lounge/salon/extra living room/hostel.

She tiptoed her way past the easel and the small mountain of canvases to its left, avoiding feet contact with unidentified panties on the floor right under the coffee table. Well, would be unidentified, if they weren't accompanied by the same shiny shirt she'd seen splayed on her best amiga's conquest for the night.

With their clothes on the floor, Abi assumed that they must still be in there and still be at it, but as the bathroom door opened down the hallway and María emerged in a freshly showered glow, the questions became a little juicier.

"Girl, I know you got that good shit going on, I do know this, but there ain't no way in hell," Abi pointed, picking the shirt off the floor, "that you fucked him so good he forgot his shirt."

"*HA!* Oh shitttt, that's where the fucking thing was," María answered, hunching over and laughing, towel barely staying wrapped, "Yo he was looking for like five minutes but I told him to get the fuck home, he must've actually just left shirtless... yo that's pretty stupid though, he ain't even have to go really."

"You probably used your abuela yell on him and didn't even notice. Shit, you probably used it on while y'all was at it. I cannot believe you brought that loud- ass, fake-ass Justin Timberlake home."

"Es muy guapo, chica, the hell you expect me to do? You know I get down with los gringos, the cute ones can't resist me," she remarked, dropping the pretense of the towel at that point and stepping into her room to get a long shirt.

"You'd think he'd be better at giving head though for all that mouth he was giving, damn waste of a tongue on that boy. Dick was pretty decent though."

"Their most useful parts are put towards the most useless tasks," Abi replied, her spark of philosophical whimsy reminding her that she hid half a joint left, from some Tuesday night shindig they'd thrown. "Yo bitch, want a hit? I'm about to make some ramen or something, I'm starving."

"Um, bitch why is you even asking me, better get that shit out," María answered, emerging from her boudoir with an elegantly ragged tee on, "I wish I could say I was more sore but he got the job done, mostly anyway. Had to pull the bunny out after he left."

"It's amazing that we have to wait until after their egos out of range for us to get off, who invented that rule," Abi espoused from the kitchen, carefully eyeing the boiling water for maximum ramen readiness. These were the good noodles that their other-other-other roommate, Yuki, had picked from the below-ground Asian superstore in Flushing, so proper respect was owed in preparation. "I bet he did that thing where he said he was too big for a condom too, as if that's a thing."

"Ha ha ha, right! He tried it while I was blowing him though so I think me almost biting his shit off sent the message. And hold up, hold up, enough of your little performance Miss *A-bi-lo-la*, what in the fuck has your sneakin' ass been up to all night? I left you alone with that big motherfucker in the little blue suit, and now you're home long after my dick-and-dash is gone. Oooooh girl, you broke you off a piece of that chocolate bar didn't ya?!"

Abi's melanin had to do all it could to keep the blushing contained, but María could sense it even with her back turned and twenty feet away. It was an ability she called "Latina Intuition," which, while sounding offensive, somehow seemed OK the way she described it. But that's a story for another time.

"AHHHHHH! Bitch did you fuck him?! Ah ah ah," she screamed, jumping off the couch and practically tackling Abi, "You better start talking ho, spill spill spill!"

"Relaxxxxx, bitch, damn," Abi laughed back, wrestling the half naked María off of her, "It ain't even like that, quit crowding me. Now sit your barely-dry ass on the couch like you have some sense."

They sat down together and commiserated over the cannabis. They were about three rotations and a perfectly smooth high in before Abi got to the events at the movie theater.

"So then we get there, right, and there's like five movies showing and three of them look like random French nonsense but he's looking at the list like he actually knows all of them, total lie."

"Complete bullshit, but we love a man faking it til he makes it."

"We do, that's facts. So like, he picks the movie, and I'm just vibing along, and then we start chilling at the bar, and he wanted to—"

"Ugh, bitch, stop, you are boring me to literal tears. Enough about the fake first date, Abi, be real: *Do - We - Like -*

This - Man?' María asked, with a clap for each emphasis.

"I mean…."

"Speak bitch, damn!"

Abi cracked up at María's ravenous persistence.

"OK, OK, damn girl… I do, I really do, ughh it was like the cutest date I've ever been on and I literally met him while I was trying to make him leave with your gringo. He was sooo sweet and he listened to me all night, he asked me the kinds of questions about acting that only people who actually care ask, like 'What do you like seeing in a character you're developing?', shit like that. I felt like I was hanging out with someone I've known for like five years and it was literally someone I just met, how does that shit even happen?

"Like, this man literally was the most respectful and fun person I've met in the last year and I literally almost told him to go fuck himself in our first conversation.

"And we're both Nigerian, which is crazy because he's like the first Nigerian guy I've met who my Aunty Mori didn't send me over WhatsApp and unsurprisingly the only interesting one. Oh and he loves kids, he said he used to volunteer with kids for a literacy organization, and he likes stand-up comedy, and reading at cafés, and people watching in the park, and he offered to give me a piggyback ride when he saw that my heels were starting to hurt, and he never even let me look at my wallet all night, and he—"

"Ooooh, girl," María said right before exhaling a perfect cloud, "you are tweaking on this man right here! I knew from the second I saw you looking at him in that club, your soft ass falling in love at first sight and shit ha-ha-ha!"

"Shut up!!!" Abi screamed, falling sideways on the couch

and shoving the nearest pillow into her face, hiding the all-too-confirming smile, "Ughhhhh, what is wrong with me, why am I always like this? I just met the man and I'm already doing this shit… Like, he's really cute, and funny but not as funny as he thinks, and he's like smart and seems responsible and he has some corporate job but like doesn't act like some kind of finance asshole, like I don't even—"

"Miss A-Bi-Lo-La! Re—and I really need you to hear this part, so I'll repeat—re-fuckin-lax girl, shit. You've talked more in the last forty minutes than you did in the whole two months of that play you was in. You're cute and all but we are too high for this. But Abi, girl, for real," María paused, reaching out and taking Abi's hand, pulling her up from her pillow fort, "I am sooooo freakin excited for you right now! You have been going through it this last year, I know how it's been and I remember all those talks we had about how you didn't know if anyone was out there for you. Let tonight breathe, let it sink in, and just take it slow, OK?

"He sounds like a great guy, maybe this could be something. And if it isn't, then he can join the rest of the poor, stupid bastards who missed out on your divine queenliness and don't know what the hell they're missing. Either way, boss bitches stay winning, always and always and always."

Abi let her deceptively wise friend's words sink in, finding comfort in the resolution to let just a little bit of realism set over her excited fantasies. She hugged her friend lovingly, the kind of pure, joyful bond that survives the best of times and the worst heartbreaks, the kind that she and María had shared for what felt like ten lifetimes and could last ten more. And with that embrace, the formal proceedings of the post-night were concluded, and the two hours of getting increasingly stoned and watching TV ensued.

After the last hit was smoked, after the last "Love you, girl" was exchanged, and with the last bit of mental energy she had for the day, Abi laid down in her bed and set on her final task for the night. It was just a little something that she'd been trying to make part of her "Get Your Shit Together" routine. Tonight, it seemed like the perfect way to end.

Therapy Journal Entry: 06/27/18

Tonight went in an incredibly different direction than expected - well, part of it at least. The part where María went home with a random guy, that was a bit expected. As was the part where the too-packed and way-too-white club was overrated and overpriced. That was all the same, in different ways, but then it all went very off script.

I honestly have no idea why I said yes. I meet a guy at a bar, a total stranger who I only started talking to because María wasn't quite sure if she wanted to fuck him, and all of a sudden I end up going to a random ass theater to watch an old Orson Welles movie. The fact that I'm not trapped in a basement somewhere in North Jersey right now is a miracle.

He's... nice, I think. No—he is nice, and a little funny, but not as funny as he thinks. I got the sense that he was fluctuating between covering up his nerves and a pre-rehearsed act, or maybe that's always the same thing... I don't know, I guess that's the point. I just met him, I don't know him, but when he asked to keep hanging out something in me just felt like saying yes. Despite the last year of my love life being best described as "dry and confusing," I never stopped thinking that maybe something interesting was out there, waiting. Something more interesting than Ali's twentieth time showing off the proper way to pronounce Ib-ee-

tha, or Derek begging for a three-way with María that seemed a lot more for his benefit than mine, or the two months of absolute nonsense that was Dwayne And The Surprise Baby Mama. That's one for another day…

I know I'm supposed to use this thing to get my thoughts in order but I guess I don't have any yet? Which makes sense! As opposed to me letting him buy me a drink at the theater bar, which defies every singular female instinct, but the only thing wrong with the drink was that he tried to impress me by picking the most- obscure-yet-inexpensive whiskey they had in the place. Tasted like absolute ass, and I made him get me a tequila sunrise instead. If I see him again I'm sure he'll learn to ask.

The movie was low-key pretty good but like, definitely the kind of movie he saw on a list and decided to save for the right occasion. Once I told him I was an actress I could see him put on the cinephile persona - every man seems to think the fastest way to a creative woman's heart is through their Top 20 list. OK, that might be harsh, he did look like he was enjoying himself, like he was smiling and paying attention in the kind of way that's hard to completely fake. He only went for the hand over the shoulder two thirds into the movie, on some middle school shit. It was cute or whatever…

Ughhh this is so dumb. He's just some guy I met at a bar, I might not even see him ever again. Just because a man walks you home doesn't mean he won't ghost you without a second thought. Niggas ain't shit, we know this, don't forget it. He probably already thinking about texting some other girl… We had a nice walk though. And we talked. And talked and talked and talked. Like, it didn't even feel like a date or anything, it felt like a walk I'd taken twenty times with a man I've known for twenty years. It felt… natural.

My drunk ass really out here catching feelings… Nah, this is too much. Let's see if he even texts back before I start writing his name down in hearts. Mama raised me better than that.

Goddamn it… it's happening again, isn't it?

A Sunday Lunch

Mr. Rahmani's was a little busier than usual that Sunday, but we were still able to grab that window table. Apparently, some family in the neighborhood was holding a birthday celebration for their one-hundred-year-old patriarch and a few of the guests had arrived a little early. Given the size of the expected crowd, we would have to wait for a little while before being graced with Mr. R's presence, so in the meantime we kept ourselves entertained with a civilized discussion on the previous evening's events.

"Dude, I swear, I have never gotten head like that in my entire life. My dick was melting like cheap ice cream in the shittiest parts of Arizona."

OK, so maybe "civilized" was a bit of a misnomer, but honestly, that was pretty tame for him.

"I'm telling you, this chick has to be a porn-star on the side or something, and if she isn't then she is wasting a God-given talent."

"I'm no Christian, man," Ravi rebutted, amused yet shaking his head, "but I'm pretty sure describing blowjobs as a God-given talent is some sort of blasphemy."

"Son of Christ here, can confirm." I figured that bit of Christian duty would make up for me skipping Mass that day.

"God made those lips, God made little Curtis, and He, in all His divine wisdom, brought the two together last night to just absolutely shit all over his Sixth Commandment."

"Not literally, I hope," Ravi replied, providing an image I did not need to have as I was halfway through my lamb vindaloo.

"All right, all right," Curtis declared, somehow without a hint of irony, "let's quit the dirty talk for now, there's a bunch of kids around today for some reason. So, what happened with you, Ravi? I don't think Kola and I saw you after we started talking to those two babes."

"I met this guy Xavier in the ATM line, he seemed fairly interesting so we went to dance, DFMO'd for a bit and then we migrated to a couch. His friends show up about an hour after we meet, all get a drink or two and then suddenly there's talk of a trek to Bushwick. I assumed it would be slightly awkward to tag along but everyone seemed nice about it so I joined. It was going fairly well until one of the girls decided to whip out some E, and at that point I figured I was in for a messy night; I declined but Xavier took some. We finally get to this place, one of those ironically refurbished warehouse rave spots, but all of a sudden one of the guys, I think he was Moroccan or something, he's passed out and everyone is trying to deal with him. That seemed like a natural conclusion to the evening, so I took Xavier aside, gave him my number and Instagram, and got the hell back to Manhattan."

"'Dance Floor Make Out' and a warehouse rave, that's a pretty good night my man. And you're back on the magic stick again, I see."

"You don't 'get back' on anything, that's not how being bi works."

"I know, I know, c'mon man you know I'm fucking with

you. I got nothing but love for the LGBT; besides, if sexual deviancy sends you straight to Hell I'm gonna be with y'all for the ride, no questions asked."

"Coming from you, man, that's almost progressive. What about you, Kola, Curtis said you two were with some 'babes' last night?"

"Yeah, Koka-Kola, what happened with that girl anyway?"

I proceeded to tell them about my evening with Abi, starting from when Curtis left with her roommate all the way up to that kiss on her porch. I left out the little incident with the strays; those conversations are just for you and me.

"Now that," Ravi exclaimed, "that's crazy. You managed to rush through all the awkwardness of the meeting up and the first date in one night, all without creeping her the hell out. Either she couldn't care less about human trafficking or she's way, way into you."

"You think so?"

"Dude, you guys went to a movie at like 1:00 AM after meeting in a bar while this guy was plowing her roommate. If that's not the start of a really cheesy rom-com, I don't know what is."

"All right, all right, let's slow our roll here," Curtis butted in, "now all of that sounded real nice and everything, but my question is, why the kiss on the cheek?"

"What do you mean?" I asked.

"I mean, after all of this nighttime magic, all those sparks flying, she gives you a peck on the cheek. What's up with that?"

Was it really just a peck, I wondered. *No, it was a little longer than that. A little wetter too.*

"I know that some girls like to do kissing only on the first night, but one kiss on the cheek? Something seems up with that. Maybe she just got out of something long-term and isn't sure if she wants something or not. Same shit just happened to you, right Ravi?"

"Well Jenny was a little different, our date wasn't like that at all. And we actually did end up making out by the end of the night, so the way the evening ends and whether or not something comes out of it later aren't as positively linked as you're making it sound."

"OK I'll concede that point, the two don't have to be related exactly, but it's still a pretty fuckin' good indicator. Look, I'm just saying that the girl seems a bit strange to me, that's all."

"The only girl who was acting strange last night was her roommate," I remarked, "because I still can't believe that you got that girl in bed after you called her a '*mamacita*' and spat a few lines at the bar while you were piss drunk."

"You know how rock stars take drugs to inspire their music? My brain works the same way with alcohol and women; it both loosens my inhibitions while simultaneously causing my game-spitting lobe to function at inhuman speeds. I can't help being a prodigy, fellas, it's in my genes."

"You do have a point there," I had to confess, "I remember when your dad used to take us around your town those weekends I slept over. Fifty-year old man making all the college girls' knees weak with nothing more than a smile and a wink."

Curtis didn't crack a smile on that one, and it took me a few seconds to remember why: his dad had divorced his mom a few weeks after Curtis and I graduated from Ignatius. He told me that his father had been cheating on his mom forever, but his mom always put up with his bullshit; at least, she did, until the day she found that he was screwing one of the local high school girls. As if that wasn't bad enough for Mrs. Branson, guess who happened to be the barely-legal mistress's homeroom teacher?

"Point is, pull more than anyone in a mile radius at all times. It's a Branson guarantee."

"Oh, I would very much beg to differ with that."

"MR. RAHMANI!" we all cheered, giddy as a bunch of schoolboys when the teacher walks in.

"Hello, my boys, how are you this afternoon? Did you enjoy your food?"

"You don't gotta bother asking that, man, you know we loved it because you know it's the best. What about you, how's your Sunday going?" I asked, observing his fancy-looking clothing and styled white mane.

"Ah you're spying my pathani, yes, it's a more formal version of my usual attire. I'm closing the shop up early, it's a dear friend's birthday and we'll be celebrating the night away."

"Yeah, we heard some lady talking about it when we got in here," Ravi chimed in, "is the guy really one hundred years old? That's crazy."

"*Bah!* The people back home are hardy, some live far longer than a hundred years. My great-great-great-great-great grandfather lived to be one hundred twenty-four, and his father before him saw his one hundred thirtieth year. That's what happens if you live a halal lifestyle and keep active, not like you lazy people here."

"Health advice aside, one hundred years is just way too

long, no offense to your forefathers. I'm thinking a nice eighty-five years will do me just fine."

"Hmm, well thank you for putting my old age into your young perspective."

"Speaking of your old age," Ravi asked, "what song is this again?"

"You don't know 'Johnny B. Goode?' Chuck Berry, my boy, an American legend!"

"Ignore him, Mr. Rahmani, I'll give him shit for that later." I fucking meant it, too.

"Don't be too rough, Kola. So, young Curtis, what's this I hear you talking about the 'lady-killing?'"

"Oh nothing, Mr. R, I was just informing these two about how I can bag a perfect ten with two hands tied behind my back and a big sign that says, 'One Pump Chump.' I believe that you said I was mistaken though."

"You said you were the best of all those around, but somehow it appeared that you were near me, so I had to inform you of your falsehood. I can't allow you to live your life in a state of delusion." Even when he was roasting somebody, you couldn't help but get that friendly grandpa vibe.

"Whoa, whoa, whoa," Curtis responded, with semi-serious shock, "are you saying that you, Mr. Pray- Five-Time-a-Day, Mr. Everything's Haram, the guy who I'm pretty sure tried to unsubtly convert us to Islam on several occasions, was just nailing chicks back and forth back in the mean streets of Lahore?"

"Some Muslims eat pork, some drink, and some forget to go to mosque; me, my vice was women. They would call me 'Mohabbat ka Badshah,' 'The King of Love'. I was good, man, too good for my own good; back then we weren't as good as you kids are with the protection, so I had a few scares, but Mash'Allah, no children came of them. By the time I was about your age, I'd calmed down with that mess and was ready to find a good girl, a woman to settle down with, my dear Hadiya. But, to answer your question, I was the top of the hill in my day, and those skills don't vanish my boy."

"Bill Russell won eleven championships, that doesn't mean he could beat LeBron right now on the court. I respect your game but I'm still calling myself the King for now."

"The impudence of youth. Anyhow, how was your evening last night? Was the club 'all the rage' like you say?"

"My man, we're gonna have to update your slang," Curtis replied, "but yeah, the club was amazing. Everyone had a good night, if in wildly differing ways; I got laid by a Cuban fashionista, Ravi ended up with a bunch of druggies in Brooklyn, and Kola had un nuit d'amour with a young lady."

"Ah, a romantic evening with a stranger, very interesting. What happened?"

"The girl Curtis took to bed," I started, "her roommate walked up to me because this guy was bombing apparently and she wanted an evacuation. Lord knows how he pulled that recovery off, but after they left we just ended up talking for a bit, I asked her if she wanted to see a movie on the spot and she said yes. After the show, we took a train then walked for a bit, and then I asked her out."

"And what else?" Curtis' head would pop off if you tried to avoid a topic he was insistent on.

"And then, she gave me a kiss on the cheek, which this clown insists is a bad omen."

"A kiss on the cheek? Ha! There's nothing wrong with that, boys, it means she's trying to be chaste, a woman who was raised a certain way."

"Oh, so the one thing worse than not liking ya, Koka-Kola; she likes ya, but you ain't gonna get none. Well that's that, you gotta drop her ass."

"Shut the fuck up, Curtis. Look, Kola," Ravi implored, "don't listen to this asshole. A lot of girls don't want to do much the first night, everyone knows that. Just because this one won't associate with them doesn't mean they're that rare."

"I agree with young Ravi, it is not a bad thing at all. Curtis, you are being far too foolish. But, none of that is important; Kola, the only important question, is how does this girl make you feel?"

Like a million bucks. Like a little kid on Christmas. Like I'm walking on air. Like all of my neuroses and existential crises were wiped away in one evening. Like an idiot for thinking this much about a mere five hours of my life. Like I'm making all the same mistakes I usually make with beautiful and funny women. Like I have no idea what the fuck I'm doing. Like I probably never did and never will.

"I mean, I like her, I know that much for sure; I definitely want to go on another date. Besides that, no idea."

"Well, take that as a start, and go on from there. Life is like walking down stairs; try to jump ahead too many times, and you're guaranteed to fall. You'll be fine, my boy—if you don't listen to this one, that is," he said as he tussled Curtis' blonde curls and grinned wide. "Well then, I must go greet some more of my patrons. You boys want some haleem? Hadiya made far too much for tonight, so there is a ton, you can even take some home."

"You just love asking us questions you already know the answer to, don't you?"

He just gave that grin again.

A Fade

As I hopped off the bus and started my walk, I took a few minutes to reflect on the last week of talking with Abi. Despite the strangely intimate time that we'd shared, the texting felt like it did with any other girl; maybe I'd just always picked good texters, but regardless some part of me was disappointed that the feeling from that night couldn't be recreated digitally. I would have to wait until Saturday to see what could be done, which meant that I would be left alone with nothing to do but imagine all of the different ways that our day out could go terribly wrong. I was in a really good place.

After a few blocks, I arrived at my destination, High Class Cuts, my go-to barbershop for the last two years. It was all the way up near the 161st-Yankee Stadium station, making it both an illogical distance (NA note: technicaly Yankee stadium is only a 20 minute subway ride from midtown - so wouldn't say illogical) from my place and way too close to my old neighborhood to justify not using my old barber. Why, then, would I go there? Because a nigga's got to do what he got to do to keep his shit fresh as possible, and Cuts had the best barbers I'd ever seen.

One of Ravi's work friends had told me about it at a bar party, and due to my admiration of his high-top, I decided to check it out. I swear the first time I walked out of there

I felt like I was about to shoot a music video, the freshness of the cut belonging side-by-side with half naked dancers and stupidly expensive cars. It was a modern-style shop but it had that old-school soul, with everything from the pictures of the famous (and hood-famous) patrons to the old-timey tracks constantly on rotation. The TV was almost always playing BET or VH1, if there weren't any NBA games on at the time, of course.

As much as I loved living with a full-blooded white American douche and an artistic, quiet Indian fellow, I have to say that having a space owned and usually exclusively filled with my own people was something I valued to an immense degree. There were conversations I was able to have and topics that I was able to explore that I just really couldn't get into with my boys, and certainly not with anyone at work, lest I risk being the cause of some office-wide, mandatory diversity training. I didn't live in an all-white neighborhood, thank God, but even with Mr. Rahmani, the cultural connections could only go so far; we'd once had an hour-long discussion about how The Prophet Muhammad viewed slaves which ended reasonably but exposed some very clear differences in perspective.

My guy was Tomás, or "Too-Tru Tommy," as he had insisted I started calling him after my first few visits. He was a big ol' southern boy, born and raised in Hollygrove, the craziest neighborhood in New Orleans. He'd moved up to New York after Katrina hit and found a job cutting hair, having owned his own shop back home. His accent was as deep and rich as the bayous he'd visited as a child to see his grandparents, and he would always tell me how much I needed to go down to the Big Easy someday. He was tall and squat, about as big as me but with years of physical labor stored in his muscles. His deft maneuvering of the clippers stood in stark contrast to the rest of him, worrying me the first time I went in but proving endearing after I saw his skill at work.

"Wellllll hello there boy, how you doin' today? You a little early now, I got me a customer still in the chair right here. Take a seat, son, I got you in bout' two minutes, maybe three."

"No problem Too-Tru, I'll grab a seat. Yo, Mr. Jones, what's playing right now?"

"Man, you don't know Herbie Hancock? 'Chameleon'? Y'all young folk missing out, this is that soul music. Listen to that funk right there." Mr. Jones was an old-timer, one of the shop's first employees hired by Mr. Conway, the owner. He had the craziest scraggly white hair on his head, and always wore the same pair of blue work shoes that he'd bought in 1984. "Bom-bom-bom-bom bom bom bom-bom-bom-bom bom bom… bet you'd rather listen to Little Thug or one of them ASAP (NA Note: potential alternative "One of them Migos boys) boys."

"Bruh, you and your old ass always hating man, whatchu know about A$AP Mob?" Tyrell, the newest dread-headed hire and the establishment's most talented shit-talker, chimed in, "I bet yo ass still thinks Funkmaster Flash runs the rap game. Can you believe this nigga, man? How you been anyway bruh, ain't seen you in a minnit? Your shit looking mad nappy."

"Shit man, I've been chilling, ain't nothing to it. I got me a date on Saturday so I'm just trying to keep this fade clean, feel me?"

"A date? Oh shit, this nigga finna pull some Romeo shit on a bitch, man."

"Where'd you go and meet this young lady at?" Tomás asked.

"At a club last weekend, my roommates and I went. It was aight, but she was something else. Still haven't figured out what we're doing yet, but we're meeting up during the day, so I'll figure this shit out later."

"Wait wait wait, hold the fuck up—you met a bitch at the club, and you taking her ass out on a date, after you already smashed?"

"Nah man, I ain't smashed yet. We chilled after the club, then I dropped her home and that was it."

"HA! Nigga you better marry this chick if you tryna be Mr. Romance-A-Hoe out here, I don't play that shit at all. Nigga out here taking club bitches on dates, if a club bitch want something to eat after I got me a five-hour foot-long right here bruh."

"Boy, shut your ignorant ass up!"

"Oh c'mon Mr. Conway, you know that shit true."

Mr. Conway came out of his back office, looking tired from a long day's work. He was a short man with a big personality, and a booming voice that made you wonder what the full capacity of the human lungs truly are. In his youth, he'd had dreams of being a championship boxer, and had even gone on to earn a respectable 11-4 record on the circuit; it showed on his face, with a slightly crooked nose and permanent reminders of some nasty blows to the cheek. That barbershop was the favorite of a host of bad, bad men, but everybody knew that Mr. Conway wasn't to be messed with unless you were planning on pulling out a piece, and even then, he was far too respected for someone to try that.

"The only thing I know is that you're out here disrespecting women that you ain't ever even met, acting like a damned fool," he shot back, keeping young Tyrell on the defensive, "meanwhile this young man over here actually sounds like he knows how to treat a lady. Sound like she's the exact opposite of them chicken-headed honeys you run around with."

"Man, whatever! Everybody knows I got bitches on rotation."

"The only thing your ass has on rotation is the excuses on your rent."

The rest of us all burst out laughing at that one, except Tyrell of course, who preferred a quick scowl and a silent acknowledgment of defeat. He may have been a shit-talking savage but Mr. Conway was the roast master, without question. The man Tomás had been working on was finally finished, so I stood up and got in my usual chair.

"So, go on and tell me about this girl, son."

"I don't know man, she's really cute, funny, talks shit, likes the same kind of movies I do…"

"She white?"

"Nah, Nigerian, just like me."

"Hmm, good," Mr. Conway, said, crossing his arms in contemplation, "too many of you young boys going after them white women, mess around and get picked up for 'disturbing the peace' when you visit the parents' house."

"Well the last girl I was messing with was white, but that didn't last long."

"Of course it didn't boy!" exclaimed Mr. Jones, "Them white women don't stay around with niggas. They'll hang around for a few months, living out their Mandingo fantasies, but ain't no Lil Becky trying to take a brotha home to Papa."

"Oh y'all exaggeratin' a tad bit now," said Tomas, "My cousin just got married to a white woman only 'bout a few months back, them folks was real kind at the wedding. Nicest white folk I ever met."

"Only thing lower than the bar for nice white folk is a nigga's credit score." Tyrell earned a round of chuckles for that one, happy that the subject of his rent had worked its way out of the cycle.

"What you come 'round fo anyway?"

"The usual man, that nice fade that you always do."

Tomás got to work on my hair and the barbershop banter continued to fill the air. I went on my phone for a few minutes to check some work emails, one of my least favorite and most frequent activities. Something about a spreadsheet, something about a meeting, and something about setting up a spreadsheet for a meeting; standard fare. I decided to save my misery for a later time and reenter the environment, finding the conversation had shifted subjects.

"I don't care what the hell you say, boy, they ain't no better black movie than *Do The Right Thing*," Mr. Jones declared with self-warranted certainty, "and that's the honest truth. First things first, Spike Lee the director, and the only nigga more famous than him for using a video camera is R. Kelly. Second, it's funny as all hell, had me in stitches the whole time. Third, and most important, it's the realest shit ever put to film, a story about hate that don't take no sides, just shows the ugliness. That's called high-grade storytelling right there."

"Man, fuck outta here with that," Tyrell replied, "that

shit's corny as all hell. I ain't saying it's wack, just corny, goofy more like it. Best black movie of all time is *Boyz n The Hood*, that's a fact. Ice Cube as Doughboy is that nigga for real, and Laurence Fishbourne killed it as Tre's pop. You talking about real shit but you ain't gonna give no love to Ricky getting shot up, that sermon on gentrification or even just the ending? Nah, that's that movie right there, no question. What do you think, Mr. Conway?"

"*Coming to America*, simple as that. Eddie Murphy, a real-life black Hollywood superstar, at the height of his powers, had me laughing my balls off for two hours straight. I still wish I could go to McDowell's. Either that or *New Jack City*, that was some good shit too. Nino was the definition of a bad brotha. What about you, Too-Tru?"

"Me? Aw hell, it's gotta be *Soul Food*, ain't got no doubt. All about the power of family, and there ain't nothing more important, or more black, than that right there. Lord knows my momma still my favorite woman, and not just cuz she make the best gumbo you'll ever find. With the superb actin' too? Yes sir, no doubt; how about you, Mr. Kola?"

"Hmm… damn, this is a hard one. I'd have to say that my favorite comedy, for sure, is *Black Dynamite*, and I'm honestly shocked none of y'all picked that already, shit's hilarious. The entire Blaxploitation era spoofed in ninety minutes of pure genius. Drama? That'd have to be Spike Lee's actual best movie, *Mr. Jones*, which would be *Malcolm X*. Now, I don't want to start no diatribe, but personally I'm a fan of Brother Malcolm—"

"Shit, boy, you don't know nothing about no 'Brother Malcolm,' talking like you was there."

"Ayo, Mr. J, why you gotta interrupt the nigga?" Tyrell questioned, clearly frustrated with the old man's antics, "just cuz your ass can remember the slave ships don't mean he can't have an opinion."

"Malcolm wasn't nothing but a troublemaking loudmouth, leading good brothers and sisters to that Islam nonsense and promising victory against the white man. Dr. King and the rest of us were out there doing the real work, suffering and marching, getting the dogs and hoses. I told y'all I was almost there that day in Birmingham, just missed it cuz my—"

"'APPENDICITIS FLARED UP!'" we all chanted in unison, having heard this same story at least one or two million times and all howling out in laughter as a result. Needless to say, we didn't have much faith in his retelling.

"Well, Mr. Jones, with all due respect," I continued, figuring he would appreciate the quick exit from the ribbing, "if I was around back then, I would've rolled with Malcolm. I'm not saying he had the right idea or that King was wrong, but if I had to pick between learning karate, packing a gun and getting ready for a race war, or getting the shit beaten out of me on a regular basis in the hopes that enough white people started to think it was fucked up, I'm going with the former. Just because it was a winning strategy doesn't mean it was an enjoyable one."

"So what you trying to say is that you'd take the easy way out?" The intensity of Mr. Jones' sentiments on the Movement had clearly gone underestimated by me, but I didn't want to engage. You have to pick your battles.

"I'm not even going to validate that with a response. Anyway, what I was going to say is that the best black movie, for me, is *Killer of Sheep*. It's a lost classic from 1978, a black and white film set in Watts County; neo-realist, non-narrative vignettes about a slaughterhouse worker succumbing to his existential malaise. The way Burnett crafts the visuals and implements the music is extraordinary, reminiscent of the true Italian masters. It's one of those films that never got the proper love until thirty years later but deserved accolades."

"Bruh, there you go again, always goin' on about that artsy bullshit, Mr. College Boy over here. Pick something that more than ten niggas actually watched."

"Tyrell, I know your ass ain't over there shaming a brother for having an education," Mr. Conway boomed, "even you have more sense in that big ol' head than that. Ignore him, son."

"Man, I'm just saying these African niggas are different, y'know? And hey, for real," he expressed to me, acutely aware of the territory he was about to enter, "you know I fuck with you man, for real, but it's the truth. There's an ugly separation there; ain't you the one that said your aunt was on some racist ass bullshit one time?"

What Tyrell was referring to was a time back in Lagos when an acquaintance of my mother's, who had never been to the states, had told us to watch out for the "bloodthirsty animals" we'd be living around in Harlem. Even after politely explaining that it was a nice neighborhood, already checked out by my father, she was still convinced that we would be entering a den of sin, my brother and I a couple of bad friends from becoming gangbangers, and my sister one bad boyfriend away from single teen motherhood. I wasn't a fan of hers in general, but I have to admit, the false notions certainly stuck for a while after my big move. I deeply regret that fact, but it couldn't have been helped; when Hollywood makes everything involving black skin look dangerous for the sake of selling thrill, the impression tends to stick. It took a few months before I was able to figure out the more nuanced reality of things, but thankfully I managed to get over the biases (NA note: We can never fully get over our own bias -food for thought).

"While I will admit there's some major ignorance across the ocean, it goes both ways, hell it ain't like I never got called some offensive shit in my time here. From the white boys at school I just had to take it as it came, didn't want the hassle, but from the kids on the block? That was just confusing. This one dude, Lamar, I swear he deadass asked me how my whole family could fit in a hut. One neighborhood girl I was trying to talk to was convinced I had AIDS, and even a few adults thought I must have been living in a war zone."

"Aight, niggas is ignorant the whole world over, I'll give you that, but still I gotta say it's a lot worse from y'all to us. Like the cousins y'all wished you didn't have."

"Well what does that have to do with me going to school or liking old movies, exactly? You already know I needed scholarships for both high school and college, I ain't on any Carlton Banks bullshit or anything. Isn't that one cousin of yours at Emory on a full ride? You gonna give him shit too?"

"If he start talking about some Italian mothafucka and weird ass movies then yeah," he replied, gearing up for his redirect, "but that's not even what I'm really talking about. When you were at that fancy white boy high school, I bet you got treated differently from the rest of the niggas. White folks see y'all funny names and they go crazy, man, like a kid with a new toy. Look, it's like this: the less American the nigga, the less guilty they gotta feel, the less bullshit you get, and with you, they must have been in love with your ass. Little jungle nigga on scholarship, talking about big books, getting good grades and playing sports? It's just like that shit from Django, that um… yo, Too-Tru, what did that Leonardo DiCaprio motherfucker say in Django?"

"'One exceptional nigger', I do believe."

"Yeah, yeah that was it, an exceptional ass nigga. White folks love exceptional niggas, especially niggas from someplace they ain't never been that don't talk or act nothing like the ones they're forced to call their, quote-unquote, 'countrymen.'"

"You think the cops have a nationality tracker in their patrol cars, or the lady following me around in the store stops after a few seconds because she hears the slight accent? They pick and choose the niggas they like but before they pick, there ain't no difference. Look, I can't take back what my aunt said any more than you can take back what those kids said, but I at least hope we can agree that the real problem doesn't start with each other… and besides," I continued, realizing suddenly that a drastic shift in tone was needed, "on top of all of that, don't get all serious just because I'm out here being cultured and shit. Maybe you should learn some of my enlightened vocabulary, T, so you can start picking up them college hotties you're always hitting up on Instagram."

"HA! Listen up, Kunta Kinte, the day I need yo help gettin' bitches is the day Mr. Jones wakes up without a big ol' stick up his ass, so pretty much never. I'll take ya word though."

He walked over to dap me up (I'm not translating AAVE for you guys anymore, figure it out), and just like that our little discourse was over. The shop quickly regained its usual rhythm, the conversation shifting to Mr. Jones and Mr. Conway going on about the lusciousness of Angela Bassett, and I settled back into my cut. Between the inevitable arguments, unwarranted clowning, and endless laughter, it's no wonder I couldn't help but feel at home in that space.

(Enter the home invaders. Peace and laughter across generations broken like tired skin from a lashing. Tale as old as time, pain fresh and new.)

A few minutes away from the final step of my cut, the ever-important hairline line-up, Mr. Conway rushed from the backroom. He shouted at us, frantically, and waved his hand for quiet. He changed the channel and stood staring at the screen as the update rolled across:

"ORLANDO TEEN SHOT BY POLICE; SOURCES SAY UNARMED BLACK MALE."

In an instant, all the levity in the room was erased. We listened on as the reporter relayed the information in fractions; some kids in an abandoned lot, a patrol car pulling up, alleged cellphone footage from a block away. They were still waiting to verify the tape, keeping us waiting for the final act.

"…Motherfuckers."

Mr. Conway said it, but we were all thinking it.

"What number do you reckon that is, this year alone? Shit, what number this month?"

"Lord knows, Tommy, Lord knows. The poor family…"

We were all just quiet for a few minutes, experiencing some terrible mixture of reactive sadness and déjà vu. No one wanted to talk: even if we had, no one wanted to hear it.

The anchor raised her hand to interrupt the reporter: "Mark, Mark, I'm sorry Mark but we have to stop for a minute, I am just receiving word that we have obtained a video of the alleged incident taken on an eyewitness's phone. We're going to play it now, viewers are warned that the content of this video is graphic in nature, please be advised. I repeat, the content is graphic in nature."

I should have listened.

"It appears that in the video the officer is attempting to detain one of the teenagers, right there - that's what he's doing as he tries to get the young man into a prone position. Now, you see there," she said as the background faded to highlight the soon-to-be victim's image, "that is allegedly Hakeem Fieldston, fifteen years old, the alleged shooting victim. We can see right there that he begins to move towards the officer, but clearly, we can also see that he has his hands out in front of him and has no visible weapon. The officer looks up from the other young man, reaches for his weapon and-"

The audio was muted. There wasn't any sound besides her voice. But I heard it.

We all heard it.

We all felt it.

The kid went down on his knees about a second after, falling to his side. The other kids on the video ran, and the recording stopped while the bystander was mid-turn. I almost wish he'd stayed, in spite of the obvious danger he was facing. Part of me wanted to see the face of the officer. I honestly just wanted to see what kind of face he had at that exact moment; it could have been the face of a dangerous, unstable officer who'd let some taunting get to his head at the worst time possible and was now experiencing a complete mental break; it could have been the face of a monster who'd just put down one more God-forsaken nigger, the definition of "Protect and Serve" in his mind; or maybe it was the face of someone who wasn't there, someone who had no idea what he'd just done or why he had done it and was even beginning to forget where he was. None of those faces would've made me less angry, less full of rage, but at least I would've known what kind of rage to feel.

"So, Tommy," Tyrell said, hate dripping from his voice, "where does that cracker right there go on your scale for 'nice white folk?'"

No one spoke.

"When's the last time you heard about a cop stopping a bunch of white kids from playing a damn game of kickball in their own neighborhood?" Mr. Jones asked to no one, "When is the honest-to-God last time you ever heard about some shit like that?"

For some reason, I actually tried to remember.

"Hey, Kola," Mr. Conway said as he looked at me, heavy eyes revealing the pain of an old soul who'd seen much worse, yet still felt the pain, "I know I might be rushing here, but if you end up having kids with this woman you like… maybe you should think about taking them somewhere else."

I hope my eyes never look like that.

I wish his eyes never had.

A Hustle

6 1/2.

Every work night I get six and a half hours of sleep. Sometimes I strive for seven, sometimes I settle for six. Six and a half seems good to me; I read it in a wellness book one time. The worst is Sunday though, those last few hours of the weekend. One more episode, one more Facebook post, one more paragraph of that article I've had open all day. It's somehow easier to stay awake the more tired I get.

14. 23.

The subway takes fourteen minutes. Walking takes twenty-three. Well, technically the fourteen minutes of subway time includes the six minutes of walking to the station, and the one minute of walking to the office, but I feel like walking to and from a train don't really count. It's insincere, in a sense. I like to walk some days, usually on the warmer days when it doesn't come with a strong chance of pneumonia (the subway's viral possibilities are mostly limited to the flu and several strains of gonorrhea). Having eleven extra minutes to spare is also a great motivator for the day, a testament to the power of your proactivity. Really puts a spring in your step.

999.

I like to imagine the amount of times I've forgotten my work badge is still under a thousand but that might be too optimistic. For something I need to literally enter the building, you'd think I could figure out an effective system for keeping it one easy location. I don't lose my apartment keys; I rarely misplace my cellphone; there were one or two scares with the wallet but all false alarms. Somehow two pieces of laminated plastic continue to evade my better senses of organization.

4,000.

"Midas' New York office employs four-thousand of the most intelligent, hard-working dedicated professionals in the financial services industry. As part of the global Midas family, two-hundred-fifty-thousand strong, we strive to deliver exceptional service, industry-leading insight and forward-thinking vision to our clients, all in the goal of creating a better, smarter marketspace."

26. 3.

This company owns twenty-six floors across three Midtown buildings, and somehow there's still never enough space in this office. People run around all day looking for any flat surface near an outlet, hoarding meeting rooms and skulking for empty desks like there was gold underneath. It's not an issue for me, my desk permanently situated and reserved, waiting for me each morning and left behind once my last drop of willpower is zapped. Sometimes I imagine it's taunting me, amused by the fact I choose to chain myself to it. On occasion I forsake my stationary tormentor and work from the comfort of somewhere between my bed, my kitchen table and the couch (usually some videogames involved by that point), but those are few and far between.

24. 7.

Hustle culture is a disease and I've started to display all of the symptoms. For those of you who are blissfully unaware of this phenomenon, allow me to give you a peek into the life of the modern young professional. The average college graduate is, as you surely know, the successful result of eighteen years of education, incalculable amounts of healthy sleep lost, and an innate craving for financial freedom from their parental units, topped with just a dash of mental trauma and sprinkled with a permanent fear of failure. You take that walking ball of nerves and false confidence, plant them in an office, and hand them stack after stack of work with the immediate concern of checking tasks off a list and a vague, more long-term notion of developing their skills. They need these jobs to afford rents they shouldn't have agreed to and lifestyles they shouldn't be living, so they stick around for a bit, waiting for their big break or something better to come along. An entire population of young, anxious would-be-overachievers who believe they're owed experiences and recognition: how do you motivate them to give their absolute, 100% maximum effort?

You turn the work itself into the lifestyle.

Monday morning turned from the death knell of the

weekend to the dawn of five fresh chances for productivity. Offices got more comfortable, less cubicles and more open spaces, the illusion of wide-open space inside the confines of writable walls littered with notes. They invented this thing called a flat hierarchy, a conceptual social structure where your boss is theoretically on the same level as you but realistically can still dismiss and disregard you on a whim. What really sells it though are the perks, that's where they sink their teeth in; when your place of work also becomes your place of dining, exercise, recreation and even sleep, what sense does it really make to go home? Why go all the way back home to eat out and sweat it off on the treadmill when you can do all that at the same place you also happen to produce the content/software/product/manna/output that defines your entire personhood?

You don't really notice it at first, the signs of your own internal decay; for me it started the first time I read an inspirational LinkedIn post that didn't trigger my gag reflex. I brushed it off as an unusual reaction to an exceptionally well-written piece of schlock, but then I found myself repeating some of the catchier bits in my head as I crunched away at a spreadsheet. The problem became more apparent after I began to spend moments of free time wondering if I was "utilizing my connections to their fullest potential," or whether or not I was "defining my brand." That one in particular always bothered me, defining my brand, the farthest rationalization of megalomania we've managed to come up with. One particularly nauseating article I came across asked me to grab a piece of paper and pen, sit down for five minutes, and come up with five words that defined my value.

Fearless
Unrelenting
Critical
Keen
Uplifting
Have to say, I think I nailed it.

200. 85,000.

I was hired straight out of university, picked up by the firm during the madness of recruiting season. They handed me a full-time job offer before I was even able to cope with the end of my days of socially acceptable alcoholism, and like every other choice I was making those days, I made my decision based on nothing but general optimism and a strong sense of resignation. I needed a job to justify the four years of tuition my parents had to pay, and they needed someone with the exact combination of grades, internship-acquired skills, diversity bonus and borderline decent personality to fill a spot in their class.

I was one of roughly two hundred associates hired in the New York office for the year, which means I was exactly 0.5% as important to the company as I believed in my own head. The starting salary was an even $85,000, lacking the signing bonus I was hopeful for but slightly exceeding my already inflated expectations. After signing away a reasonable two to three years of my life, the rest of the semester turned into a blur, some combination of coordinating the apartment-hunting effort, showing up to class late and blacking out for three out of five nights during Senior Week. Graduation came and went, and I found myself with three months to kill before move-in day. Most people use this time for vacation or creative exercise, something they might feel they won't be able to do anymore once professional life starts. Maybe it was the acceptance of inevitable misery, or maybe it was just the surprising calmness of a whole summer with nothing to do except wait, but none of those urges hit me. I was anxious but not about the last days of suspended adolescence; I was worried that I wouldn't be able to hack it, that I'd end up back at Mommy and Daddy's with nothing to show for my supposed brilliance.

I was worried it would all be for nothing. Especially what happened that night.

#NULL!

Bill Gates may be a philanthropist whose generosity puts most multibillionaires to shame, as well as a certifiable genius, but he also invented Microsoft Excel, which means that he's basically the devil in my book. I'm obviously aware that the program revolutionized the modern workspace and is far, far easier than what came before it, but none of that shit helps make the hours go by faster as I input number after number, function after function, table after table. I know that I'll never understand the pains and trials of childbirth, but I still can't imagine it's quite as brutal as spending hours trying to figure out what's going wrong with an Excel function only to realize that it was, in fact, the simplest mistake possible for anyone who isn't an abject moron.

I still remember the first time someone asked me to

help them make a growth-share matrix, my head nodding rhythmically as I racked my brain for some idea of what she was asking for. I would later learn that the best way to approach these situations is to simply ask a damn question or two and use Google to fill in the rest, but at the time I saw questions as signs of weakness and weakness as a quick route to getting fired. For those of you who expect this part to include some definition of what a growth-share matrix's, refer to the previous sentence.

50. 50.

When it comes to the topic of coworkers, I can genuinely say I lucked out. Given all the nightmare stories I always hear, all the tales of harassers and power-mad bosses, of ass-kissers and professional office politicians, the fact that I only hate half the people I share an office with is amazing.

To be clear, I don't hate them in the sense that I wish someone would burst in the door and give another good case against the Second Amendment, I just mean that they bother me deeply on some level due to factors both within and outside their control. Take for example my first manager, Bradley: Bradley was the type of blue-blood asshole one would absolutely expect to find at a place like Midas, but would still very much like to avoid. He hailed from some corner of New England that likely had the stench of obscene wealth and Native American blood all over it, and when he wasn't going on about some big client he'd managed to impress or hot date he'd managed to lay, he would start yapping away about his goddamn regattas. The fact that it's perfectly acceptable for rich WASPs to get away with using a fancy Italian word to describe a simple boat race might be one of the things I hate most about this country, or at least indicative of it. He'd done crew in high school and at Cornell, and had thus learned over the years that if he just sold it hard enough, he could in fact turn being an amateur boat paddler into an entire personality. One time, after offering me backhanded praise on a presentation to the project team, he asked if I would be interested in hitting the erg machine with him sometime. After I politely declined, he proceeded to explain in great detail exactly which of his three girlfriends had the best blowjob skills.

He was probably the worst of the bunch.

Probably.

There was my mentor, Hiroshi, a senior associate with a specialty for speaking fast and saying little. If you're having trouble imagining that combination, then just imagine short, choppy sentences jampacked with information and leaving zero room for interpretation. Eventually I just started to record every tenth word and hope I could piece it together. Normally that word "mentor" evokes some measure of familiarity, a sacred bond between a wise elder and a passionate youth, but that wasn't exactly how the relationship had come about. I was assigned to be his mentee by my transitional coach, who had been assigned by my positional coordinator, in collaboration with my performance management leader and under the rigid oversight of my HR counselor. Like any good product one hopes to put to use, no expense in money, time, or pretense was spared to make sure I started on the right foot and stayed firmly on the path of profitable productivity. His role in all of that was to help answer any questions I might have about what it takes to succeed, and to his credit, he always enjoyed those one-on-one conversations; he also enjoyed not responding to emails and randomly messaging me with inspirational life quotes. Some people are just born to be confusing.

There weren't any other real standout nuisances, the rest of them blending into a generally annoying entity that I could tolerate with extreme discrimination. As for the other half of the office, there really isn't anything to point out; my office was full of talented, smart, creative and energetic professionals. We pushed each other, encouraged optimal performance, and celebrated wins with genuine excitement; the other 90% of the time, however, we mostly just sat around performing tasks that ranged from mundane to critical and hoping we were doing just enough to earn a raise and promotion.

2.

If you asked me to describe my job to a stranger, there are two versions I could give: the rehearsed and the realistic. I could spit out such magnificent phrases as "helping organizations create improvement infrastructures," "facilitating procedural progression into advanced stages," and "evaluating client needs to discover hidden opportunities for growth and positive change." I could sit here and tell you that my job is to work towards the client's best interest and deliver on Midas' promise of exceptional service.

I could serve you that steaming pile of horseshit, or I could tell you that financial services consist of helping businesses make more money by telling them things they could probably figure out for themselves. There's a lot more to it, obviously, but not as much as one would like to think.

0.

Is this what I want to do with my life?

Is this it?

It all ends up here?

What about saving the world? OK, fine, forget the world, but what about the kids? Going back home to Nigeria, making a difference? Didn't you want to build schools or feed people or, I don't know, end the violence; didn't you want to give back?

That voice was always different from the usual ones, more incessant, with a higher pitch. It hit different tones and frequencies, puncturing the continuum of my mental flow until it ruptured my comfort and forced me to examine the damage.

Is this it?

One of the best companies around, good pay, a future I could actually plan around. Everything I've been promised for doing as I was told.

Is this it?

My parents came to this country so that this life could happen for me, and that's what I did. What else is there? Life isn't some "dreams come true" B-movie, there's not some great fate to be discovered. Study, work, save, spend, and die; simple as possible.

Is this it?

Is this it?

Is this it?

I'm still waiting for my answer.

A Dream

A field of flowers. There were more colors than my mind could conceive of, every point on the rainbow. It was an endless terrain, stretching past the horizon and doubtless beyond that. The sky was blue, but, well, a brighter blue, as if only a thin inch of atmosphere was separating me from the blackness of space. I looked down and saw a path forming itself, so I began to walk. The path kept forming and I kept walking, marching mindlessly, eyes forward, focused solely on movement. Time passed, although I can't say how much.

As I followed along, it dawned on me that something was deeply wrong. The air was starting to turn, and the colors were starting to fade. The path had stopped forming. I was stranded, and everything was collapsing around me. I ran. I ran nowhere and far away, only to realize I'd barely moved. The flowers continued to fade around me, but they didn't decay; the color vanished but the form remained. A translucent plastic graveyard. I ran again. I knew I couldn't afford to stop, so I just kept at it, hoping that something would dawn on me before my legs gave out.

In the middle of my sprint, my foot caught on something in the ground and sent me tumbling. I stood up, turned back, scanned the ground and noticed a protrusion from the ground. I got to work digging out my treasure. It took me a few seconds to realize what I'd uncovered. It felt like hours.

I screamed.

It was a skull. Cracked on the side. Shaped like my own.

It was him.

He looked at me.

He spoke.

Help. Me.

I screamed.

The flowers vanished.

A Dress

She awoke the way she always awoke, eyes-half red and mind half-functional. If the mornings were a person to her, they'd be something between a childhood bully and an annoying neighbor. There were always too many things to do: too much time to spend on her hair, too many clothes to pick from, too little fucks to give about whether or not to wear make-up that day. And those were on the days when she got out of bed at all; the ones in bed were easier on the soul, but much more of a drain on the mind.

11:00 AM--not awful, I suppose, she convinced herself, still better than waking up in the evening.

For all the times that she averred her hatred of actress clichés, her room contained an entire treasure chest of them: playbills from Broadway shows, an extravagant vanity mirror with lights, a decorative changing curtain, movie posters featuring her inspirations on her wall—Angela Bassett, Diana Ross and Whoopi Goldberg, in particular—and, la pièce de résistance, a picture of the Hollywood sign, right on her door to see every morning on the way out. The walls were her shrine to her own ambitions, her room a temple of worship for the divine muses of her craft.

She tumbled out of her lavender sheets and pink and white bed to put a few dents in her too-long list, and turned towards the door to make her trek to the first arena of battle, the bathroom. Usually, waking up this late would mean that the place would be ripe for the taking but this morning, like many before, one of her comrades had been just one step ahead of her. Marinating on the pointlessness of even waking up at all, she went back to the kitchen and decided to start with food instead.

She lived in that constantly conflicting space between loving every inch of her body and scouring the internet for weight loss tips. On those days when the mean girls in middle school had called her one too many a mean name, she'd come home, crying and distraught, like children are wont to do; yet somehow, every time, by the end of the night she'd managed to remind herself that only one opinion mattered. Her fragility was integral to her strength, her ability to feel the pain giving her the fortitude to rise above it. As she stood there, trying to decide between making a strawberry-banana-kale smoothie and cooking up some eggs and bacon, one of those many middle-school melancholy memories hit, but she shrugged it off, casting it aside for recollections of those times she made the boys' hearts stop in the years to come after. She was the goddess of her own world, as all women tend to be. She picked the smoothie, not because of the harsh words, but because a choice is a choice.

As she made her nutritionist-approved meal, she began another one of her daily rituals, flipping through her phone apps like pages in a bad comic. There were posts to like, updates to notice, photos to heart, and texts to respond to, including some from a particularly interesting if slightly full-of-it guy. Her morning was for her, though; she decided to bless him with her time later on in the day.

"Hey babe, good morning."

"Bonjour, Pierre. How's it going today?"

"UGH, everything is terrible and I want to die but also I want ice cream. It is hotter than a Beyoncé video out there. Honey, are you just getting up? You still have your morning face."

"If by 'morning face' you mean 'post-rest glow,' then yes, thank you for noticing; if not, you can keep your little Frenchie mouth shut."

"Moi? Ah, ma chère Abi, tu es terrible!"

She tossed a strawberry at him just to punctuate her point. While María was the social planner for her entire existence, Pierre was her go-to for in-the-house clowning around; it made sense, given the apartment dynamics. María worked a regular schedule at Lavanya Bari, slaving away for a woman she so lovingly referred to as "Meryl Streep in The Devil Wears Prada but desi." Samaira would be around sometimes but usually spent most of the day bumming around with the other local comedy acts before the nighttime sets started-- when she wasn't on the road, that is. Pierre worked directly from home, so he was always around, lounging in different sections of the apartment as he powered his way through the creative process. The two bandmates, Yuki and Claire, were either in rehearsal, in the city hustling for gigs, or, as had just started recently, in each other's pants, even if they both insisted that it was just casual experimentation. Point is, they weren't around too much.

Abi, on the other hand, tried to balance out her laziness with aspiration; while her mornings scarcely included the early hours, she kept her days busy. Having just finished a show and waiting to hear back from a few callbacks, she spent most of that time doing the one thing she loved as much as acting: putting smiles on faces. She'd started volunteering at the local shelter a while back and had become a star in no time, beloved by both workers and patrons alike. That smile, those damn white diamonds, she'd make them shine for people living their darkest days and bring a little light in each time. She did more than just smile for them, however; she loved listening, hearing their stories, getting to know them as people. In her mind, the way to keep herself humble and grounded was to remind herself of the humanity of others, constantly and consciously. When she asked them for their stories, they thought she wanted to hear about the mistakes they had made, the problems they faced, the suffering and the torment. When she requested stories of their first kisses, their Christmases, the places they've been and the things they've seen, they were shocked. She treated them like she desperately wanted to be treated; as subjects of interest and appreciation, evocative and powerful in the tales that they told. I guess she figured that if even one of those people ever left a conversation feeling a little more important, a little more valued as their own being, then she'd done a job well done.

One shower, ninety minutes of hair and make-up, and seven tried-on and tossed-away outfits later, she was out of the door and on her way to greet a new day, if a little reluctantly. Her only plan at that moment was figuring out a way to stave off the depths of boredom; the goal was to make it to the evening and go for a little shopping with María. A lofty ambition, indeed, but she was nothing else if not persevering.

She dropped by her usual cafés and made chit-chat

with the gathered ensembles; the writer two rewrites and a plot away from his best work, the elderly folks reading their newest pickup from the bookstore, the poets and painters and philosopher-fakers, all lounging about in an embrace of the new-age intelligentsia.

She stopped by to see Ms. Kenchington, a former flowerchild turned party girl turned Manhattan theater scene personality who had somehow ended up a confidante to an aspiring African actress. The woman had moved to the states from the English countryside at seventeen and proceeded to embrace everything the 60's had to offer; the drugs, the sex, the music, the air of revolution and the blood of martyrs. She'd seen everything and had been everywhere; she'd even managed to get herself on board Led Zeppelin's plane, The Starship, for most of their 1975 North American Tour. If the actresses on Abi's wall were her temple goddesses, then Ms. K was more like a benevolent yet chaotic cult deity.

"So, how'd that last commercial go, love? The one for the mobile phone or whatever it was."

"It was fantastic! The director said I was the best one all day, so I'm excited, and she was lovely too. I still haven't heard back for that *Mr. Robot* part so that's a drag, but you can't win them all."

"Oh, hush now Abi, you know you'll get it. I can feel success in your aura today, you're glowing, darling, absolutely glowing. You know what you should do? We should do a ritual cleansing together, clear out your negative chakra, you'll feel like a brand-new being."

"Hmm, that would be… something! It definitely would be something. Oh, where's Gilbert by the way?"

"Oh, he's skulking around somewhere, morose as usual. Honestly that cat worries me sometimes, maybe he needs more feline company."

Abi had a crazy cat lady joke on the ready, but she figured that maybe it wasn't the right call: "The more the merrier!"

After she left Mrs. K to her contemplations and meditations, she stopped by her favorite ramen joint and picked up a quick bowl. Like any ramen restaurant in the city worth mentioning, the entrance was below ground, the cooking was out in the open, and the dish was beyond description. Yuki had told them all about this place after finding out that her mom knew the owner from their high school days in Fukuoka together. The noodles had the perfect width-to-softness ratio, the short rib was practically in liquid form, and he used this black garlic aoli that could be easily confused with edible cocaine. The whole thing was soaked in a creamy pork broth and an egg on top, looking like a dream and tasting like a dream you don't want to wake up from.

The next few hours were spent at home, dishing with Pierre about what's-his-face and discussing the mysteries of love in general. He always erred to the side of the romantic while Abi believed in cautious optimism; they both valued love, they just expected different things from it. Having just gotten out of a fling with a married man, Pierre's faith in true romance was in a particularly precarious position. Abi, on the other hand, was far more comfortable, and far more reserved as a result.

"Soooo, do you like him or not? Kolawally, or whatever his name is."

"It's Kolawole, and for the freakin' millionth time, he's all right. Who cares about him, what ended up happening with your big, tall dash of Arabian spice?"

"Honestly babe, I just don't understand; one minute he's Mister Smooth and sexy man of many lovers, and the next he's a guilt-ridden cheater. It was like he suddenly snapped out of a month-long trance. He started getting emotional, talking about his husband; ce n'etait pas ma tasse de thé. Needless to say, he and I are no longer on speaking terms."

"Well honey, that's what happens you mess around with a married man. Should've known better."

"Oh bitch, hush, you know you'd break off a piece of that sexy director you were always gushing about: Monsieur Axelrod, oh là là! Don't judge me."

She tried to find the argument but she was honestly at a loss for words. She decided to opt for throwing a pillow at him instead; her argumentative tactics were top notch.

María finally gave Abi the call to meet her down in Soho, ending another bout of absent-minded distraction. She loved shopping with María, mostly because it was their favorite shared activity, but also because her best friend was blessed with the fashion taste of a *Vogue* editor but with the budget consciousness of an immigrant mother. She was looking forward to getting a brand new, drop-dead gorgeous top.

Not for any particular reason, of course; nope, not for any reason at all.

A View

"So, do you think the cop's gonna get indicted?"

"I don't know, it seems like they almost never do, even with the videos. I was at the shelter when we got the alerts on our phone. We watched the video after we got home."

"I was out at the barber's, it came up on the TV. I've never seen that place so quiet, but I guess words wouldn't have been of much use. How do you describe something both familiar and unfathomable?"

"'Evil' would be my word of choice."

It was only our fifth or so conversation but I was already beginning to appreciate her penchant for poignancy.

"Yeah, guess that pretty much sums it up, doesn't it. Maybe he'll get the indictment, maybe not, but he's not going to jail. The system never convicts the system, unless someone's paying someone."

"Can't you drop the cynical schtick for a minute? We should be about action right now, not apathy."

"Well I would like to think that I'm more realistic than cynical, but maybe you have a point. I don't know, maybe I just have fatigue; I was in that shit for Trayvon, Mike Brown, Garner, Freddie Gray, Philando Castile… who was that one from South Carolina?"

"Sterling, Alton Sterling. And don't forget Sandra Bland."

"Yeah, them too, and every other black body in the dirt

that CNN doesn't pick up; hell, I got heated when I learned about Latasha Harlins."

"Which one was that?"

"1995, a Korean store owner shot this fifteen-year-old girl in the back of the head because they got into an argument after the lady thought the girl was stealing. She had the fucking money in her hand too. Judge sentenced her to a $500 fine, five years of probation, and some community service. My sister's that age... how much you think they'd charge for her life?"

We let the question hang in the air, the answer eluding our desperate grasps.

"Point is, all of those years of fighting and marching and protesting, and a fifteen-year-old still gets an execution sentence for looking at the police the wrong way. How am I not supposed to be tired?"

"You're supposed to be tired, and then you're supposed to get angry, and then you're supposed to fight. You need to catch up on steps two and three with the rest of us. My homegirl Rhonda is hosting an organizing meeting on Tuesday, you should come."

An organizing meeting? Really? A meeting to plan more meetings? What's next, a book about another book?

"And what is Rhonda planning on organizing exactly?"

"Transportation down to Orlando for the marches and setting up a victim fund."

Huh... maybe I am the asshole here. Interesting.

"I'll think about it."

"Good, I think you'll like it. Maybe you can even take that off that perma-smirk for a little while. Speaking of taking things off of you," she paused, the cheeky setup providing just the right kind of segue, "I like the fade, it's a good look on you. You ever think about trying to grow it all out?"

"This hair? Nah, tried it in high school once and I looked like a complete clown; my shit grows out to the side too much, end up looking like George Jefferson. That's not exactly the look to go for, as I'm sure you can imagine, so no, I don't do that anymore. What about you, how often do you change up your style?"

"Boy, have you not seen that Chris Rock documentary?"

"What was that?"

"*Good Hair*, it's a documentary. Watch that first and then figure out whether you want to talk about black woman hair. But, long story short, I got this about three months ago and I'm probably going to keep it for a while."

"Well, like you said, it's a good look."

"I know."

She smiled that damn smile again.

The day was going well so far, the heaviness of that particular conversation aside; we'd met up at around one for lunch at this Indian-Mexican fusion place she'd been wanting to try for a while, and from there we had gone to Washington Square Park to observe some of the madness. Summer weekends in the city are always a gold mine for people-watching, and we were able to bear witness to some truly fascinating specimens. I'll try to give you a highlight reel:

A family of about nine in matching tee shirts and camouflage hats, the father looking like what would happen if Stone Cold Steve Austin had a lumberjack beard and was about six-foot-seven, and the mother seeming to have been crafted at the same factory where Fox News gets its female correspondents from, right down to the exquisitely crafted cheekbones. I would go into detail on the seven children, but I honestly think they might have been septuplets; seven young boys with barely discernable differences in height or facial expression. They were basically like the hardcore version of the Romneys.

Five elderly Asian women in a tour group gushing over two burly men in flannel and camouflage playing bluegrass for tips. The ladies dancing like it was nobody's business and flashing the cash in what looked like the hilarious opening scenes for a comedy about male strippers.

A tiny man, painted from head to toe in white plaster, standing on top of a miniature Roman column and holding a golden orb while he posed, standing on one leg and staring over the horizon. The only reason that I know this was a tiny man is because I thought he was an actual statue and went to take a picture of him. When I did so, he proceeded to wink at me mid-shot, filling with a terror that I hadn't known prior to that day.

A very old, very married couple, very loudly arguing about where the McDonald's was and disagreeing over whether to ask for directions. The wife laid out a very compelling case, citing relevant examples such as "the time you got us lost in that Italian village," and "the time we missed the plane for little Noah's bar mitzvah because you took the wrong exit" and, my personal favorite, "the time you took the wrong turn on that road in Corsica because you were staring at that girl's ass." The husband, meanwhile, taking a more action-based approach, proceeding to follow up his eventual success in finding the McDonald's with the cockiest, widest, slyest "told you so" grin I've ever seen in my life. I think there was a clear winner there.

Two dudes who were dressed entirely too much like the Columbine shooters. There's nothing funny to add on here, those two just looked creepy as hell so we left. I don't play that shit.

"So where are we going to again?"

"Well I figured we could go up to Central Park, hit up th Met? Or maybe get upto the Guggenheim."

"No, no let's stay in the Village," she agreed, "I love it around there, and it's been forever since I've walked around. There's this one place, Grey Art Gallery, that Pierre told me about."

"Pierre?"

"One of my flatmates, dummy, the comic artist."

"Ah, right, Pierre. What's his graphic novel about again?"

"It's about this bully who makes a kid kill himself and then sees his ghost everywhere. He can't decide yet if he wants it to be a redemptive story where the bully learns something, or whether the ghost is going to be the main character and learns empathy for the bully. Either way, it's some pretty messed up stuff. He is finished with the design work though."

"Jesus, that just sounds all sorts of depressing."

"Hey! We should go to Strand after this! What do you think?" We'd only hung out for a few hours total but I was already noticing something; she had a habit of doing a little hop every time she got really excited about a new idea. It reminded me entirely too much of my now-dead pet rabbit Thumper, and I mean that in the best way possible.

"Yeah sure, I love that place. Last time I was there I picked up *1984*."

"Had you never read it before? Come on man, that's some high school freshmen shit. Step your game up."

"Yeah, yeah, whatever; it was one of the top entries on my 'Books I Should Have Read By Now So I'll Just Keep Pretending' list, and so I finally picked it up a few months ago and got through it. You must have a few of those yourself."

"Hmm… I guess the worst offender would be *The Great Gatsby*. I don't know how or why but I never got around to it."

"Oh, so you're going to sweat me over *1984* while you've never read F. Scott Fitzgerald's seminal work? That story is the encapsulation of the American Dream, in all its glory and horror."

"*Wowww*, 'glory and horror', and I thought I was the thespian here"

"Hey, I just realized that I never even asked you what your play was about, the one that you finished a little while ago."

"Oh right; yeah, the show was called *Sins of the Sea…*"

She went on to describe a pretty remarkable tale, although not remarkable enough for me to spend five pages explaining it to you. It was something about two cousins and their mutual love interest engaged in a WWII England love triangle. They come together as kids, grow up, join the war effort and the whole thing ends with the guy getting shot down by a Nazi U-Boat and the girls reconciling over a hug. The power of forgiveness is a wonderful thing.

Abi played the main girl, Penelope's, Commanding Officer Annalise Baxter, a particularly brash, yet sweet instructor who eventually becomes a confidante. She explained the complexities of playing a woman officer, getting the tone right, and a few other acting bits.

Oh, and this part: "Man, I killed that shit! I'm telling you, there wasn't a dry eye in the house when I was out there, either had them laughing or crying. Annalise only gives out the realest, truest, deepest advice, like the big sister everyone needs and only appreciates after they get all their shit together, which is essentially just me in real life anyway. You know, maybe I should have been in the army, I was really convincing as an officer? Shit, ain't like I'm gonna run eight hours a day though, fuck that noise; anyway—"

It went on like that for about eight more minutes, trust me you don't need any more to get the point. She finally finished her recounting of the play, right up to the encore, and then went on to mention: "I'm sure I could get a recording of it if you want. Maybe we can watch it together sometime?"

I appreciated the intimacy of the request while recognizing my own reluctance to sit through the melancholy-sounding affair.

"Yeah I'd love to. Um, one thing though…. Where the hell are we?"

We both took a second to look around, trying to figure out how far we'd walked and what part of the Village, if any, we were in. It was then that I remembered.

"Hey Abi, I really think God's trying to troll us right now."

"Huh?" She replied, confused.

"Come on, I'll show you."

Less than two minutes later we were at Pier 45, overlooking the Hudson. After getting lost because we were talking about a play mostly set near the ocean, we had found ourselves looking out at a river, on a beautiful summer day without a cloud in the sky.

"Ah, now I get it."

"Well, it may not be as scenic as an oceanside cliff, but I still like the view. Want to go sit?"

She agreed and we went and found a nice spot next to some very comfortable sunbathers.

"Whole lot of paleness going on round here. What do you think, should I bust out my bikini too?"

"Hmm... the guy in me wants to say yes, but the gentleman in me wants to say yes politely, so I'm totally torn on the issue."

She laughed at that one and proceeded to roll up her shift, exposing her plump midriff and leaving her booty shorts to cover the rest. I decided to join the crowd and get my shirt off, letting the sun's last round of rays for the day blast me. We laid down in silence, really enjoying the turn of events.

"Hey, Abi."

"Yeah?"

"Why do you think Sophie forgave her?"

"What do you mean?"

"Like, why did Sophie forgive Penelope? I know Arthur died so they were both upset, but it didn't change the fact that he still cheated on her with her cousin. Arthur never reaches out to her or gets forgiveness from her, so why does she give it to Penelope the minute she sees her?"

"Hmmm… I think that that's just the way life is, y'know?"

"For someone who speaks professionally you're not great with your own words."

The punch to the arm she gave me hurt a bit, but it was

worth it.

"Shut up! I mean that's just what life boils down to sometimes; forcing ourselves to connect with people even if it doesn't make sense, just because we all need the connection. The girl just lost the love of her life after finding out that he and her cousin, basically a sister to her, both betrayed her. She was broken, totally and completely, and then out of nowhere that same girl shows up. People need other people, especially at our lowest; she just needed somebody to hold on to, to share the pain with. You asked why she forgave her, but I don't think she did; I think she just couldn't bear to have any hate when she was so desperately in need of love. They probably took a while to get close again, and it would definitely be awkward, but we need love more than we like to hate, and that's why it always wins in the end."

I took a few seconds to really let her words sink in. I imagined myself in Sophie's shoes, totally broken, robbed of the two people I held closest in the world, one physically and one emotionally, and then seeing one of them return to me. Would it really be possible to hold that hate, letting it clog the hole that can only be healed with love? Would I be able to live like that?

The more I thought about it, the more daunting a task it seemed.

We laid there for hours, chatting about happier things and watching the sun make those purple kisses to the horizon. Once evening rolled around, Abi had to keep a date with María, but she told me in no uncertain terms that we would be hanging out the following weekend.

We kissed by the waterside, and held hands on the subway.

We kissed on the subway, and held hands on the walk to her place. We kissed in front of her place, and I let her hand slip out of mine.

I could have held on to that hand until the sun came again.

A Good Night Kiss

If she'd told me she was religious and that she didn't want to offend the Lord, I would've understood; if she'd told me she was still a virgin, I would've understood; if she'd told me that she just wanted to take it slow, even though she started fucking the last guy five minutes after she met him, hell, even that I would've understood. What I couldn't understand, and what I was trying to force myself to, was exactly what she meant by "Soon, I promise."

Soon? It's been weeks. Soon, when? Tomorrow soon? Next year soon? Heat death of the universe soon? What the hell does "soon" mean? For that matter, what exactly is she promising me for, like she doesn't want to for some reason? If she didn't want to then why did we hang out all summer? What the hell's going on?

One overly-price-hiked Uber ride later, I was at Abi's, standing on the same steps where we'd shared a few of our most intimate moments so far. After running through my usual internal monologue, I made a vow not to worry about Curtis' nonsense and to have a good time with Abi and her friends. Weed, some food, a free rock concert and then some bar hopping; all the ingredients for an epic night were laid out in front of me, and all I had to do now was not fuck any of them up. It was a tall task, but I set myself to it.

Remember Abi's two loft mates that I told you about,

Yuki and Claire? Their band, "ØD/GIN," as luck would have it, managed to book a last-minute replacement gig at Mercury Lounge, the NYC indie rock scene equivalent of a final interview. Yuki, a surly Japanese girl with bright blue hair and a perchant for perfectly ripped jeans, was the lead singer and played rhythm guitar. Her roommate Claire, a dirty-blonde, tatted-up Canadian, played the electric. The other two members only lived about ten minutes away, so there was never any issue with rehearsal, an essential condition in the race to make it out of the dive bar scene and start getting some serious looks on the circuit. This would be their first major gig, so naturally they told literally everyone that they'd ever met about it, living mates included, and by extension, myself.

Thankfully for both my patience and my knees, Abi's building had an elevator, and since I was riding up to her floor alone, I decided to give myself a little pump-up speech. As I was getting myself hyped up and trying to keep the demons quiet, the door opened, and a middle-aged couple came in, mistakenly thinking it was going down but politely waving off their mistake. Why am I bothering to mention one of the most mundane things that happens on a day-to-day basis? Because the lady, nicely put together and clearly ready for a night out on the town, was standing right next to me with what I hope was in fact her husband's fresh cum, just scattered all over her blonde hair.

The levels of awkwardness I experienced in those twenty seconds were enough to last twenty lifetimes. I'm honestly getting a queasy feeling in my stomach just writing about it now. The thing is, the entire time, while I was trying to keep my eyes away from staring right at her and my nose distracted from the distinctive aroma, I couldn't help but race through a list of questions in my mind: Do they know? Is this some sort of weird kink? Does only the husband know and this is his idea of a prank? Does she know and she's just doing some power trip shit, daring her husband to make a scene in public? Do they do this shit every day or am I just the unlucky asshole who got in the elevator the same night they decided to do some shit they saw in a bad porno? How fucking long do the elevators take to go up three floors in this place?

God, deciding that I'd been punished for some sins long forgotten, let me off that elevator right when my sanity was at its brink. Figuring that meeting all of Abi's friends for the first time and smoking would be weird enough without mentioning cum-hair lady, I decided that I would just keep that incident somewhere way back in my repressed memory area, the same place where I keep most of my middle-school interactions with girls and that one weird thing that happened when I was wrestling in high school. I finally got to her door, 13B, and knocked.

A very tall man, with some spiffy khaki shorts and a spectacular black-polka-dotted white button-down, opened the door to welcome me in.

"Vous êtes Kolawole, oui? Bonsoir mon ami! Je suis Pierre, Abi m'a beaucoup parlé de toi!"

Clearly, Abi had told her loft mate that I spoke French; what she had neglected to inform him was that I only took enough courses to pass a requirement for graduation, and that any attempt to converse with an actual Frenchman would leave me with little more than frustrating confusion. We continued our francophone conversation as we settled into the living room. Their apartment was laid out similarly to ours; with a large couch surrounding a TV across from a kitchen and three bedrooms on either side. But their place was a much different flavor than ours, with all of the urban photography and sports memorabilia swapped out for abstract paintings and new-age wall adornments. We sat down as I attempted to remember everything that I'd learned that one night before the proficiency exam in May all those years ago.

"Ah merci ! Abi m'a parlé de vous aussi. De quelle région de la France êtes-vous?"

"Je suis né à Nice mais j'ai déménagé à Paris à l'âge de sept ans. Je suis passé en Amérique pour l'université et je suis venu ici depuis."

"Ah, je comprends maintenant. Mon ami est allé à Nice une fois en vacances."

"Vraiment ? Ah, je manque ma ville natale, la beauté, l'histoire, l'art, c'est tout…"

"Hey KoKo!"

Oh, thank you sweet Baby Jesus, I was running on fumes there.

"Hey there, short stuff."

"Sorry, we were helping Sami pick out an outfit for tonight and she was not being cooperative. She and María always get into it over clothes. Anyway, what do ya think?"

She posed in her black bralette with sexy black jeans and boots, all put together with a red and black flannel wrapped around the waist. I have to say, she was easily the best-dressed girl I'd ever been involved with; I guess living with a professional fashionista like María has its perks.

"Outstanding, ten out of ten."

"Like a star that dropped from the heavens and landed in '90's Seattle," Pierre added, clearly a fan of extra emphasis, "Magnifique, darling!"

She accepted our praise with a dainty bow, and as she was settling down next to me María and Samaira came out of the bedroom. María had gone with a stylish golden romper for the evening, and Samaira, who was exactly as crazy-looking as I had imagined from Abi's stories, was rocking a sleeved blue sequin top over white jeans.

"Hey Kola, long time no see!" María said cheerfully, clearly not ready to ask me anything about Curtis but knowing that after a few drinks at the show she would be ready to annoy me all night on the topic.

"Hey María! You look great - well, you all do. And you're Samaira, then?"

She had a super-short brunette pixie cut and a face sharp enough to cut diamonds. She was right in-between her two female companions, height-wise, but while Abi was the definition of curvy and María looked like all her body fat went to her breasts and thighs, Samaira was a waif with a petite frame mismatched against a large personality.

"Yo, so you're Abi's new squeeze, right? She never shuts the hell up about you, made you sound like the second coming of Christ or something."

"As a Catholic I should be a little miffed at the causal blasphemy, but a compliment is a compliment. You're a comedian?"

"I like to imagine so, but maybe everyone's just always laughing at me and not with. Wouldn't that be a thing to find out."

"Eh, wouldn't be too bad, at least you'd have been getting paid for it."

"HA! Yeah, that's one way to put it; my dignity for peanuts, an unfair trade entirely in my favor. Just got an agent last month so maybe that whole 'financial stability' thing might start up, but we'll see. Speaking of which, if you happen to find yourself in Blackfoot, Idaho next month, come check me out, I'm doing three nights to kick off my first big road tour."

"I can think of a few places I'd rather than be than Idaho… Guantánamo Bay might be up there. Maybe Topeka, Kansas."

She went on to inform me that Topeka, Kansas was in fact a stop on the road tour, and that devolved into me writing down all her scheduled New York shows. Girl really knew how to fill up her seats.

The bottles of liquor started to make their appearance and suddenly we were having one of those lovely apartment sessions. The conversations flowed and moved, pulling people in before they moved on to the next thing. I found myself switiching back and forth between María's scathing takedown of the new Versace catalog and Pierre's intense *Peanuts* fascination (his favorite character is Linus, in case that means anything to you).

"Alright mofos, pizza is on the way and the Netflix is cued up. Who's ready to get higher than a straight white male's sense of entitlement?"

We all plopped ourselves down as Samaira began packing a fat bowl made in the likeness of Mickey Mouse. As she was getting the recreational tools ready, María and Abi began trying to pick what to watch. The two performed the standard streaming service ritual of starting at the shows that were ready to be continued, gleefully expressing how great it would be to try something new, scrolling down every single category listed and only barely scrolling through any of the selections, discussing what new shows or movies would be a good idea to watch, realizing that they'd spent far too much of their time not actually watching anything, and then, eventually and inevitably, picking something out from the shows that were ready to be continued. The result of that process in this instance was *Stranger Things*.

"Hell yeah," I exclaimed, "my two favorite things: competent child actors and tastefully forced nostalgia."

Abi sat back down and cuddled up to me while María sat on the other end, instructing Pierre on which wine to bring back from the well-appointed kitchen. Once Samaira was done with her preparations, we were ready to light up and begin our evening. I've never been a huge smoker myself, aside from the occasional bad weeks in college; I liked being high but between the constantly shifting statutes and the amount of effort involved in obtaining illegal drugs, I never cared enough to make it a habit. Samaira had gotten some primo shit, straight out of Jamaica according to what her dealer told her, and it was working rapidly. My high always starts the same way: first, the sides of my face get super tingly, enough to the point where a light breeze will make me feel like I'm in a wind tunnel, and then after that my right eyelid gets erratic. If the stuff is really good then sometimes I start to feel it in my hands; they start turning into jelly and then all of a sudden, the tapping of my fingers becomes a fifteen-minute drum solo. If it goes any further, then I get into "dancing-light" mode where colors start jumping around in front of me, but by the time I hit that level I'm already so high that I can't leave whatever piece of furniture I'm sitting in/lying on, and at that point I just resign myself to watching the magic happen.

Fortunately, between the five of us we simply didn't have enough to smoke for me to get that high, and by the time the food had arrived, we were already on our third and last bowl. Abi was blazed off her ass, so much so that I was genuinely thinking I would have to carry her. Pierre and María both seemed to be well on their way to cross-faded territory as the combination of wine and weed was beginning to work its magic on their brains, soaking and smoking simultaneously. Everyone dug into the food and as the drugs began to take their final effects, we entered the most-dreaded stage of the high cycle: fake-deep contemplation.

"Don't you wish you grew up in the 80's, man? Kids had so much fun then, and all the cartoons and toys were better," Pierre pondered, slowly becoming the physical embodiment of a Buzzfeed article.

"Nah man, fuckin' Reagan and shit, and like… Soviets and shit," babbled Samaira, making an excellent case for why drugs should never be the preparation for civilized discourse. "Star Wars was still good then, though, so there's that."

Conveniently forgetting the Ewoks there, pal… oh, and also the AIDS crisis. That sucked too.

María and I seemed to be the only ones in the room content with sitting down and just watching the show, and that surprised me more than anything else. I'd gelled with Samaira and Pierre rather quickly, but I honestly didn't think that I would have much in common with Mar í a, except for our inexplicable attractions to Curtis, of course. She seemed nice but I didn't care or understand much about fashion and she didn't seem to be much of an easygoing person. It was in that moment, however, that I realized we shared the most powerful bond possible: a never-ending desire for some goddamn peace and quiet when the TV is on. Better friendships have been built on far less.

Finally, at around 9:20 PM, Mar í a's phone alarm went off and it was like a light switch went off in her head. Suppressing whatever drug-induced fog she was under, she popped up and started rounding up her troops, telling us all to get up and check all our shit lest we forget something. In the meantime, she decided to order the Uber ride and set up the splits. I would later learn that María had grown up in a household with six brothers and one sister, all younger, and therefore was very much used to giving out commands to inattentive minds. I also later found out that the fashion industry is a lot, lot more than a bunch of ladies sitting around an office trying to figure out which clothes looked the prettiest; that shit is cut throat, and María's status as one of the rising stars in her company was as much a result of tireless effort and cold-blooded competitiveness as it was her eye for fuchsia skirts and white sunglasses. While Curtis had been given his unofficial status as leader of our group simply to placate him, María was a different beast altogether, a calculated, no-bullshit queen bee masquerading behind a warm smile.

My high began to settle a bit after we had all gotten into the car. Suddenly remembering that other people not immediately near me also existed in my life and that I needed to maintain the illusion of caring about that fact, I whipped out my phone to check for updates. Four texts. All from Stacy.

And just like that my vibe was killed.

She was going out to this bar with her work friends and wanted to know if I could come along; she even mentioned one of them was a big fan of the same anime show that I told her I liked, trying to mask an invitation to mess around at a bar as a chance for making new friends. She wasn't a very good liar, but I admired the effort.

So, there I was, in a car with the girl I really liked and all her friends, en route to an amazing night not fully guaranteed to end with sex, while an old hookup that I knew wanted to ride me like a bronco was blowing up my phone. If I was a little more baked at that moment I would've probably seen a Little Curtis and a Little Ravi pop up on my shoulders and start offering wildly contrasting advice. Little Curtis would probably tell me to just keep texting her all night, keep her revved up; I didn't have to hop out of the car or anything, but if Abi eventually decided that tonight wasn't the night, at least I would have some fun no matter what. Little Ravi would no doubt counter those arguments and tell me that what I was having with Abi was special and that I shouldn't fuck that up over a girl I didn't care about; in only a few weeks, we'd gone from strangers to nicknames and meeting her friends, and in my experience, that rarely tended to happen. They'd both go on like that for a few minutes until they would eventually get bored and start talking about soccer or something funny, and would then slowly dissipate, leaving me alone with my thoughts once again.

I put the phone away and hopped into Samaira's and

Abi's riveting conversation on Korean barbeque. Samaira was espousing the deliciousness of the lettuce wrap technique while Abi was insisting that the only way to truly enjoy the meat was straight from grill to mouth. It was a fascinating debate, but my distractions required attention. I really didn't want anything to do with Stacy, at all, but I also *realllly* wanted to have sex. A horndog I am not, but every man has needs. I decided that I was going to just let the night run its course, and all I knew for sure was that I wasn't about to ruin anything as a result of my chronic indecision.

We arrived at Mercury Lounge about twenty minutes after we left the apartment, when the line was at its peak. Fortunately for us, Yuki had remembered to put our names down on the list so we got in right away and found a great spot on the mezzanine with two tables to push together. The venue was as small as advertised, a plus in this specific instance as opposed to a minus. The floor was devoid of seating and the bar was to the side of the main hall; this place was strictly about the music, whenever there was a show anyway. The lighting was intimately dim throughout and the décor had a decidedly abstract feel to it that could be felt against the oranges and golds of the walls. They were playing "Ballroom Blitz" and as I let that electric rock and roll hit me, I could feel the night's energy building up.

Being the guest in the group and figuring that I should start earning some good graces, I volunteered to go down to the bar and get the first round for the evening. They all gave me their orders and Abi graciously volunteered to come help me carry them back up.

"So, what do you think of the gang?" she asked.

"Oh, they're great, no question; a little loud, but somehow there's more of them and it's nothing close to what I live with."

"Yeah that reminds me, María is still pretty pissed at Curtis. What's his deal anyway?"

"Still pissed? What are you talking about?... Oh God, don't tell me he knocked her up."

"What?! No, you idiot, she's pissed that he stopped texting her since the last time they hooked up a few weeks ago."

"They've been hooking up since after the club night? Well, that is honestly news to me," I replied, somehow both intrigued and completely indifferent at the same time, "Anyway, you should probably let her down easy; Curtis always brags about his women in explicit detail, so the fact that I didn't know isn't a great sign for any long-term prospects."

"What a pig. And I figured that but María said he seemed really into it, after he texted her first the next day she figured-"

"Wait, wait, wait, wait… he texted her first?"

"Yeah, the next day at around like noon."

This motherfucker had been texting his hookup from the night before, the one thing he literally always used to say was the number one sign of a "beta bitch," while he was giving me shit at lunch for only getting a kiss on the cheek. The hypocrisy was staggering.

"Huh. I am honestly shocked to hear that. OK, well I still don't see where the emotional connection came from on her end."

"Hey, trust me, I said the exact same thing; I really think she fell for him though, Lord knows why. Oh!" she exclaimed, doing her little bunny hop again and grabbing my arm,

"There's the bar, right there!"

We got the drinks and I gave the well-mustachioed bartender a nice tip. He was an older gentleman and he looked like a man who only owned mahogany furniture, and also kept a collection of antique pipes in the study, only for show and never to smoke. As we were walking back, Abi said something to me that almost caused me to drop the drinks: "It would be kind of funny, if our roommates started dating so soon after we did."

Dating? We're dating? When the hell did we start dating? Wait… goddamn it what am I saying, of course we're dating you fucking idiot. You took her to a movie the first night you met her. Then all that shit you said to her on the pier that day, no wonder she fell for you. Damn, I'm pretty smooth, huh? No, stop, focus asshole. It's like I lost track of time or something… Jesus Christ, I might actually be stupid. I always suspected but— OK, *Ok*, we're dating now, she already said it, it's too late, just keep calm and don't fuck up the rest of the night, we can reevaluate tomorrow. Maybe Mr. Rahmani will have some wise words for me.

"Yeah, wouldn't that be something." I snuck a glance at her, looking for any signs that she was weighing my response. She wasn't showing any, but suspicion is my natural state so I remained on alert.

We made it back and handed out the drinks, and after a few more minutes the announcer finally got on stage to get the crowd ready for the show. Their manager had done an excellent job that evening and the result was a fully packed room. The place was cramped and even up on the mezzanine it was getting a bit too warm for comfort. I was no stranger to being surrounded by sweaty strangers, but it never gets any more comfortable. The crowd was giving off the perfect energy, hyped but not rowdy, trashed but not trashy. Everyone was ready for a show, and as the DJ switched up to Rage Against The Machine in the final lead-up minutes, it was like a switch went off. The mood was infectious.

When the band finally got out from the back the place erupted. If I had to guess, I would say that one third of the crowd were friends of the girls, another third were genuine fans, and the rest were just there to check out new talent to listen to. The third demographic would be the most important to impress, especially the bloggers, influencers and record label folk undoubtedly among them. Yuki came out first in a maliciously cute schoolgirl uniform, black and dark red with pink skulls on the skirt; Claire decided to go with the no-shirt, bound chest look up top, a great choice for displaying the ink, and strategically tattered black jeans, no doubt borrowed from her lover; Eliya, the wonderfully mean-looking Israeli drummer who was wearing an extremely-form-fitting camo tank top and a half-shaved head look that I didn't normally find attractive but was suddenly warming up to; and finally Kelly, the blasian bassist wearing an obnoxiously large, ludicrously red top hat to match her cropped red leather jacket. The ladies sauntered onto the stage, already drunk off the crowd's applause (and probably tequila), ready to blow the roof off. Eliya gave the double devil's horns and Yuki did a few cutesy twirls before sticking her tonge out and giving the finger. They took their places and Yuki began the countdown.

Those girls blew the roof off that place and everyone in the building was losing their shit for two hours straight. They opened up with this one song that started with a sugar-sweet melodic intro with humming that lasted just long enough to make you think you were at the wrong show, and then, out of nowhere, the instruments unleashed a barrage of pounding rock. Yuki's petite self, dressed like a combination of Harley Quinn and an anime schoolgirl, ripped the mic wide open with a loud, grungy growl, and suddenly the floodgates opened. For all the excitement I was feeling as a quasi-acquaintance of the performers, I couldn't match the mania happening below me, the concertgoers who were off their feet and out of their minds. They went high-octane and then just kept finding new heights to hit; there were three mosh pits before they'd even played six songs. Everytime I thought they were going to take a mellow turn, they just turning up the intensity; it would have been exhilarating if it wasn't so exhausting. Each instrumentalist got a solo, of which I have to say that Claire's was by far the best; while the band leaned stylistically toward a mix of Nirvana and AC/DC, she had clearly grown up on a strict diet of Slayer and Norwegian black metal, and it showed. She looked like she was ready to unleash the demon army at any second, but she kept herself at bay and played out her part with no additions.

A standing ovation was the least of what they earned but they were happy for it, and even though I was one of many begging for an encore, I also figured they probably truly didn't have enough material to work with.

When we finally caught up with the band after the show they were in deservedly high spirits, not only because of the rave reviews they were getting on Twitter, but because two of the concert attendees just happened to be label reps and they just happened to invite the band down for a visit to HQ on Wednesday. The girls were on cloud nine and ready to celebrate.

"All right mis amigas, and you two, too, who's ready to fucking party!"

"Yasss girl, let's get the fuck out of here," Kelly declared, "Eliyah can't drink for like two more weeks because of the damned antibiotics, so she's gonna drive all the shit back to our building. Are you sure you won't need any help, babe?"

"Nah I got it," she replied, wolfing down a cheeseburger at the same time, "I need to get some rest anyway, that set killed me, man. I'll see you when you get back, and I'll see you two wild bitches on Wednesday. We're gonna knock the dicks off of those suits! Go on K-Pop, I'll leave here when I'm done with dinner."

"All right babe, I'll see ya later. Let's roll y'all!"

The energy was still infectious, and I sure as hell wasn't ready to be cured.

An Invitation

Those damned steps; there we were, Abi and I, at those damned steps again. I'd come to hate those steps, to see them as more of a barrier than an entrance. Each step she had taken on those steps was another step away from the next step of our intimacy, a step in the wrong direction. I would go so far as to say a step on my heart, but love wasn't what I wanted in that moment. It wasn't what I was avoiding, and it wasn't what I feared, but it wasn't what I wanted; I wanted her, all of her, every inch of her, every part. I wanted a night of passion and pleasure and pillow talk and pain and perspiration; I wanted her, more than I could handle. I wanted her as soon as I once again realized that we'd reached her stop, I wanted her when I leaned in to kiss her, to embrace those lips and be near those white diamonds. I wanted her even more when she kissed me back, wrapping her arms around my neck and getting on her tippy toes to put less strain on my neck. I wanted to hold her, squeeze her, take her; I wanted to toss her up in my arms and take her up to her floor, into her apartment, onto her bed; I wanted to see and taste and feel her, all of her. I wanted *her*.

I didn't want her to say she'd had fun but she needed to go to bed; I didn't want her to take that first half a step up the steps, leaving my arms and entering somewhere I couldn't follow. I didn't want to let her hand slip out of mine, and I didn't want to say goodnight, and promise to text her the next day. I didn't want… Stacy.

I didn't want Stacy, but I didn't want to not want her; I wanted to want to want her. I wanted to be able to just turn around, start walking, pull out my phone and see if she wanted to fuck. I wanted to be able to shake Abi off and go and screw some girl who was so eager that she'd sent me six additional unanswered texts, totaling up to ten on the night. I wanted to want to just go and fuck this girl senseless, leave, and then go back to talking to Abi… but that wasn't I wanted.

She stopped.

She turned around.

She told me she'd gotten a recording of that play. She asked if I wanted to come up and watch.

She looked at me. She wanted me to come upstairs and watch the play.

She wanted me to come upstairs.

She wanted me.

"Yeah, sounds fun. I definitely want that."

A Misunderstanding

"That was literally the longest day of my life, I want to be very clear about that."

"I said I was sorry, didn't I?" she replied, begrudgingly, "How many times am I going to have to apologize for this?"

"Ask me again after the first billion and we can take it from there."

"I'll start keeping a counter, first thing in the morning."

Mr. Rahmani's wasn't technically open on Sunday nights, but the old man usually let us chill if we were around and wanted some quick bites. He always had these fried chickpea things, pakora, ready to go for us, partially because he loved us but mostly because making them for us was the only way he could sneak a few for himself without his wife finding out. Abi and I were snacking on a few while Mr. Rahmani and some of his neighborhood pals were watching some movie about Ramayana.

"I still can't believe we made it through all that alive; you know I was hungover all the way up until, like, 3 PM? The fact that I was able to go through the whole Metropolitan Museum is astounding."

"Well, if it helps, you really made a good first impression, my dad absolutely loved meeting you," she said, thinking her unbelievably cute smile could get her out of trouble.

"You know, I'm sure if we were in a cheesy rom-com

those words would mark some big, really important moment for my character, but what I'm actually feeling is confusion. One more time, just so the next time I roast you I get it right, remind me how you forgot that your dad was coming for an all-day visit, that you did, in fact, plan three weeks ago."

"It's hard to keep up with shit, OK? Damn! I've been really focused on my next few auditions, I had to help Pierre deal with this whole big love life crisis, and my spin class has really been keeping me busy- "

"Spin class? Really? You're using spin class as an excuse? Is saying 'I fucked up, Kola, please forgive me' really that hard?"

She pouted, a response I'd come to understand as an indignant admission.

"Honestly, I respect that, but it doesn't change the fact that I had to spend upwards of seven hours going to almost every single damn museum in Manhattan with a fast-walking, even-faster-talking man who thought, again, just so you remember, that I had just gotten back in town from Lagos to make a surprise visit to—and here's the kicker—my girlfriend of one whole year. The funniest part is that your lie doesn't actually change the part of the situation that he was upset with."

"OK, in my defense, what the fuck else was I supposed to do? It was either say we were on the road to marriage or get screamed at by my dad in front of all my roommates."

"I think the best answer to that is: put a reminder alarm on your phone calendar, and then wake the guy you brought home up before said father arrives."

She did her damn pout and made those puppy dog eyes,

melting me away despite all my resistance.

"Ugh… look, just because I'm not capable of being angry with you doesn't make this what you did any less ridiculous."

"Doesn't it though?" she contended, popping another pakora in her piehole.

"No," I answered, snatching the next one out of her hand, "it does not. I am happy about one thing though, now I know that I have a knack for acting. I made a pretty convincing one-year boyfriend, if I do say so myself."

"I will admit your improvisational skills were pretty good; that 'date' we had to see the *Fela!* revival on Broadway was a great touch, albeit shameless pandering."

"It's all about understanding your audience. And since you did give me a compliment, I'll say that I'm sorry for spending half an hour in a cab going along with his jokes about how awful of a cook you are, no matter how funny they may have been."

"I was going to try and pretend to not be deeply, permanently scarred by those remarks, but thank you for apologizing, I appreciate it."

"No problem, short stuff. I'm sure you and your mediocre fufu will make some guy very happy one day."

She threw a pakora at my head. I decided to grin and let it slide, practicing a little deescalation.

"That reminds me, we should go say we're sorry to Mr. Rahmani again for the ruckus last night."

"I thought you said that he loved late night customers."

"Late night customers are an entirely different thing from a bunch of heavily intoxicated twenty-somethings."

"Speak for yourself, pal," she chided, "I was perfectly

fine."

"So, when you spent half the car ride back to your place singing the *Fairly Odd Parents* theme song, that was you being sober."

"Bull. Shit. No way that happened."

"Well, you're half-right; it did happen, but you were babbling so much that I could be confusing my nostalgic cartoons."

"What, the fuck, ever, bet I'm still better at singing than you."

"Oh, I don't know about that, I was a choir boy, after all; my teacher said I had a classic voice."

"Yeah, Louis Armstrong-classic, maybe," she tacked on, poking her tongue out at me, "and anyway, at least we weren't as drunk as the rest of them."

"Who was it that committed assault again?"

"Claire when she smashed the glass bottle over the guy who was creeping on Yuki."

"Right, and then we…"

"Then we went to some surprise midnight concert that Kelly wanted to go to, and then after that was the Chinese thing."

"The Chinese thing?"

"These three playboys from Beijing were feeling María and invited us all to this rooftop party."

"Oh, no, no, no, this one I remember perfectly. Your jealous ass almost killed a couple of little Asian girls because they were getting friendly with me. I thought it was about to be a massacre."

"…I will neither confirm nor deny those heinous

allegations leveled against me," she responded, embarrassed rage slowly building up behind furrowed brows, "but what I remember is Yuki basically bullying the DJ into letting her take over for a few tracks, and that's when the party got lit. She's basically an over-the-top anime character brought to life."

"Haruhi Suzumiya in the flesh; OK, then what happened?"

"Pierre got a text from this guy he's been fucking for a while so he decided to just call it a night and go back to his place. The rest of us got even more trashed on all the fancy shit they had at the open bar, but naturally we all started getting the drunchies. Your ass suggested Mr. Rahmani's and then we all went and pigged out on halal goodness. He didn't even charge us, said you had a friend discount."

What Mr. Rahmani referred to as a "friend discount" was him frying up all of the leftover meats from the day, toasting some half-stale pita, heating up some day-old rice, dumping spices and sauces on the whole thing and then serving it to his boys and any of their friends upon request. In one sense, it was very sweet, but in another sense, it felt like we were farm pigs being fed from a trough. Then again, given how drunk we usually are at that point, it's probably not an undeserved comparison.

"All right, that all checks out. So, all of that happened, then we went back to your place, undoubtedly made enough X-rated noises to wake up the priests in St. Patrick's, woke up, did it one more time, powering our way through the hangovers just to get a quick nut, all before you left to go to the bathroom and saw your father standing in the living room talking to Pierre in French."

"You pretty much summed it up, yeah."

We both stopped to take a second and appreciate how absurd the turn of events had been. A wild concert, an even wilder night out, hopefully even wilder sex, and then a day spent pretending that we were on the road to becoming an old married couple. It's strange though... it didn't feel too unnatural.

"OK, I think that's enough for one day. Twenty-four hours straight with you was a lot of fun, all things considered, but I do have to get to work tomorrow and get an actual meal."

"...You know, I think there's still some of that pizza left... we can finish that episode we were watching too, if you want."

She'd given me a lot of looks in the weeks we'd had together: angry pouts, blank stares, giant smiles, sarcastic smirks, all sorts of faces. This, however, was the first time that she decided to bite her lower lip and raise an eyebrow at me, and in that moment, all I could do was pray it wouldn't be the last.

Wrapped around her finger, right where she wanted me.

A Delay

Ten. Fucking. Hours.

On the night before my birthday, I got stuck on an Amtrak train for ten fucking hours.

I'll get to the story in just a second, but I really, really, need you to understand the exact length of time that I was dealing with here. Like, imagine how long it takes you to explain Wi-Fi hotspots to your grandparents, and then double it. Didn't quite get through? OK, then try imagining how long it takes a twenty-something woman to edit an Instagram post of her bottomless brunch and then subtract five minutes. Got it now? Alright, back to the plot.

I had gone to D.C. that weekend in a desperate attempt to consolidate a long list of social obligations into one jam-packed extrovert extravaganza, mostly in the interest of releasing myself from "bad friend" guilt for at least six more months. They never tell that after you graduate the most annoying part of staying friends with everybody is just the actual physical distance. A lot of them ended up in New York with me, but far too many stayed in D.C., like moths to an egomania-fueled flame. Social media and texting helped do most of the work, but there are some things that only real-world interaction are good for.

I stayed at a nice enough AirBnB, aesthetically basic but with enough amenities to make up for it. I didn't have any time to visit the old campus but in the span of three brunches, five parties, seven coffee meetups, three bowls of weed and one incredibly awkward surprise catch-up at the Trader Joe's, I managed to connect with just about everyone I wanted to see that weekend. The highlight of the trip, funny enough, was the one activity I did by myself; Sunday morning I went to see the recently released Diana Wilson film, *Dandelion Bonfire*, a powerful, striking coming-of-age tale about a woman recounting her rural Great Depression-era childhood in rural Tennessee. I'm not usually one whose heartstrings get tugged, but that one got to me, and it got to me hard. The woman just has a gift.

Like I said, it was a good trip, worth the fare and the time. Well, most of the time.

It should go without saying that anytime someone dies is a tragedy, especially when that death is accidental. Now that I've said that, I feel far less guilty declaring that the wasted guy who decided that a train track was the right place to take a nap is on my top ten all-time most hated strangers list.

The first hour and a half after the train stopped were bearable, if only because I had no idea what was going on. Train delays aren't uncommon, mind you, so it wasn't like there was panic. By the time that we got into the second hour I started to feel a dread coming on, encouraging me to get up and start walking up the car. I joined a group of fellow passengers and learned what was going from some middle-aged guy in a gaudy leather jacket. I tried to take the optimistic route, imagine that the police might be able to wrap this up quickly, but from the few incidents I'd witnessed in my time, I knew that was a goddamn lie.

Aside from the fact that my perfectly planned birthday was imploding before my very eyes, I was equally upset at being stuck in an enclosed space with strangers for an indefinite amount of time. It was like all of my most mundane nightmares combining into some horribly boring reality. On the one hand, I was in no mood to talk to anybody, and on the other, I was in no mood to watch television for hours without any idea of when I'd be free. An impossible decision lay before me in that moment: mindless conversation or mindless entertainment?

Thankfully, I didn't have to end up choosing.

"Do you mind, young man?"

I looked up and saw her, red and white shawl wrapped snugly around her and her light grey coat. She had a wizened face full of a distinct sweetness, her artificially snow-white hair causing the ebony to play out in her visage. If the accent wasn't enough to tip me off that she was African, the face certainly did the trick, which might explain why I was so quick to flip into my state of deference normally reserved for my loving but iron-fisted grandmothers.

"Yes, ma'am, of course; which seat would you like?"

Say what you want about beating your kids, but it's great for manners.

"Oh, no need to get up, I will sit right here." It was one of the two-seats-facing-two-seats, so she took the opposite corner; I'd had my laptop playing on the one across from me, but I quickly removed it and placed it on my lap. "Thank you very much, young man. I did not mean to disturb you but I just wanted a little company during all this mess and you seemed to be the only friendly face here."

Friendly face? Me? Seriously? I mean, I guess I've been laughing at these old Dave Chappelle videos for a while now but I would hope that she can differentiate laughter from a joyful disposition.

"No problem, ma'am, happy to have the company. My name is Kola, by the way, Kolawole Idowu."

"Dhakirah Nkrumah, pleasure to meet you."

She had a charmed voice, something resembling the regal, and it had a comforting effect on those who received it. The learned nervousness that I was channeling into politeness turned into real calm, and as we began to engage in pleasantries, a genuine interest in the conversation grew.

It would certainly prove to be interesting.

"So you're really with the GCEG, huh? I've heard so much about you guys."

"Yes, I really am; would I lie about such a thing? I am on the Board of Directors, so part of my duties going up to New York once every few months and begging for donations. It's not the most dignified work, but I revel in it! Ah, anyway, what about you, eh, what do you do with yourself?"

"Business consulting, over at Midas. Started when I was fresh out of school and haven't strayed off the course."

"You make it sound like you are a racehorse, running on a track and being whipped by a tiny man," she exclaimed, far too accurately for my comfort, "Is that your life, really? I do not imagine it's that bad."

"Well, not bad, no, but not exactly the 'fulfilling life path' I keep hearing I'm supposed to be on. It's a good job, and they've been good to me for three years; no reason to leave but mostly inertia causing me to stay. A trap of my own ambitious design."

"Interesting… you speak like a learned man but you think like a fool, it is rather confusing."

At that point I honestly couldn't believe this woman wasn't my actual grandmother. It was goddamn uncanny.

"OK, look, Ms. Nkrumah, I'm really not in the mood for a lecture on my mostly-reasonable life choices. Aside from the fact that it's a little much, especially for two people who just met and won't ever speak again, I'm content with where I'm at. It's just gonna take a little while longer."

"A little while longer for what, exactly? And hush with all that stranger talk, we are African, dear boy, and I am your elder. The words I speak are important by their mere existence."

"Ugh… yes, ma'am, you're right. And I'm waiting a little while longer for, well, you know, everything to click, y'know? All this shit I've been doing my whole life, all these checkmarks I've hit. Good school, good job, good friends; I've got everything I'm supposed to have, and eventually it's gonna feel like it. Until then, I'm just going to drown my anxieties in pointless distractions."

She gave me one of those seemingly condescending stares I'd grown so accustomed to.

"You are wasting your time, child, and time is something precious. Too many back home do not have it, and too many here don't see the value in it. You cannot be out here wasting time on 'pointless distractions,' eh? You need to sort yourself."

I was ready to chuckle at my chiding and let the conversation find its end, but she had a different idea.

"I got it! You will come work for me; there, problem solved."

"Um… what?"

"We have a new project coming up, starting next summer," this amazingly bold woman said, throwing me further off with every word, "USAID gave us a five year grant for education intervention activity in rural Nigeria, Mbaise in Imo State to be specific. We will have two main offices, one in Port Harcourt, and one in Lagos, working in coordination. It is perfect; you are in business consulting and you also majored in International Development, it is a natural fit. I am sure I can find you a position with us."

You know that feeling right between surprise and disbelief? It's a sweet spot, perfectly balanced from both sides of the credulity spectrum. I literally couldn't believe what I'd just heard but I also couldn't believe how instantly happy I was to hear it. Then I couldn't understand why I was so happy at all; after all, it was insane. Insane and appealing, but mostly insane. Mostly.

"I'll… I'll think about it."

"Yes, yes you will. Here, take my card, I am going to find different seating. You were lovely, but I also just want to sleep in peace for a while. Hopefully the train starts moving again. I expect to hear from you soon, very soon. Enjoy your night."

She grabbed her things, re-wrapped her shawl, and strode down the train car. We'd been talking for four hours, and moving for two. It was 3 AM in the morning. I needed to sleep.

Am I really going to go back?

Am I really going to follow that dream?

Am I really going to see him *again?*

I didn't get much sleep.

A Dance

Snow in November is not something one expects but can still turn out to be a magical affair. Climate change isn't good for much but it certainly makes the seasons more interesting.

The Metrograph was playing *Persepolis* that night, so we'd made a whole plan to catch the evening show and then grab a few drinks at this weird absinthe bar one of Abi's castmates told her about. It was the first time we'd been back since that first night, and we could instantly remember why we'd had such a lovely time. When you can fall in love again with a film you've both collectively seen seventeen times, the venue has to have something to do with it.

We had thought about cancelling due to the forecast, but we weren't going to let some iced water ruin our plans. Walking worked fine.

"I think I'd do pretty well in a repressive regime, can't lie. My natural flair for the *fabulously* dramtic might get in the way but I know I could play meek and mild-mannered pretty well."

"I love how you think constantly avoiding the eye of religious police is the same thing as acting quiet. You'd have that hijab off the second you realized no one was complimenting your hair."

"Um, duh, I can't hide all this from the viewing public, but I ain't stupid either; I'd just do what they were doing, sneaking out to parties and stuff."

"*Ohhh*, right right, the part where that guy freakin dies trying to escape the cops. Yeah that all looked real fun."

"Yes, exactly, the *guy* dies; guy, as in you, as in not me, who's just gonna be with my girls chilling and pretending nothing was going on. It's literally the one benefit of patriarchy and I would fully take advantage of it."

"You're the worst, babe, never change."

She grabbed my hand and gave me one of her trademark, too-cute-for-words smiles.

"I know."

The snow wasn't melting but I sure as hell was.

As she reminisced about her family's first trip to Disney World and all the youthful shenanigans that occurred, the snowflakes floated by our faces. The roads were empty and covered, so while we had the chance, we decided to walk in the middle of the street. I always like getting the central perspective, especially on nights like these, with the moon out in full and the streetlights working in harmony. It was late January, the winter's high point, and while the wind wasn't biting enough to warrant a night in, the snow didn't make for much in the way of convenience.

A six-month anniversary; part of me couldn't believe it. It wasn't that six months was some extraordinary length of time, or that I never thought we would make it that long, nothing like that. I guess I just couldn't believe the idea of it, half a year with the same person, this one individual out of billions. I'd had long term women in my life before Abi but to be six months in and have everything going amazing, well, that was a different story.

We texted every day and called every other night; we

moved around furniture in our bedrooms to allow for fully optimal joint-viewing pleasure; Abi kept a running list of restaurants she simply had to take me to while I kept one of films she couldn't go another day without watching. Her laugh was my call to relaxation, her smile a light in the fog. Being with her made me wish for summer, for longer days to spend and more passionate nights to savor. She was warmth- -my protector against the cold winds that sweep up the unfortunate, the miserable, the lonely. She was my little slice of happiness, wrapped snugly around my arm and refusing to let go. She always loved walking like that.

Six months.

Another six months.

Another six months after that.

The longer I dwelled on it, the stranger it seemed, but still not for the typical reasons. I began thinking about other things… other people. Stacy, the last one. Marcela, the first one. Rebecca. Khaliyah. Zaya. Trish. Imane. Sandra. JoAnn. Pamela… no, Penelope, it was Penelope.

Abi.

All those possibilities, all those collections of moments, had all come into my life and gone. Truth be told, a few of them were fated for death from their inception, little more than farcical happenings. Some of them had been thrown off course for reasons beyond my control and comprehension, placing my happiness in the hands of cruel Fates, indifferent to my suffering. Then, of course, there were the tragedies, the ones that seemed perfect, the ones that I thought would go beyond my youth and stretch out into a time ahead of my comprehension. Jealousy, emotional distance, trust issues, no support; I'd played both the victim and the villain many a time, so I won't dare ask for pity. The tragedy is never in who hurt whom or who lost what; it's in the hurt and loss themselves, the witnessing and weight. There's a reason they don't have happy heroes in those stories.

Six months.

What had we done in six months?

Our bedrooms were more like two halves of the same suite, our phones reduced to relationship management devices more than any pieces of master engineering. When she took it upon herself to sign us up for a ballroom dancing class, I responded by insisting that she let me have Sunday afternoons for football-only usage. I ended up meeting her mom eventually, and a few days after New Year's we got dinner with my parents; with an overall record of four approvals and zero drama, we'd sailed through that storm without a scratch. At some point, "her friends" and "my friends" had undergone that strange transition to "our friends," and any event we went to tended to feature a healthy mix. If I had to guesstimate, I would say we went through… thirteen TV shows, twenty-six movies, two album release day listens, four opening nights, ten gallery exhibits, and one extremely painful open-mic night, hosted by Samaira herself as a favor to the comedy club owner.

We talked. Politics. God. Race. Sex. Good. Evil. We challenged each other to share, to break past those walls, confront the fears plaguing us. She told me about how she was still sure, despite all the good things that were going on, that it was all just too good for someone like her, that she'd end up a failure and that her dreams would die with her spirit. I told her that the only reason I tried to interact with people was because I couldn't escape the feeling that left alone with my thoughts, insanity, depression, or, God forbid, worse, would start to take over; my social skills weren't even a mask, they were an active deterrent. We shared things far less serious than that, guilty pleasure songs and problematic favorite celebrities; we shared things far more serious, things I won't even put to words here. We shared ourselves, our beings, our humanity, and in return, we gained access to the others; live and learn, learn and live.

We'd shared some of the best parts of ourselves; we'd watched as the very worst revealed themselves without warning or control. We'd fought, a lot, and deeply. Things were said, feelings were hurt, dreams questioned, and ideas challenged. There were times where I was convinced I was dealing with an impulsive, immature dreamer with no real responsibility or care in the world, someone whose judgment only travelled in one direction and who had no problem nagging me to death all day out of boredom but then would pretend like she was the busiest woman on Earth when it suited her. I'm sure there were times when she would wonder what she was doing with a self-centered, unresponsive, can't-take-anything-seriously-to-save-his-life smartass, someone far less funny than they would like to believe and who would rather throw himself off the Empire State Building than take a helpful suggestion. I'm sure there were times where "hate" would not have been out of the question. Few and far between, but existent nonetheless.

Six months.

Six months to answer one question.

The question.

The only question that matters.

If it wasn't for what happened that night, I don't know if I would have gotten my answer. It came out from the old liquor store, end of the block, two bad windows and the blue neon sign. We were under a streetlight, and in that moment, the brightest star couldn't compare.

Fly me to the moon
Let me play among the stars
Let me see what spring is like
On Jupiter and Mars

Our eyes locked, both of us in equal amounts of confusion and amusement over the sudden appearance of Mr. Frank Sinatra, both in unspoken agreement about what the musical moment demanded. Her hand in mine, mine in hers.

In other words, hold my hand
In other words, baby kiss me

We swayed with the tune, bodies locked and minds ad delirium. It was all just a bit too much, a bit too perfect. The solitude, the atmosphere, the perfect amount of wine in our bloodstreams; it was heaven on earth, however brief. We danced out of celebration.

Fill my heart with song
Let me sing for ever more
You are all I long for
All I worship and adore

Her eyes. Six months. Six months together, and that was the first time that I'd ever really seen her eyes. They were *beautiful.* Deep, rich hazel. Bright. Round. Inviting. Sweet. Her eyes; why had I never seen her eyes like this? All the hugs, all the love made, and yet, never once like this.

In other words, please be true

I couldn't stop staring. I couldn't stop thinking.
In other words
I didn't want to stop.
In other words
I never wanted to stop.
I
Love
"You."

Reality snapped back in an instant before the final note even played. I couldn't believe what I'd done, what I'd said. I couldn't believe that it was me. I couldn't believe that I was still looking into her eyes.

She was silent. Stunned. Shook.

I needed a response more than I needed oxygen.

The snowflakes kept falling. They were pretty that night.

Still silent.

I'm sure it was no more than five seconds, but I swear I could've died and come back ten times that night. She kept her eyes locked and her mouth agape, until suddenly closing both. There were three seconds of that, each of which was more terrifying than the last.

Suddenly, she moved in. Her lips, my shock. Contact. She pulled back.

"Took you long enough, dumbass."

She smiled. That same damned smile.

The music had ended, but the celebration had not.

I could have danced there all night.

A Withdrawal

Art becoming realized always creates a temporary rift in space and time. It can feel small at first, or maybe it's so small it's negligible, but once the eery feeling of recollection sets in it's something you can't stop. The longer you sit in the moment, the closer you get to accepting the ridiculousness of interpreting reality through fiction, and once you accept the comedy, the tragedy can set in.

In total, Abi had seen *Rent* about three times on Broadway, twelve times in film version, and a few thousand in her own visualized adaptation. The soundtrack had been on repeat for the majority of college, culminating in the selection of "La Vie Boheme" as her team name in the annual theater program Beerlympics. It was her show, that one special show every actor has that despite the complete, clear impossibility of being true, they fully believe was written for them and them only. It was the tale of love in the face of despair, the necessity of art in a dying world, independence, revolution, pettiness, shame, dignity, hope, and the omnipresence of failure. All deeply human sensations, and all swirling in Abi's head as she put pen to paper to fill out her rent check.

The whole setup, at its core, was medieval: their landlord insisted on having tenants deliver the checks to his unit on the top floor, like peasants bringing tribute to a medieval lord. Most owners have the basic business sense to reserve the top-level places for those willing to shell a few extra dollars for a balcony, but egomania does strange things to a person. Without a family to speak of or even a pet, the old curmudgeon—whose completely-forgotten name added some self-imposed mystery to the fun—was barely ever seen, only confirming signs of life by the super continuing to get paid.

In the umpteenth iteration of this most sacred ritual, Abi opened up her phone to verify the collections had come into her account. With a total rent of six thousand and four roommates to speak of, she was responsible for receiving twelve-hundred dollars per person and having the last fifth ready to come out of checking. She couldn't remember exactly which bet she'd lost against Pierre to end up with the job but she regretted it each time.

It wasn't so much the monthly reminder texts she had to send or even the five-flight walk to drop off the check; the shitty part were those brief, delicious hours when her bank account would swell far past its usual size and offer a glimpse into financial stability. A number far larger than its real value that took her to a different, safer place. A place without that flinch of hesitation before agreeing to go out for brunch; without the subway ride that would have made much more sense as an Uber ride except for the part where it didn't.

No matter how many late nights, early mornings, or out-of-the-way day trips it took, she never had to do the unthinkable and put out her hand. Every dollar Abi earned was dragged from the city concrete but they were hers and hers alone. It was a promise the day she'd lowered herself to taking that first and last loan from her parents to make the security deposit, a promise she'd written down in her beloved rose gold notepad the day she paid her parents back with interest. It was the same book that contained the theaters she would one day perform in, the cities she would visit, the lives she would live; a book of dreams and promises. A sacred document that she turned to for strength after a long day of odd jobs and audition prep.

To say that the offers hadn't been coming in would be implying that they actually existed, somewhere in the ether, and she just wasn't having luck. While that may have been the objective truth, Abi was living in a longer, slower hell of the whole acting universe seeming to have transported out of her reach. The one commercial she'd booked the previous year for a doomed office-share company had been returning less and less in royalties, and the last of her show checks from *Sins* had run out.

She'd returned to her one of her New York all-stars, the phenomenal Janae at the Bollheim Temp Agency, for some quick-money gigs. Over a two-week span, Abi had walked about nineteen dogs, podcasted her way through six hours of receptionist duty, and even tried her hand as a mailroom worker for some law firm. Walking the halls of White Man, White Man, & Jewish Man was a fascinating exercise in constant interaction while somehow maintaining full invisibility—an interesting time, but not one she wanted to repeat.

Like every month, the money was earned and saved and dipped into very slightly to pay for one extra night out, the details of which were always a little fuzzy. Like every month, casting lines were waited in, audition reels were recorded over video call, and every email from her agent was like a light flashing in the dead of night in a slowy darkening forest.

As she crossed the final letter on the check, the last few seconds of a monumental three-minute task, Abi felt that she needed a break. Luckily, she knew someone who was just as free to talk—and do other things—as she was. She picked up the phone and hit her most recent FaceTime call.

"Hey baby girl, how ya doing? Just caught me getting back from the gym."

"Oh OK, sorry! I can call you back when you're showered and everything."

"Nah don't worry," Kola assured, "definitely didn't do enough to work up a real sweat. I'm getting way too damn lazy, need to tighten up. Can't have the oga belly popping out quite yet, ya know? What about you, what are you up to?"

"Ohhhh, not much, just finished the rent check up and trying to figure out the best way to kill a little time. Figured you could help me with that…" she proposed, in her decidedly sultry voice.

"Mmmm, well now doesn't that sound like a lovely time. But I can't, babe, not tonight, I need to do some bullshit slide deck. Honestly not even sure who it's for or why we're doing it, but it's on my work stream and I'm betting someone's year-end bonus is on the line."

"I thought the whole point of working an office job was that the work gets done in the office."

"Well, if I'd been better at managing my work, or if I gave a shit about this nonsense engagement, that would be the case. I'll make it up to you, babe, promise. I'm sure you can find some way to kill your boredom in that wonderland apartment of yours."

"Pierre is doing some weird kombucha tasting thing, Samaira's on tour somewhere in Maine which, you know, hilarious, and Yuki and Claire are probably making out on the bottom of some dive bar in Queens."

"Fuck-buddy goals honestly. Well what about Mar í a?"

"Yeah I don't know what's up with her recently, she's always running around and getting in late. I don't think she's seeing anybody because she hasn't said anything, and she's literally told me about every dick she's come in contact with since move-in day. Detailed reviews too, in case you were curious."

"I'm honestly amazed you think I've lived with Curtis for three years and haven't seen his dick yet. At least six different occasions, only one of which was consensual on both ends."

"Do I even want to ask?"

"I'll defer to US military protocol on that one. Hey, I'm sorry but I got to start setting up dinner. You alright though? You seem down."

"Oh I'm fine! Thank you though babe, no just need to get some sleep, gotta make some rounds tomorrow, see if any good auditions are coming up, you know how it is. Good luck with your slide deck though!"

"Thanks babe, love you!"

"Love you too!"

The beeping signaled the end of the call and the return back to the bright, messy, too-lived-in bedroom. In a few hours it would be another day alternating between running around town and lazing around the loft. Waiting, watching, waiting for the show to begin, for opening curtain in front of the crowd that lived in her ambitions. For the theme song to start blasting while she took the next step on the walk to stardom.

Abi put the check in the marked white envelope and placed it on the corner of her vanity table. There was nothing else to do, no one to kill time with. There was barely even any weed left in the apartment to blow the rest of the night on. In the silence, she wondered if this could be one of those nights, one of those moment-of-inspiration, life-changing nights where the inspiration to get one's shit together stampedes over all the laziness and fatigue of modern living. When plans get written up to the sounds of 80's synth music and vision boards are formulated. She even thought about making this the night she finally tried to write her own play, her own story.

But then she had a better idea.

"Alexa, play 'Take Me Out' from *Rent The Musical*."

"Oh, and what's the weather? Gotta get the right outfit."

In a few hours, it would be a new day, a better one, and a belly full of tequila and yuca fries sounded like the perfect way to start it.

A Good Boy

"Aren't you going to call Abi? You usually do it around dinnertime, don't you?"

"Nah, not tonight man; we got in a big fight the other day and I'm not really in the mood to deal with her right now."

"The perfect couple got in a fight? Love is dead, a tragedy."

"Shut the fuck up, Ravi."

Curtis had gone out to the gym for a late-night workout so it was just Ravi and me in our place. I was feeling a little less than talkative due to Abi's most recent nonsense, while Ravi, in an unusual turn of events, seemed to be cheery as all hell. The normal state of affairs in our group was the full ensemble, Curtis, Ravi, and I all hanging out together and enjoying (mostly) each other's company. Curtis and Ravi on their own would get wrapped up in any variety of pseudo-debates about one thing or another; and a conversation between me and the Bombastic Blond would usually involve a myriad of profane insults. Both dynamic duos worked well, but if I had to, I would have to say that Ravi and I were the best pair. Curtis required talking more than he had the breath required to do so, but Ravi and I could spend hours on the couch, just watching something or listening to good music, with the occasional constructive conversation. In three hours of watching *Sherlock* the only other conversation that we'd had was about whether Martin Freeman's John Watson has any of the textbook symptoms of Stockholm syndrome.

"Look, every couple gets into fights. It's honestly kind of insane that you two haven't got in a super-big fight already, borderline unrealistic."

"Do you and Xavier get into fights?"

"A few here and there, mostly about him though. He's always weird whenever his ex-husband gets brought up and I keep trying to talk to him about it but he just refuses to get into it. It's like he doesn't want to get to that level or something."

"Don't you think you're better off leaving the past alone?"

"Not when it's something that big, no. I mean, there's just this huge part of his past that he never wants to share with me even though I pretty much share anything he asks about; it's like he's not as emotionally invested as I am. It's not irrational to expect an equal level of comfort with each other, or at least it shouldn't be. I told him as much, but he still won't broach the subject, so I've just decided to let it be for now. And let's not change the subject here, this is about your failing relationship, not my blissful slice of heaven; so how have you not gotten into fights?"

"We've gotten in fights, man, tons of them, we just always resolve them before we leave the conversation. Didn't I tell you about Stacy?"

"What about her? I thought you stopped texting her a while ago."

"I did, but then I ran into her again a few weeks back, and we started talking again." I could already feel Ravi's judging sideeye, "Not like that, obviously; just friendly shit, basic small talk. I told her about Abi within five minutes just to get the message across, but she took that as well as I could imagine, and then she asked if we could get a drink sometime. Innocent enough, right? Well, Abi lost it when she found out about that, and then she went off on me for like, fifteen minutes on how I had to call her and tell her no."

"Well, did you?"

"Of course I did! The fuck else was I supposed to do, debate the finer points of hanging out with an old hook-up? I said she was being crazy but that only made it worse, shockingly enough, so I just capitulated; live to fight another day, y'know?"

"Well, in Abi's defense, it takes a special kind of idiot to think that an ex wants to hang out platonically, especially one with a drunk texting record like her."

"Oh come on, man, just because we used to fuck doesn't mean we can't grab a drink and talk, right?"

"Oh, *of course,* man! Yeah, you two can just meet up and talk about all those super interesting things you both used to talk about, like 'Who's Coming Over to Whose Place' and 'Hey, Did I Leave My Watch on Your Kitchen Counter?' Riveting stuff, truly."

"I genuinely hate you, Ravi, just really need to get that out there."

"Love you too, pal," he responded, picking up the controller and scrolling through the Netflix cue, "look, I don't think I really need to explain why hanging out with Stacy is a dumb idea. Not worth it, and it's not like you're one for extra social obligations."

"Yeah, yeah, alright; I honestly don't care either way. I think I really just wanted to win this one; if someone's keeping record of our fights then I am way, way, wayyyy under .500. Really need to get those numbers up."

"You're going to be a borderline playoff contender at best. So what else have you been fighting about?"

I told him about the time that she got mad at me for not replying to ten straight texts in a row after I complained that I'd done "nothing all day" at work; about the time when I whined at her over cancelling dinner plans she told me to make, only to find out she was feeling bad from her period, leaving me racked with unearned male guilt; about the time we got into a yelling match over who lost the tickets to the Giants game, in the middle of the parking lot, before eventually buying from a scalper and sitting through the game under a moody cloud. And then, there was the latest fight.

"So, the thing is, she's still getting royalty money from a commercial she did back in the spring, but she got cut out of the last one after three days of shooting and the other one didn't take her; essentially, she hasn't worked in months. So, all I said was that she's lucky that she only has to do one job every once in a while to get by, and then after that, things got *baddd.*"

"Did you not expect that saying she was only semi-talented would result in hurt feelings?"

"Oh, come on, that's not what I said at all. I literally just meant that it's cool how you only really need to land a few really good gigs per year to make a living, as opposed to having to go to work every single day. She hasn't even had an audition in weeks. Meanwhile, there are like thousands of other wannabes who can't get a spot in a commercial for a local insurance company, and an entire city full of them in

La La Land. I know she's freakin' good at acting, so I don't understand how she could take an amused observation for an insult."

"Maybe, and it's just a thought, but maybe it has something to do with not respecting how hard she has to work just to *get* an audition. It's not like they just hand those out to anybody. And she probably didn't love you bringing up her latest career disappointments as 'cool.' Just because you acknowledge her talent and relative success doesn't make your comments any less dismissive."

"Wow… be honest with me, man, are you some kind of wise old man trapped in a millennial body?"

"Absolutely, and don't tell anyone or I'll put a curse on you."

"You're certainly a wicked witch, huh? Alright fine, I'm wrong and everyone else is right, what else is new; thank God I apologized already or this would be even worse. Anyway, the point of all that was that we do in fact have fights but no big ones yet, which apparently you think is a bad sign."

"It's not a bad sign, it's just a potential red flag: if two people are serious about getting to know each other, big differences are bound to come out in big fights. Unless you two are super, super similar and basically share a brain, there's going to be a big one. I just hope it doesn't end up being the last one."

The guy really had a way with downer endings.

"OK, fine, you win; I will now be hoping for/expecting a major fight sometime in the near future. Thanks for the pep talk, Ravi, you're a delight as always."

"Any time pal, any time."

We went back to our standard practice of complete peace and silence and letting the TV take our minds off our problems. For as little as we talked, he was always a rock for me, someone I knew I could turn to when the problem was too big and my lifelong partner was too obnoxious.

As you can imagine, that was very much most of the time. Including five minutes after the conversation you just read.

"I'm home, you fuckin' clowns. And I got something with me."

"Another positive STD test?" Ravi offered.

"A new set of baseless delusions to prop up your fragile ego?" I begged to know.

Neither of us had actually bothered to turn around at this point, being basically immune to Curtis' bluster, so when we got our reply, I have to admit we were a little taken aback.

"Woof! Woof woof!"

Our heads whipped around towards the door, and there it was, four feet on the floor and tail wagging in the air.

"Curtis… why?"

"Great question, Ravi; gentleman, I would like to introduce you to the newest member of our gang, Hopper! Hopper, meet your new friends, Ravi and Kolawole."

As our new Chocolate Border Collie friend, his white and brown coat wonderfully offsetting his beautiful blue eyes, began to explore its new surroundings, Curtis attempted to explain his actions. There was some asshole at work, Hank, one of those people whose entire personality is based on how many socially aware activities they engage in. Volunteering for local election campaigns, teaching inner city kids, composting; all those incredibly good things that allow incredibly annoying people to feel better than everyone else. On Monday during the previous week, everyone was eating lunch in the office and Hank was going on about something involving rescue animals. Curtis, clearly frustrated to the point of absentmindedness, decided to blurt out that he'd just adopted a dog and strangely enough, didn't feel the need to brag about it. Now, this wasn't exactly a random bit of nonsense; he'd had a few dogs in his life, all of them beloved. Once he said it out loud, he realized there was a bit of truth to the outburst, but he had a more immediate issue: working his way around the lie. If he were a lesser man, he might have stumbled or, even worse, gotten guilty and confessed, but thankfully dishonesty was Curtis' native tongue. He invented a convoluted story about building pet codes and unsure roommates (rude), saying that he'd be picking the dog up at the end of the week. He told them to all expect some incredibly cute Instagram posts, which got the exact reactions he wanted from both his female coworkers and his obnoxious officemate.

Then he just had to go out and actually get the damn thing… without telling us. Or actually checking the building code. Or buying any dog food.

The man is something else.

"So, you bought a goddamn animal from some random asshole in Brooklyn just so you could take a few obnoxious pictures?"

"Whoa, whoa, calm down Kola; yes, I'll admit that the idea came about from me running my big mouth, there's no question there, but it's not like I'm throwing him out onto the street afterwards, I'm keeping him. I mean, come on! He's so damn cute! *Come here boy! Who's a good boy?*" The dog came over and received his loving hands, the instant bond between the two difficult not to find adorable.

"OK well, what does the building code say?"

"Well, technically, it says no pets, but-" he said, anticipating our impending yells, "we're in the clear, Mr. Gurram said it was cool. You know he loves me ever since I taught him all about rock music. Guy loves his Lynyrd Skynyrd, man, what can I say."

"Another convert to the church," Ravi remarked, standing up, "All right, I'm going to grab the laptop and research how to take care of a dog, since I already know I'm going to be doing most of the work. Kola, please play with the unintelligent animal for a bit and then also get to know Hopper."

As Ravi left the toom the dog made its way into the kitchen. While Curtis was yelling at Ravi through the door, somewhat-justifiably offended, I observed the creature as it moved around. Watching a pet get used to a new home is always an interesting experience; all that energy and longing for love wrapped up in a tiny little body and begging to be released. He seemed like a smart little guy, able to get the general layout of the land quickly. He walked into all the rooms and traced along the perimeter of the apartment before eventually settling back into the living room. Upon his return, I decided to tune back into the conversation.

"Did you even buy any dog food?"

"I'm going to leave early and do all that shit tomorrow, figured I could just give him a steak tonight. First night here and he's getting a gourmet feast, lucky little scamp."

"What about housetraining?"

"It's not a fucking puppy, you idiot, of course he's trained, he took a shit on the way over here. Look, is it so hard for you to just admit that for once there's absolutely no real reason to criticize me and that I know what I'm doing?"

Ravi had come back out just in time to shoot me a look, inviting me to join in for a resounding unison: "Yeah, kind of."

"Well, fuck you too, guys. Anyway, the dog's staying, end of story; now, if you don't mind, I have some incredibly adorable photos to take."

It took him an hour and a half of shooting, editing, and caption consulting—yes, consulting, he asked a trusted advisor—but the guy got eight-hundred and sixty likes, so what the fuck do I know?

A Red Hat

2:47 AM, November 9th, 2016:

"CNN projects: Donald Trump wins the presidency… Donald J. Trump will become the 45th President of the United States."

Sixty seconds that I will never forget, in my entire life, no matter how desperately, painfully, or intensely I wish to do so.

First things first, let's get the fun stuff out of the way: I wasn't able to vote because I wasn't a citizen yet, but if I could have voted, it would have been Madame Secretary Hillary Rodham Clinton.

OK then, so for the seventy-five or so percent of you that didn't just close this book and immediately light it on fire, let me go ahead and paint the scene: like many fine citizens of this nation, Ravi and I had decided to attend an election night party one of his coworkers was putting on. Curtis had been invited as well but he had vehemently declined, stating that he had much better things to do than watch, and I quote, "the next lying piece of shit who's going to be stealing my money give a long speech." I already knew he was a proud Libertarian (his dad kept a place down in the New Jersey woods that can only be described as a drug den/weapon arsenal, and Curtis had accompanied him there on many a weekend visit in his formative years), but I figured he'd at least come for the free booze and Columbia coeds. Leaving our friend to stew in his tax-hating juices, we headed on up to the stylish 116th Street apartment and settled in with the rest of the guests, a group that mostly consisted of grad students and the younger people from Ravi's office. As usual, it took me a little while before I was relaxed enough to find a social engagement for the evening, but I ended up striking a conversation with a law student from Melbourne named Alex. Pleasant guy; never talked to him again a day in my life, but still, very pleasant.

After about an hour or so the main event of the evening finally began and we all settled in for the festivities. Ravi scored a primo couch spot with a girl he'd been chatting with for a few weeks, while Alex and I decided to post up in the back with the copious amounts of remaining alcohol. We knew we were in for a long night, and we knew that we definitely wouldn't want to be sober for it.

It was the understatement of the goddamn millennium.

For those of you who aren't denizens of this great land, coverage of the presidential election night essentially has four interspersed segments: announcing the locked-up states that no one cares about because they've been voting the same way since Nixon, running through every single mathematical possibility for either candidate's victory (occasionally they talk about the third party candidates but only to amuse themselves and pass the time), pundits talking at each other about exactly how badly the other pundit's candidate would ruin the country they love, and the genuine, almost surreal panic that accompanies every single-digit point shift in key battleground states. The fourth course this time around would consist of Colorado, Florida, Iowa, Michigan, Nevada, New Hampshire, North Carolina, Ohio, Pennsylvania, Virginia and Wisconsin.

As you can imagine, the panicking was abundant.

7:00 PM:

"So, Kola, how long does this usually take, mate? I still got a paper that needs a bit of finishing."

"Relax, man, usually it takes all night but this time should be relatively quick. See, she's definitely going to win Wisconsin and Michigan, 99.9% for Pennsylvania, Virginia and Florida, and she'll probably take Ohio and Iowa to boot. Combine with the states we already have locked up, maybe even Georgia and Texas, and it'll be all done before you know it."

8:00 PM:

"Can someone check those Florida numbers, please?" one entirely pink-clad woman asked to the room, hand showing just the slightest signs of shaking as her cup swayed, "Try the Associated Press or something."

"It's only 75% in," Ravi replied, "give it a few more minutes. Besides, it's not the most critical battleground; she doesn't have to crush him in every state, and we still have the Blue Wall."

As a few more of those locked-up states rolled by on the screen, something almost inconsequentially small began to find its way into the room. I won't abuse my gift of hindsight and say anything concrete was beginning to dawn on us, but it was almost like the air started to seep out, gradually but still noticeably to the discerning eye.

9:00 PM:

"Alex… where's the rum? Why is all the rum gone?"

"Oy, mate, you know you finished the whole damn thing, yeah?"

It took me a few seconds of scanning the table for this

supposedly empty bottle, until I realized rather disconnectedly that I was in fact holding it in my other hand.

"Huh, look at that. Well where's the vodka then?"

"Hey, everyone, please relax, OK, he's not actually gonna win Florida," said a very self-assured, very skinny man rocking an "I'm With Her" t-shirt, "They must've just gone through all the white trash votes. Once the last 9% comes in from civilization she'll be home free."

"What do you guys think he'll do after the loss?" asked a woman who looked entirely too much like Lena Dunham for me to not mention it, "This guy I know who used to date my favorite barista said he already registered a name for his Trump TV network."

"Oh God, like Fox News but with half the brain cells."

"Zero divided by two is still zero!"

10:42 PM:

"Why do they keep talking about how Ohio's picked every President since the 60's? Like, who gives a shit about the 60's besides old white people?" said Ravi's workspace neighbor, who I would later find out was named Rebecca Blanche, "it's just farm country anyway, of course he wins with those people."

Despite the righteous indignation her voice conveyed, the sounds of the room were mostly those of trepidation. It was still too early at that point, there were still plenty of votes to count, and I can honestly say that at this point the reality of the situation had settled upon me, and so, with Alex having left to finish his paper and Ravi's girl having moved on to some Brazilian guy, I dared to drunkenly yet quietly broach the unanswerable question with my good pal.

"Yo, Ravi... what do you think it's gonna be like? If he wins?"

"Well, let's see," he replied softly, spirit breaking under the weight of his darkest nightmare materializing before his eyes, "we'll live in a world where a borderline racist, proudly misogynist, confirmed Islamophobe is leader of the free world and will probably launch a nuke the first time a foreign leader calls his dick small. How does that sound to you?"

"Sounds like I should get on a plane."

"Forget the plane, if these clowns get their way we'll both be out of here on a boat."

10:53 PM:

There's no sight quite as fascinating as a room of people who are all sharing the same thought. All those individual personalities and voices, all transfixed on one phenomenon, and all experiencing the same exact reaction, but expressing it rather differently. One guy was on his laptop, furiously flipping between ten different election trackers and his Twitter feed; Becky was pouring what I can only guess was her "totally last, I swear you guys" glass of wine; a bunch of people were standing up in the center-left of the room discussing plans to move to Canada; and as for Ravi and I, well, we did our usual television routine, complete with blank stares.

"You know, it's funny, when I first moved here the only things I knew about Florida were that Mickey Mouse had a house there and it was full of some kind of unholy monster called an alligator."

"Not in the mood, Kola."

"I mean, seriously, I thought the cowboy was bad in 2000, but this is something else."

"It's not over yet, OK, she can still win in— what was that?"

"Pretty sure that Becky chick just smashed a wine bottle on the ground… shots?"

"Shots."

1:35 AM:

I'll be honest, I was blacked out by this point. Ravi says that once it became clear he had Pennsylvania, there was a crescendo of shrieking, weeping, and profanity, a long bout of depressed silence, and finally, a mass exodus into the sobbing streets. We would have left as well but between the host actually being one of the departing partygoers and us being too drunk to realize the place was empty, sitting still just made more sense. I don't think I was actually asleep at that point, but it wouldn't have made much of a difference.

2:47 AM:

The host still wasn't back, Ravi was asleep, and I had only woken up to go to the bathroom. As I stumbled in a drunken haze looking for my phone charger, or any phone charger, the pundits were going through their song and dance, half the panel engaging in delighted mockery while the other delivered apocalyptic musings. Ravi was just recovered enough to drag his feet so I figured we could make the walk home. We had to go, but I ended up sitting down for a few minutes to collect myself.

Some part of me wanted to go insane with anger. Some part of me wanted to analyze how this could happen in the nation I'd come to know as the greatest on earth. Some part of me wanted to grab the nearest bottle and see exactly how far my liver could go.

Ultimately, all those parts of me ceded to the part that remembered the day after the election, is, in fact, not a national holiday, and that my client meeting was, in fact, still scheduled for 10:00 AM. I splashed some water on Ravi's face, got our collective shit together, and hailed a cab, ready to go home, get some sleep, and wake up to my brand-new America.

Itua Uduebo

A Box of Flowers

The following excerpt was transcribed from an audio recording taped in the New York office of Global Children Empowerment Group 501(c) on November 18, 2017 and has been obtained with special permissions by an involved party.

"There was one day in year four of primary school - so I was 9, I guess - when I decided to walk home from school... I realize that's not the strangest thing in the world for Americans but in Nigeria everyone in the suburbs had a driver, along with a maid, a house in a gated cul-de-sac and armed guards. Our guy wasn't particularly watchful so I knew could sneak out of the lot. My friends and I had been to the neighborhood near the academy before for snacks, and - I'll admit - cigarettes once or twice, but to walk all the way back to my part of town? I can't even try and tell you what I was thinking, if I was at all; those are the kind of fun things boys do, I guess.

"I'd seen the poverty before, it's virtually inescapable when you live in Lagos, but there was always a sense of distance; I was either passing by and glancing out a car window or popping in briefly to partake and exit at my leisure. After four hours of wandering, the reality of my situation began to dawn on me, the fact that I was lost and had no way of getting to the police or even getting back to school grounds; a phone would

176

have been the next best thing, but not being able to remember my phone number wasn't helping. Worn down from the panic and walking, I decided that any amount of danger was worth getting some rest, so I found an abandoned spot next to what I didn't know at the time was a heroin den and slept.

"I don't know what would have happened if he didn't fall on me. Maybe I would've slept a little while longer and gotten picked up by the officers eventually, maybe I would've gotten kidnapped and sold off for a quick buck; I don't like to think about it. I woke up, startled and groggy, grabbing my bag out of instinct and preparing myself to run. Once I was able to see my assailant, however, I was more confused than anything else… it was a hard sight to process. He looked just, and I mean, exactly, like me, so much that I honestly thought I was dreaming. It was odd, like that thing they do in the cartoons with the mimicking doppelgangers except it was less, well, animated. It wasn't until I took a second glance that the differences started to show: my cheeks plus a few scars and cuts, my eyes featuring more redness, my feet minus the nice shoes the nanny had cleaned that morning. I stood up and discovered we shared height and figure to match, albeit for a slight limp on his end that gave me an extra inch. We stood there in silence, one taking in the other, absorbing the peculiarity of the moment. I looked behind him and saw that he was accompanied by a cart of wares, trinkets and odd bits he must've spent all day trying to sell. I spotted little wooden carvings, patchy fabrics, pieces of scrap metal… and then there was this box of flowers. Fake flowers, plastic, but they still had this, I don't know, artificial beauty, a certain vividness. I was transfixed by the collection, even as it sat amongst the refuse.

"I walked over and picked one up, a slender violet, and stared for a while. He didn't seem to mind neither my intrusion on his property nor my completely ignoring him. I asked him, in the Queen's proper English, where he got the pretty flowers from. He replied, in rough pidgin, that he found them, and needed to sell them. I asked him why he wasn't in school. He said his mother was sick, so he stopped going. I wanted to ask why his father didn't buy her medicine, but even then I knew enough to know better. I looked at the flower again, felt the unnatural smoothness in my hand, and wondered, in what simple terms I could muster up, how I could find something so inauthentic to be so perfect. I placed the violet in my pocket, and started talking to him again.

"He had this softness about him, something disarming; a look in his eye I didn't see in a lot of the other boys. I told him what was wrong and he said he knew where the police were, he could take me. As he took me through back alleys and past the countess merchants lining the dirt-clothed street, the stars glowing as brightly as the gas lamps adorning countless windows, a charmed silence blossomed between us, a stoically immaterial embrace. I didn't think much at the time, being slightly more concerned with my own survival, but it's not so hard to imagine I was the first kid he'd played with in a while, and he was certainly the most interesting kid I'd ever met. The way he talked about the dilapidated buildings and greeted the shopkeepers, you would think he was living in a wonderland, full of colorful characters and picturesque sights. His imaginative power was infectious and soon it started to affect me; what had only hours before been an endless mess of gray and brown transformed into a darkly hued tapestry, and the unfamiliar faces became welcoming and warm. For a little while, honestly, I completely forgot I was lost.

"We got to the police station, finally, and walked up to the nearest pair of officers. Two things happened next, one of which I didn't see happen, and the other something I'll remember until I die: one officer looked at me, in my uniform blazer, prestigious academy patch blazed upon the breast pocket, and yelled at me to know what I was doing around here. The other officer took a more… more physical approach, with my new companion. I… I already knew what a baton was for, but to actually see it go upside a little kid's head, well, that's something else entirely.

"I screamed as he collapsed, shocked and confused, honestly thinking I was next, but while he lay on the ground in pain, all I received was a disturbingly calm questioning. Stunned into automation, I provided all the information I could, the junior officer was sent in to make a call and I was told to sit in the car. My body complied but my eyes were still locked on his motionless body, rising and ebbing just enough to show breathing but still producing an unwelcome amount of bleeding. I meekly begged the officer to help him, said that he didn't do anything wrong and that he needed help, cried that he was nice and asked why they hit him, why they would do that.

"He… he answered me. He said something that I, honestly, don't want to repeat. Something that taught me a harsh lesson, engraved it into my gray matter: some people's lives just don't matter. Some people, for a lot of people - or maybe I should say a lot of people to some people - mean nothing, and they mean nothing because for some inconceivably evil reason, everyone's come together in a universal, subconscious, unanimous declaration that they mean nothing. The children paid in pennies and rice to make the shoes that your favorite NBA player sells for $500.00 mean nothing; the kids who look up at the bright, blue sky and only see the next drone strike, missile, or chemical attack mean nothing; the boy selling flowers by the road to keep his mom alive… that night, he meant less than nothing. The second that officer saw him, he didn't see a meaningless child, he saw a threat, an imminent danger to someone who mattered, a child from the other side of town, the part of Lagos he was probably working double shifts to buy a house in. In me he saw a life, a life in the den of the lifeless that he was charged to keep under control, and the second he saw one of those things near me, he acted… in his mind, he probably thinks he's the one who saved me. My hero.

"They put me in the car, drove me home, told my parents what happened and left me to alternating rounds of joyful prayer and furious punishment. The next day, I went back to school, went home, this time under a much more watchful-eyed driver, and life continued. I never tried to find him, never tried to go back to that area, never even tried to remember him. The only things I couldn't forget, no matter what I did, for all those years, were the sound of the baton, crashing against his skull, and the flowers: plastic, perfect and pointless.

"I guess, in the grand scheme of things, I realized… um, wow, I apologize that was… an incredibly long answer to the… I'm sorry, what was the question again?"

"Kola, the question was: name a time you were inspired to make a difference."

"Make a difference, right, OK… well, then let me say that the reason I used that example is that—"

End of excerpt.

A Reasonable Explanation

One of the first things I had to get used to when I moved to America was the snow. For those of you who may not have done so well in grade school geography, Nigeria is right along the equator, so things like "winter" and "cold" and "not needing a fan on at all times" didn't really exist in my childhood. I certainly never had to deal with frozen water piled as high as my head before that first winter in New York, so you can imagine my reaction. I understood the science behind it, but I didn't like it, and I absolutely admit that I tried my best to pray it away a few times. While all the other children would lose their shit over the mere possibility of a snow day, I would be in my room, wrapped in an afghan, drinking hot tea, reading my latest library pickup and counting down the seconds until it was over.

It took a couple more years, and a few well-earned snowball fight victories, but eventually I did learn to love the snow. I loved the way the streets, normally a moving mosaic of different colors and shapes, would come together in a chilly white harmony. I loved the way the flakes reflected the lights, bathed in yellow while they joined their fallen comrades below. The cold stopped bothering me as much, and I even began to like those big puffy jackets—I used to call them "black marshmallows"—that my mom insisted on buying. I was never as comfortable as my native friends, but I got used to it.

Those thoughts of winters past were on my mind that December night as I entered the NYPD 17th Precinct Office amid a light snowstorm. Abi and I had decided to have a snowfall sex session that night after some naughty texting escalated, so I was already in her (place) when I got the call. At first it was hard to make out what Curtis was saying, the panic over being stuck in a holding cell breaking his usual speaking patterns, but eventually I figured it out.

"You fucking idiot, what'd you do, piss in the middle of the street? Only you could manage to get picked up for public indecency when it's too cold to even be outside."

"Look, the 'what' isn't really important, OK? Just come get me out of here and I'll pay you back later."

"Tsk. Whatever, I'm with Abi right now so give me a little while, you'll survive, as long as you don't piss off the wrong serial killer that is."

"...."

"Hello? Hey, I'm joking, I'll be there soon enough."

"Is Abi on the phone right now?"

I looked over to see her talking as well, but I couldn't make out the words. They looked hurried and confused.

"Yeah, she is, why?"

I could hear him start putting panic into his breathing, not the fearful kind though, the kind you get when you're trying to work out the exact perfect way to handle something you weren't prepared for. His mind was rushing to think of any possible excuse; alas, none was to be had.

He breathed a sigh of defeat and proceeded to tell me the truth.

As Abi and I began putting our clothes back on and figuring how to get to our destination, a lot of emotions were flying through the room from both ends. She was feeling some mix of betrayal, anger, confusion, disgust, and disappointment, all wrapped around with a hint of sexual frustration over not getting to finish (finish *again*, just to be clear). I, on the other hand, was mostly concerned with my main feelings, which were the uncontrollable urge to laugh my ass off and the dread of having to listen to Abi's opinions on the matter.

Curtis and María, unbeknownst to us, had not only been screwing each other's brains out since that very first night back in July, but had in fact been dating for two months, and had neglected to share this with either of us. While I found every single part of that sentence to be hilarious due to the extreme hypocrisy implied, Abi was in a rage. Apparently, this constituted some sort of major breach of trust between her and María. I wonder how she would have reacted if she'd been aware that I'd only told my parents I had a girlfriend at Thanksgiving, just shy of three months after the incident with her father. Well, that's not true; I don't need to wonder, I know the answer already and it involves some combination of castration and waterboarding.

"Why are you not more upset?! Your best friend kept a secret from you for like, months!"

"I mean… I don't think it counts as a secret if I never asked and I still don't really care. I'm just going to roast him for a few minutes when we get there. And how is that the part that you're upset about: they were literally fucking in a seminary graveyard. If he wasn't going to hell before, he pretty much booked it with that."

"You know I'm not that much of a Christian, I just keep it up for the folks."

"Well as long you're with me you're gonna have to do double duty on that front. My mom thinks you're coo-coo for Christ and I would rather not have that conversation again."

"Wait, when did you even tell your parents about me?"

I really did consider telling the truth, something inside me compelling me towards honesty's virtue; alas, I'm but a mortal man, fearful and weak: "September, I think, right after that thing with your dad. I was pretty much ready after that day."

"Aww, *baby!*" She cooed, giving me a flurry of cheek kisses. They started getting a little longer each time, but just as I was beginning to lose concern over the driver staring at us, we arrived. Abi's scowl came back immediately.

As much as I didn't *love* the idea of being surrounded by so many police officers, I knew I needed to keep my cool and focus on exiting as soon as possible. The indictment of Officer Connelly in the Hakeem Fieldston shooting had triggered a response larger than many expected, and the protests had been consistent and sustained. Between the police, their supporters, and the activists, everyone was on edge, and everyone was waiting for what would come next. I actually ended up going with Abi to that organizing meeting she mentioned, and what I saw had left me both inspired and concerned; the people were passionate and ready to do the work for change, but some of the ideas seemed a little, well, radical for me. I would never form an idea about a movement by the random outbursts of a few individuals, but even some of the most egregious discussed notions—armed insurrection, communism, and what can really only be described as white disenfranchisement—didn't receive quite as much pushback as I would have liked. I decided that I could support the effort, but the activist circle wasn't something I had interest in.

The waiting area was full of parents that night, both the tragically clueless and the even-more-tragically unfazed. It began to dawn on me that I was basically Curtis' responsible older brother and it was a realization that I personally wasn't very thrilled about. María and Curtis both required separate bail payments, so Abi and I had to go through the whole thing twice before finally getting them out. Needless to say, it was not a joyous reunion in the middle of the waiting room.

"Do you have anything to say to yourself?" Abi asked María, sounding more and more like my mom with every passing second of annoyance.

"Oh, get over it, chica, you know damn well why I didn't tell you. Bitch, you are so judgmental, you would never have kept your mouth shut about it."

"With good reason, María! It's bad enough you're out here defiling churches with this fake-ass Johnny Bravo, but you've been dating somebody for weeks and you didn't tell me?"

"Johnny Bravo?"

Both women looked at Curtis and he was able to get the message pretty quickly.

"Well," I said, with a casual air of deference, "we'll leave you two alone, then. Come on jailbird, let's go ask those two cops if they have any cool shootout stories."

"Where in the hell do you think you're going, Kola?" Abi replied with an oddly off-putting scowl, "How are you not upset with him right now?"

Because that would require caring. At all.

"I mean… I don't know, keeping our shit private isn't exactly a brand-new phenomenon for us. I didn't even remember to tell him that we were going to the same college for like a week."

"Yeah, I remember you fucking told me after some house party, after I mentioned something about pledging. How'd you forget that one exactly?"

"Curtis, I just bailed you out of jail for plowing your secret girlfriend on church grounds, you don't get to talk shit right now. Matter of fact, no, you're on a one-week shit-talking ban, effective immediately."

"But -"

"One week, ban, no exceptions. Don't blame me, blame the justice system."

"Isn't that supposed to be my line?"

"Well I can guess you can just call me OJ then. Where my glove at?"

"That reminds me, what was your score this week? You're playing Albert, right?"

"He won 108-97. Fucking Pats offense man, one week Brady drops four TDs and the next they play it safe and run all day, I'm seriously getting pissed at this poi- "

"WILL YOU TWO SHUT THE FUCK UP?!?"

It was at that moment that Curtis and I remembered that we weren't the only two people in the room as we often imagined we were. Apparently they'd kept on talking the whole time, and about something that was actually relevant.

"Hey, María, babe, relax," Curtis responded, proving once and for all that he absolutely lacked the ability to read a room,

"You two do your little thing while me and KoKo-Puffs here go outside."

"¿Qué? Are you crazy? Why are you not defending me here?"

"Because he's a fucking idiot, which is why I cannot believe your stupid ass is falling for him." Abi was about as good at deescalation as Nixon was in Vietnam.

"Hey, piss off, short stuff," he answered, proving once and for all that he absolutely lacked a fear of death, "and quit nagging. You sound like my aunt."

Oh God, why?

"Are you going to let him get away with that?" Abi asked, about two seconds away from pointing her actual finger in my face. Normally I would try and say something slick or, more realistically, mumble half a joke before succumbing to discomfort, but for some reason I just wasn't having it that day.

"OK, that's it, all of this is insane. This is not a conversation worth having anymore. Curtis, don't ever say anything like that to her again, I mean it. María, I don't know what you see over here but all power to you. And Abi, let's not try to control our friends' love lives, all right? Now, as for the secrecy, it's over, no point being upset anymore. How about we all go out and get a bite before the snow gets too bad and we have to spend all night with the drunks and muggers?"

"Nigga who the hell died and made you in charge, and I am not trying to control anything, I just demand an apology for being lied to."

"Bitch, nobody lied to you, OK? I told you I was messing around with some guy, I just didn't tell you his name. And you want to talk about secrets? OK, fine; hey, Kola, what do you know about someone named Abdullah?"

If it wasn't for all that melanin in her face I swear the color would've flown from Abi's as soon as María uttered the name.

"María, don't you fucki-"

"Um, I'm sorry, what? Who the hell is Abdullah?"

"He's just some old college boyfriend, OK? He moved to the city a few weeks ago from Chicago."

"Hermana, finish the story, or I'll finish it for you."

"You little… we got drinks, OK? It was that weekend you went to visit your aunt for her birthday. *Nothing* happened, like, at all, he didn't even try any dumb shit."

"HA! Getting played by a Saudi prince, tough stuff man."

Usually I don't resort to tapping another guy in the nuts, but in that moment, it felt earned. As Curtis doubled over in amused pain, I pressed on my questioning: "So why did you not tell me this, then?"

"Great question Kola; remember what you told me, huh Abi?" María asked, grinning with a level of mischief that I'd only ever seen on… well, on her boyfriend.

"For the love of God, fine, you bitch; I said that I didn't want to tell you because I knew you'd take it the wrong way and it wouldn't do you any good to get heated over nothing. But that is not the same thing as this, María, and you know it."

"*Hipocrita!* It's the exact same thing and you know it, right Kola? Don't you feel betrayed by her lack of faith in you?"

Honestly, I still don't know if María was right or not; there really wasn't any part of me that thought Abi had done anything with the guy. I wasn't angry, but I also wasn't thrilled that she'd lied to me, especially after how mad she got about Stacy. I could have thrown that in her face and called her out for hypocrisy, but I figured that my odds of getting an actual apology were far lower than the odds of this evolving into the next week of my life. I was mostly concerned that the dude was better looking than me or richer or some other trigger for my male insecurity, but without anything to go on, all I could do was imagine the worst and then dismiss myself as being irrational. I decided that the most constructive thing I could do was to use this as an opportunity to end my suffering.

"Look, clearly trust issues are a big theme for today, but can we all just agree that it's a lot easier to be honest with each other, especially if you're so stupid that you end up getting arrested as part of your lie? I don't give a shit about Aladdin or whatever his name was, and Abi, it really doesn't matter that she kept Curtis a secret. I mean, come on, look at him; can ya really blame her?"

If he wasn't in critical condition, he might have had a response for that.

"*Ughhhhhhh*, fine, whatever," Abi conceded, "look I don't know what the fuck is going through your head but I'm over the lying part. Just please, for the love of God, let me know if/when/if he fucks this up so I can gloat."

"Deal, mami, and I'll be sure to be there for you the next time you complain about Kola and his stupid—"

"AYE! OK, damn bitch I get it, shit… awww, I can't stay mad at ya, come here!"

The hugging-it-out woud have been a lot cuter if I wasn't intensely terrified about what María was about to say next. I never actually got my answer, but I maintain my suspicions (it was definitely "haircut," just had to be).

They didn't hug it out or anything, but it was evident that the problem was over for the time being. By the start of the New Year, Abi would go on to bitch about Curtis and María a combined total of ninety-eight times, stopping just one short from completing Jay-Z's legendary mantra.

"Hooray!" Curtis groaned sarcastically, still recovering from my attack, "one big happy fucking family. Now, can we please get out of here? The officers are starting to stare, and I think it's safe to say it's not because of me."

"Pinche cabron! This is all your fault, we were supposed to go get Chinese food, but your nasty ass just insisted that we take ten minutes to get busy in front of a church. Dios mío, si mi madre oyó esto…"

"Whoa, whoa, ten minutes?" Curtis questioned, genuine hurt poking through his bravado, "Be mad all you want but let's not start spreading alternative facts here."

"Fine, eleven then, whatever. Point is, I'm still hungry. What about you two?"

"Wouldn't recommend that."

We all looked back at the officer who'd appeared behind us: "The snow got crazy since you guys have been in here, no way you're going to be able to get through it for a few hours. You're better off in here than outside."

"Um, thanks, Officer," I replied, "but unless there's food in this joint we're better off making the trek. We're all starving."

"We've got a vending machine. How does that sound?"

Normally I would have taken a minute to observe the oddness of our proposed meal, but hunger has a strange way of dulling the comedic senses.

I'm sure that there are far worse ways to pass through a blizzard than feasting on candy, Pop Tarts, potato chips and trail mix before passing out in an NYPD precinct office breakroom, but for the life of me I can't imagine one more ridiculous. We didn't get to leave until the morning, and by the time we were getting out, we were all tired to the point of pure exhaustion. The white blanket reflected the new day's light and bathed the scene. It was glowing. There was only one thing to do at a time like that, and Abi knew exactly what it was: "Hey Babe, heads up!"

Right in the face.

Twenty minutes later, I had another snowball fight win under my belt, and three opponents vanquished at my feet. Nothing tastes better than a bagel and coffee after the triumph of victory.

A Holiday Special

My family lived in the city right up until my last year of high school; after my dad got a few big contracts for his architecture firm, we moved out to the suburbs of Bronxville, New York, and settled into the peaceful life. My heart and soul still belonged to the concrete streets, but I got used to coming back home on break to trees and friendly neighbors. There were trees and bushes on the lawn, and a giant mass of woodlands in the back, decaying yet teeming with wildlife. For those of you who've never dared to make the perilous journey past 242nd Street, the deer population of New York is the absolute undisputed king of its territory. Even if they could understand the concept of property rights, I doubt they would care very much. Aside from deer, there were a few pests that took getting used to: mosquitoes, ticks, skunks, Jehovah's witnesses, and people who unironically care about the local parent-teacher association.

I'd never had a good reason to spend Christmas apart from my family, and given that Abi lived in Queens, there really wasn't any way I'd be able to get away with that one. To be clear, it's not like I was looking for an excuse to not see them, it's more that some residual leftovers from my rebellious teenage years wanted an excuse to do something they didn't want. It was far in the back of my mind, but it lingered, like a fly buzzing around at night when you're already in bed and have no intention of stimulating any muscle activity.

Christmas was on a Monday that year, so I decided to come in for the weekend and head back on Tuesday. An hour's ride was all that separated my urban domain from the now-bare trees and hilly roads, but it somehow still felt like an eternity. At that point, I'd been home a total of eight times for the calendar year, the last one being Thanksgiving. My brother had brought home his girlfriend for Thanksgiving, but they'd been dating since the end of the previous summer, so it was a bit overdue. I don't know what would happen if my sister would bring home a guy, but I've watched enough family comedies to have a decent idea.

I didn't have a car at the time, so my dad picked me up from the Metro North station in the early evening. The only man in my life who made me look small, he gave me one of his patented bear hugs and remarked on how long it had been. I used to hate those hugs for a while; in my teenage years, they were always a bit too close, too loving. The personal space that I wanted so desperately to cultivate for myself would dissipate every time he wrapped his arms around me and squeezed as tight as he could, occasionally even planting a kiss on the cheek. I always got over it by reminding myself I had no idea what it was like to be a parent, but I also knew that by the time my kids were in their twenties it would be nothing but handshakes, loving pats on the back and the occasional three-second hug. Just like the good old days.

"So how have you been, son? You look well! How's work?"

"It's all right, same old mess. They put me on a new client this month and I get to work with this big-shot director, so that should be nice. Other than that I'm just chilling."

"Sounds important, eh! You should be excited, in my day associates never even got to speak to directors, let alone work with them."

"It's all about inclusivity now, don't you know? Flat hierarchies and stuff like that. Anyway that's it for work, and everything else is fine. What about you, how's the firm?"

"'Another day, another dollar' as they say in this country. We just broke ground on that new church for the diocese and I'm meeting with the Ethiopian deputy ambassador next week to discuss new work. Oh! Speaking of Africans, how is that girl of yours?"

Oh God, here we go.

"She's fine, and, again, I am sorry for not telling you guys until Thanksgiving, it honestly just slipped my mind. You know I'm not the best at communication."

"Not good? Ha! Son, you're horrible at it, amazingly so in fact. I wonder how she even stands you."

"OK, it's not like I fled the country or anything, let's calm down here. And things are good with Abi, next week we're even doing dinner, my turn to cook this time."

"You cooking? I know you, son, you're too absent-minded; you'll start watching TV or be on that phone like you always are, next thing you know the kitchen is on fire, again."

"I was, like, nine when that one happened, exactly how long am I going to have to hear it for? And you want to talk about absent-minded, but I seem to remember that it wasn't me who smashed the balcony table."

"Eh?! Never happened, what are you talking about?" This was his favorite trick, a classic I'd grown far too used to.

"Benevolent gaslighting" is what I would have to call for it, if that term isn't too much of an oxymoron.

My dad filled me in on the family while we drove. My sister, Adesua, was killing it in school as was absolutely demanded of her, but there were also some rumblings under the surface; she'd just turned fifteen and was beginning that second stage of adolescence. Remember how when you were fifteen you thought your opinions actually mattered, and that the best way to get treated like an adult was to act like a toddler? She knew better than to throw any tantrums, having gone through the same conditioning as her two older brothers, but she also knew she could get away with certain things that for us would have resulted in dire consequences. Once, while I was home for spring break, she slammed the door after a miffed conversation with my mom. I sat there, waiting to hear my mom barge into her room and start the whooping, only to see nothing occur and the issue get resolved later through—and I still can't believe these words came out of my mother's mouth— "talking it out." The small, socially conscious part of me that was happy to see progressive child-rearing methods win out was absolutely dwarfed by the part teeming with resentment over how soft they'd gotten. If I had ever slammed the door on my mom she would've bashed my head through it, and then my dad would have taken my head out, and then just slammed the door on me. And then the real punishment would have begun.

Life isn't fair.

My brother, Abu, on the other hand, was in a much more stable place in his development. Two years into college had done a number on him, changing an annoying young punk into an annoying young man with a refined vocabulary, facial hair, and an obnoxious fondness towards his beloved fraternity brothers. He went to NYU so it wasn't like he was living the Animal House life, but he was definitely enjoying himself. It wasn't like he was slacking off though: he'd started off wanting to become a doctor, but had quickly dropped that dream in pursuit of something a bit less soul-crushing: business management. Unlike me, he inherited my father's propensity for formulaic equations and calculations, while I had taken on my mother's in-depth thinking and way with words. My sister was smarter than the both of us, and we'd always been sure she'd end up the best of the bunch, but only time can tell with those things.

As for my mom, the second I walked in the door it was like having her little boy back for the first time in decades - never mind the fact that I'd just been home for Thanksgiving. I'd been taller than her since I turned seventeen so while my dad's hugs felt like being trapped, she felt more like having a dog jump on me, more obnoxiously sappy but less physically uncomfortable. The second thing she did after hugging me to death was to thank the Lord for bringing my father and me back safely. This wasn't because the roads were icy or there was some sort of terror alert; thanking the Lord Almighty came as naturally to my mother as the breath in her lungs and the twinkle in her eyes. She was a woman of God to the bone, and thanks to her, if it wasn't for all those Sundays where I was just a bit too hungover in college, I would have had a lifetime perfect Mass attendance record. Not only did we go to Church every Sunday, but we said the rosary every Saturday, prayed every morning, were told to pray most evenings, and were put into a God-awful Christian summer camp for four years in a row. You could get me hopped up on any drug you wanted and I guarantee you that I would still be able to recite the Nicene Creed in original Latin without missing a beat. The combination of Catholic guilt and African child-rearing is a truly terrifying thing to go through, but she wrapped it all up in a warmth and glow that made it seem almost pleasant. I will never be as devout as my mother, but she's certainly always been a model of how to live the life of the faithful, without being annoying about it.

My room was in the basement, a big mini-apartment that had resulted from my father's complete and total refusal to let unused space go to waste. Curtis always said that an architect's mind is always at work, and every room becomes a game to see how everything can go better together. The end product of ten weeks of my father's labor was a nice room, sizable closet, and a comfy bed, conveniently next to the PlayStation 4-TV-couch trifecta where my brother and I effectively lived. When we weren't attempting to destroy each other's dignity in FIFA or watch each other drain our lives away in the world of Skyrim, we would be lounging about and chilling our way through some show or movie. Our sister used to love coming down to invade our space, taking some odd joy in disrupting the boys I'm sure, but now such activities were certainly beneath her. She preferred the comfort of her own room, texting with God-knows-who about God-knows-what.

That first Friday evening back was low-key, just the way I liked it. Abu and I played a casual three-out-of-five FIFA set that saw me losing off a horseshit penalty call, we all had dinner and I caught up with Adesua on whatever topics she was actually willing to talk to me about. I called Abi and we talked for about an hour, the highlight of the conversation being the utter dismay in her voice when I confirmed that my fifteen-year-old sister was, in fact, a lot taller than she was. I couldn't help but start laughing over her fake-but-also-not-fake crying voice.

Saturday came and went, mostly consisting of me catching up on some reading and helping out around the house. That night mom made ayamase—rich, spicy green bell peppers crushed and stewed with goat meat, beef, tripe and boiled eggs—with rice and plantains on the side, one of my favorites, second only to the wonder and glory of jollof rice. My mom also decided that tonight was the night she was going to bombard me with questions about Abi, and between her not-at-all subtly bringing up "long-term commitment' (the kind that comes with white dresses and judgemental relatives) and my sister teasing me, I was just loving all the attention. My brother had a look of relief over his own girlfriend not coming up, and my dad had his eyes glued to the NBA highlights on TV, displaying once again the ideal fatherhood model that I aspire to. I repeated my pretaped answer over and over - "I like her a lot, but we'll wait and see" - to no avail but at the very least it wore her down. If persistence is a virtue then my mother is the patron saint.

Sunday was the Lord's Day, and with the addition of Christmas Eve Day anticipation in the mix, the spirit of Christ in the air was even more palpable. Getting ready for church for me usually involved a three-step process: (1) waking up far too early for noon mass and promptly going back to sleep, (2) being woken up at around 11:15 AM and being told that I would be the reason we were late that day, and then (3) being ready five minutes before my siblings and fifteen minutes before my parents. Abi texted me in the car ride over, a string of Christmas-related GIFs flooding my screen. Her three brothers were all back in town and they had just gotten out of their morning service, decked to the nine in traditional Yoruba garb. We preferred our Western attire to the robes and long shirts, to blend in better with our fellow vanilla churchgoers.

Mass was packed to the brim, excessively loud and grandiosely decorated, as to be expected to anticipate the Birth of Our Lord (technically I should have also gone to the Vigil Mass later that night, but I managed to get myself off the hook), but it was still a spectacle to behold. I may not love the day-to-day work of being a Christian, but I must admit, something about a grand Mass fills me with wonder; the way the voices all rise and ebb together in hymnal harmony, the power of the organ, the way the light plays with the sacramentals of the altar and black shadows blend with the gold and marble. The music in particular has its own aura to it; my years in choir had introduced me to the beauty of church songs, but as the years went on my appreciation turned to utter fascination. "City of God," "Ubi Caritas," "Ave Maria," music that transcended the limits of belief and faith, that moved the heart to something much more real and yet much more fantastical. It wasn't what I chose to listen to in my personal time; it was always far too special for that. Music that grand has to fit the proper occasion.

Even if you just can't believe that God himself is present in the moment, I truly think it's impossible to deny the supernatural beauty of it all, the way the heart stirs in the presence of the Mass scene. It always helped to pass the time along.

Sunday lunch was always an institution in my home, and one of my most beloved parts of coming back. Corned beef omelettes (canned corned beef, not that Irish shit), baked beans, Irish sausage (yes, that Irish shit), fried yams with onions, buttered bread, and fresh juice; my mouth always waters just thinking about it. I was always torn between wolfing it down out of instinct and savoring every single bite, but regardless of which route I took, I always ended my meal satisfied.

After the fantastically familiar lunch, I had to deal with one of the tasks of the special occasion; I'd already bought the Christmas gifts beforehand, but for some reason my dumb ass thought I'd be able to just take care of wrapping them at a later date. Days turned to weeks and eventually there I was, four naked gifts and no idea where the paper was. I started to think about all those Christmas Eve nights of my youth spent wondering what I would get the next day, anticipation and fear of disappointment all rolled up into an over-excited ball. Those times back in Lagos when I was a kid and I would put my ear to the bedroom door, trying to figure out if it was Santa's steps or my grandpa's cane. There was one time I actually left cookies and milk out, but instead of a morning surprise I got a light scolding from my mom for attracting flies. Even the celebrations in America had a certain magic to them, my older age notwithstanding. The feeling may fade, but it never really goes away.

I found the wrapping paper tucked away in my dad's study and I took care of the gifts. I had to wait a few hours before putting them under the tree, and by the time I went up in the middle of the night, the mat under the tree was already full. I wanted to sift through the boxes and objects to find my bounty, but I just put my gifts down and left; it's nice to keep some of the magic alive.

Christmas Day! Carols and prayers and holiday-special cartoons. A new watch, a new belt, a new tie, a new book (*The Sympathizer*, Viet Thanh Nguyen, 10/10). A Manchester United jersey. All my gifts were a huge hit, which, honestly, was pretty new for me so I was pretty excited. They were gushing over them, especially my dad who couldn't wait to set up the vinyl player and run through the full Fela Kuti collection I'd picked up. We talked, we laughed, we sang, we reminisced; we celebrated love, of both the Lord and one another, and basked in its glow. My brother and I played the new games, my sister spent hours navigating her new phone. We snacked on sausage rolls and scotch eggs until the main celebration in the evening, a feast fit for a king. A round, marvelously browned turkey, a thick honeyed ham, braised short ribs, fluffy, light mashed potatoes with the smoothest gravy, couscous, cranberry sauce, beans greener than the grasslands, carrots, corn and peas, a creamy lobster bisque that you just wanted to swim in, garlic bread and more dessert than I knew what to do with. We all gathered round to watch the NBA games, and then we watched our favorite movie, *Pirates of the Caribbean: The Curse of the Black Pearl*. Not the most Christmassy tale out there, but you go and find me another classic adventure-comedy with ghosts, tropical islands, and Johnny Depp's accidentally perfect slurring.

Everyone else was ready for bed after the movie so I

volunteered to wash the plates for the night, feeling generous and safe in the knowledge that I basically only had to do it once a year. My mom stayed behind to watch one of her late shows for a few minutes, and to have a few extra minutes of her lovingly-titled "Mommy Time."

"I hope you had a lovely Christmas, dear! I wish my baby didn't have to go back tomorrow."

"Heh, well there's not much I can do on that; projects can't manage themselves, unfortunately. I'll try to come by more often. How's that book going? You said you just finished writing that long chapter."

"Oh, it's wonderful. I got your Auntie Yemisi to take a look at it, so I'm waiting for her feedback, but by the grace of God I should be ready to move on to the next steps."

"Well that's good, then. What's it called again? 'Life Lived with Love of the Lord' or something?"

"That's the title, yeah. I can't wait to get it out there. Speaking of things that can't wait..." she said, pausing so I could get my groan out of the way before she started chuckling, "relax baby, I'm just teasing. I know you'll figure out your love life by yourself. Just don't take too long, okay?"

"Yeah, yeah, whatever. Anyway, aside from you badgering me about that particular topic, it was a really good Christmas."

"All my children home, safe and sound, Lord be praised for his gifts. I'm just thankful that everything is going according to His plan for you. Make sure to stay in touch more often from now on, OK? You're still terrible at communication; it's a wonder how that girl stands you."

It was at that moment I realized that the day these two met would be the death of me, images of a two-on-one beat-down popping up in my head.

"All right mom, point taken. Go get some sleep, I'll still be here in the morning."

"All right son, good night. I love you."

"Love you too, mom."

Love you too.

There were a lot of times when I said that out of reflex. Times when I just said it to end a conversation, and times when I said it despite some lingering anger. That wasn't one of those times.

A Dinner Date

"OK so that one is what, again?"

"I told you babe, it's called gnocchi, they're like little potato dumplings. You really should learn more about Italian food besides spaghetti and lasagna."

"Oh, look at you, Ms. Cosmopolitan! Well, truth be told I've always preferred Chinese as my ethnically basic cuisine of choice, so I never bothered much. Besides we didn't all get to do spring break in a villa like you. Tuscany, wasn't it?"

"Oh, Toscana, il mio amore! And wait a minute, it wasn't like I bought the damn place out, I only got to go because my bougie-ass white girl paid for all of us. Italy's cool and all but the warm sun and sky ain't gonna keep my pockets filled."

"I still can't believe you had a rich white girlfriend actually named Becky and you managed to contain your jokes for four years straight. That's some serious mental fortitude if I ever saw it."

"I had to call on the ancestors a few times, but I managed to keep it together; besides, even though she was on the morning-fog side of woke, I enjoyed her company. I definitely enjoyed spending her daddy's money, tell you that much."

"Her staddy or her 'Daddy'?" I asked, hoping to shock her into spitting up some of the expensive wine that she'd been pining for. It almost worked but she really did have amazing composure, which I suppose I should have expected from an actress.

"Boy, you better cut that shit out!" she snapped, trying to turn her chuckling smile into a scolding frown, "We are in a nice-ass restaurant tonight, and I don't want to be 'those' black people. How'd you even get us in here?"

"Ravi's boyfriend, Xavier, knows one of the day managers and he got us a spot. Probably remembered me complimenting his scarf that one time, the prick."

"Have I met him yet?"

"Yeah, he was there at the New Year's party, the one that Pierre was getting all nice and comfy with before Curtis told him that he was with Ravi. Your boy has a taste for older men I take it."

"Oh, you have no idea. And yeah, I remember him now, he was talking about Heidegger or Kierkegaard or something. Seemed a bit too pretentious."

"A bit too pretentious? This from the girl who got into a full-on discourse at a bar with a Columbia lit professor because she said that Ionesco's early work was, and I quote, 'derivative at best.'"

"OK, first off, I will literally never allow the work of Eugène Ionesco to be slandered in my presence, and I refuse to apologize for it. And second, that was not a discourse, I cleaned that bitch's clock in about five minutes, so don't get it twisted."

"Mm-hmm, whatever you say, sweetheart; anyway, yes you've met Xavier before. Speaking of couples, how's María handling life with Curtis?"

I don't even think that she noticed the couple at the other table who looked over when she groaned so loudly.

"I still can't believe she's with him; look, I know he's your best friend and all, so you like him, but I honestly just don't trust him. The douchiness I can get used to, slowly, but how can I expect a player like him to not cheat on my girl?"

"A 'player,' huh? Man, I hope he never hears you say that, might be the last bit of inflation his ego needs before it pops. Look, say what you want, but he's not a cheater, OK? His dad cheated on his mom all the time, and he hated him for it; if anything, he's radically honest with the women that he's with. Unless he was flat out lying to me, he told María the very first night that he's not the boyfriend type, and she said all she wanted was to break off a piece. Obviously, they both changed their minds, but he never made any false promises."

"So, you really don't think that the first time some random girl shoves her tits in his face he won't lose control?"

"I'll put it to you like this; Curtis would rather go to a girl's house, break up with her abruptly in person and take all the punishment she could dish out than cheat behind her back if he knew that he was going to end up fucking some girl putting the moves on him. He's a dick, yes, but he has a code."

"Ugh, fine, if you say so. We'll have to wait and see. And to answer your original question, they're out watching a movie, hopefully not getting into anymore sexual shenanigans."

"Did you just say shenanigans?"

"Yeah, so what?"

"You sound like my fifth-grade teacher, Ms. Rosenbaum," I remarked amusedly, "She would always say shit like that. 'Cut out the shenanigans, Kola, post-hence!' It would've made sense if she was a grandma, but the woman was like, thirty-two."

"Shenanigans is a bit less dated than 'post-hence' though, don'tcha think?"

"I guess, but still ridiculous though. Sounds like something your old character might've said, from the last play."

"Shit! Right, I forgot to tell you! I got that spot in *Luke Cage*!"

"No fucking way! Congratulations, baby!" I leaned over and gave her a big ol' kiss, long and loving, "I'm so proud of you. It's a speaking role too, right?"

"Yep!" she replied, glowing with pride and possibly wine, "and I am going to fucking kill it. This is honestly one of the best gigs I ever booked; I'm playing the sister of this drug dealer that Luke gets to turn himself in, so now he needs to protect me. First off, I get to be on set with Mike Colter, which, oh my God, I can't even begin to describe without making you insanely jealous. Like, imagine if Victoria's Secret was a client."

"Imagined, fully contemplated, odds calculated, and now I'm just upset. Please go on."

"Anyway, the best part is the actual lines, y'know? The character is scared, obviously, but she's also tough and keeps lashing out at Luke, saying shit like 'All that muscle and you can't even get up the damn stairs in time,' stuff like that. Real bitchy, very on brand for me."

"This is the part where I'm supposed to disagree with you, right?"

"No, it's the part where I already know you disagree with me so I don't even acknowledge the other possibility. Also, shut the hell up. Anyway, it's only one episode but it's actually a big chunk of screentime, plus at the end I get to do a big, teary-but-not-too-teary goodbye scene. That's the kind of shit that casting directors eat up. Basically what happens is that Luke meets this girl at a—"

I couldn't help but feel a little guilty as I smiled through her story of how her latest opportunity came about; she was in a rush to tell me everything, and I was still keeping my news a secret. GCEF had called about three weeks after the interview to offer me the position. It was a surreal moment, mostly because I was so sure I'd rambled my way out of the job, but once it hit me that I'd actually gotten what I'd gone out for... I turned them down.

What else could I do? It was far too sudden a shock to the system, the idea of actually dropping everything in my life and going back halfway across the world to a country I hadn't seen since preadolescence. By the time I had hung up the phone, I was already questioning why I'd even gone out for the position in the first place; I knew why - I had thought about memories still replaying themselves, but I scolded myself for not succumbing to logic sooner.

I decided it would just be one more addition to the small list of things I wouldn't be telling Abi about anytime soon, along with the reveal date of my relationship to the parents and my general indifference towards Beyoncé. Some things are better left unsaid.

"Lucky lady, you are," I noted, brushing my lingering guilt aside to avoid spoiling the mood, "isn't it rough though, having to do a rush job?"

"Eh, it's not too bad, mostly because the lines are so intuitive. Also, I am like, the world's greatest line learner, it's spellbinding. I think it's how God made it up to me for making me so mediocre with pauses and body language."

"He giveth, He taketh away."

"Mostly giveth in my case, obviously." She struck a little pose for the imaginary cameraman hiding in the restaurant, and for the handful of annoyed fellow patrons who were still serving the side-eye.

"Alright Rita Hayworth, calm down. This all sounds great and I am definitely, three-hundred percent super crazy freakin proud of ya, but I do have something serious I have to ask: how many good boyfriend points do I gotta get for you to get me an autograph from Rosario Dawson?"

"Hmm... I'll tell you what: I'll give you ten points every time you let me pick the movie, twenty points for every bad joke you laugh at, fifty points for taking me shopping, and then a hundred every time you..." she paused and then proceeded to slowly slide her hand below the table, simulating a light bobbing motion and biting her lip before proceeding to flick her tongue out. At first, I was in love with the sight for reasons that I shouldn't have to explain, but then something caught my eye that made it all even better.

"Mmm, alright, so a hundred for that," I asked in my best impression of a young James Earl Jones, "Now tell me what you want me to do for two."

"Let me see," she replied, teeth flashing a wicked smile, "two-hundred points every time you grab me by the waist, pick me up with those strong hands, throw me down on the bed, take or tear off whatever needs to be taken or torn, and give me some of that sweet, hard, thick—"

"Are you two ready to order?"

The waiter, who had been perfectly close enough to catch

the best parts of the exchange, had the face of a man being paid far too little for the trouble but just enough to bear with it. Everyone in customer service can relate to the stone-faced, painted-on smile used to escape unwanted interactions. The absolute mortification from Abi stood in stark contrast to his fixed expression; I made a mental note to give him a nice, fat tip for his trouble.

"Oh yeah, I'm ready. I think my girl's still choosing though, I think she's having trouble picking a meat dish." If her little legs were capable of kicking me under the table I'm sure she would've, but some people just weren't blessed with comedically convenient bodies. "Are you leaning more towards chicken or beef, babe?"

She really did know how to glare: "You know what, I think I'll go with pig. What's your best pork dish?"

After a few choice recommendations from the waiter and a few more moments of daggered wordplay, we eventually placed our orders: a split spiedino alla romana to start off, an order of linguine marechiar for me and one plate of stuffed pork chops with vinegar peppers for her. It was the kind of place where they bring the desserts around at the end, so we were looking forward to that as well.

"Where's this wine from again?"

"Chateauneuf du Pape, from Cotes du Rhone, so the southeast of France. I think María went there once."

"Another place in France I have to visit I suppose. Shit, I really do need to travel more, it's been a while, I haven't been out of the country since that wedding in London."

"Well, you don't need to leave the country to get a new experience; ever been out to Cali?"

"Yeah, once; went out to Los Angeles. Didn't agree with me very much but it was all right."

"Um, are you serious?" she asked, "Los Angeles is basically perfect, and I would literally murder several small animals just to get 10% off a decent studio out there."

"So the ony reason you're not out there right now is because no one's come up with an animal-murder-for-rent game show yet? Sounds like we need to call NBC."

"That's about 20% of it, yeah, but the other part is a bit less murdery. Like, Los Angeles is the place where dreams are reality, where you can discover the real you. New York is the place that beats you down to the toughest version, the hustle-holics, the subway survivor. Life isn't supposed to be a damn struggle all the time, and even if that's too optimistic, why the hell does it have to be something we celebrate? I dont't care if I sound like a wimp, I think life needs to feel a little softer than all this, a little easier. Just warm and sunny and… free. That's definitely the word I'm looking for: free."

"Scale of one to ten, how mad would you be if I said you were acting like a punk-ass bitch right now?"

"Twelve, and I'd stab you with this fork."

"Is it weird that I know you're not joking but I still find it adorable?"

"That means the brainwashing's finally kicking in."

"Look, I get what you're saying, I just disagree. New York just makes more sense to me."

"OK, but why?"

"Hard to put into words."

"New question: if someone said you could have everything you ever wanted in life, everything you ever dreamed of, and all you had to do was live in LA forever, what would you say? Serious answer."

"….I would honestly have to think about it."

She raised her eyes in an exaggerated manner, as shocked by my answer as she was amused by this unlikely fault line.

"Wowww, you really hate that place, huh? Shit, I'd move to Arkansas if that was on the table. You better tell me this obviously-traumatic story sometime, I am far too curious. Oh!" she exclaimed as one does when prone to distractions, "Sir! Can I I ask a little question about the pork rollatini? I might need to change my order."

We went on with dinner, drank and ate and shared the time together. It was one of those perfect nights where two people just exist in each other's space and enjoy their shared universe. I loved every second of it, almost as much as I loved the person I was sharing it with.

Almost.

Funny enough, I never did tell her about what happened in Los Angeles. Like I said, some things are better left that way.

Thankfully, that's what I have you people for.

A Rooftop

I wrote this on a rooftop. The stars were out, those specks of light dancing above the skylight. I didn't know why I was there, what I was doing in that town. Something pulled me there, dragged me to that wasteland. Something pulled me here, and yet nothing was making me stay. I was stranded in a city of four million people. And I hated it. Every single second.

I just couldn't figure out why.

It wasn't the sunshine.

I was born in the sunshine; the October birthdate might make you think otherwise, but that's only if you live in a place that understands the concept of seasonal weather. Lagos, Nigeria is not one of those places, with 365 days of various brightness levels. I was born in the sunshine, and if I get my way I'll die in it, asleep on some abandoned Caribbean beach. The beauty and power of the Sun has always been a fascination for us, the heat and warmth and life that this one, cosmically-insignificant celestial body provides for the only intelligent life in the universe (so far). That seems like a natural level of respect and adoration for something that our lives literally revolve around, but when you put it in a larger context, it is something extraordinary.

All of that being said, I'd have to say that moderation can sometimes can be an overvalued commodity, even in regards to sunshine. Everyone loves a bright summer day, that big yellow star planted against a clear blue sky, but everyone also loves a Double Quarter Pounder meal with large fries (you can lie to yourselves all you want). Loving something doesn't mean it's something you should have every day. The cold builds character, and a little bit of darkness in the daytime keeps you on your toes. Call it an extreme oversimplification, but I believe there are certain fundamental parts of the human experience that can only come from miserable, god-forsaken weather.

If, however, an inhuman, detached, completely artificial version of reality is what you're looking for, then I have the solution to all your problems: Los Angeles, California.

Maybe it was the expectation.

The firm had sent me out on the client team, one of my first company trips. The prospects of my journey were tainted by the prospects of work, but that wasn't stopping me from dreaming of the beaches. During my seven-hour denial of God's will, I mostly just thought about how that trip would be in fact, my first ever trip to the West Coast, a place I'd only ever seen on a screen or in a history book. This state of non-visitation also would have (and still does) apply to most of the country as well, but there was something different about Los Angeles, something special. It was the land of oceans and fresh air; of beaches, of glamour and beauty and fame. Days never ended and dreams always came true; it was a concept built off a series of unbearably happy endings. In truth, after all those years of living in New York, and even after the D.C. experience I received for university, I felt that being out there, even only for a few days, would somehow complete my

American experience, if such a thing even exists.

Maybe it was the traffic.

Following a quarter of a day spent defying the laws of physics, I arrived in LAX airport at midday, and proceeded to encounter my first piece of California magic: Interstate 405. Due to the fact that some madman decided the best way to build a city was to maximize suffering, Los Angeles traffic can best be described as waterboarding but for drivers. The roads exist to be clogged, it's their natural state; the collective psyche of the city might collapse under the weight of an easy commute. They make some claim to possess public transportation but upon further review, it turns out to only be true in the same way that an Instagram model's photograph is technically of her real body. I was stuck in that taxi for three hours, a timeframe which my driver informed me was somehow better than the usual. As I sat there, for the first and last time inside that most self-satisfying of vehicles known as the Toyota Prius, I felt a sudden urge to break out into song and dance. I felt like maybe this was that scene in the movie where everyone gets out of their car and joins an extremely coordinated musical number, with bright clothes and random style changes, and then once it's over they immediately go back to their cars and go right back to being miserable. That's the part I always like about musical numbers, the after, the end of the song and the return to quiet, rhythymless monotony. I think that's where I'd thrive.

Arriving at the Lakewood hotel was a mercy a lowly sinner such as myself might hardly deserve, a gift from whatever god I'd been praying to in the form of whispered expletives. The place was nice, but not too nice; "economically enjoyable" might be the proper term.

The week's work came and went, as those things tend to do, and I found myself sitting on the lobby waiting for my airport shuttle. I don't know why the thought even crossed my mind, but an idea started to form in my head that maybe, just maybe, spending the entirety of my "West Coast Getaway" in a series of client-site hotels wasn't ideal. It was a Friday mid-morning, I had no immediate weekend plans, and I had enough PTO to spare a Monday of jet lag recovery. I didn't even consider how it would look to my colleagues before I was looking for flight switch options online.

Maybe it was the Hollywood sign.

It was a no-brainer for my first stop, those nine golden letters standing as grand fixtures. Even for someone who had never given the performing arts so much as a glance, that sign was an institution, a monument to ambition and success, to fame and all the beautiful horrors that accompany it. I'd had a vague notion of their importance in my youth, a fascination with American films born from Disney magic and brought to maturity by every obscene action movie and dirty comedy I could pick up at the market.

I'd always imagined the kind of courage it must inspire, the desperate bravery that one needs to chase a dream that seems determined to outrun the hopeful. It wasn't something I wanted to possess. I've always said that cowardice is only a detriment when bravery is required; it was a place people, people from all over the world, looked up at and saw themselves in, or maybe just that most fabulous version of themselves. It was… it was…

A sign.

Just a sign.

Which, yes, I know, I already knew, but there's just something intensely bizarre about the disconnect between your idea of a place and the reality manifest. All those things that sign had stood for were still connected to it, vividly, but as I stood there under the warm evening sun, all I could see was a lit up sign slapped against the side of a mountain. In a weird way, it was more intimidating than inviting, a blinding reminder of fame's heights and the climb required to reach them. For the first time, I found my lack of artistic ambition to be something of a blessing, thankful I hadn't been tempted to make the long journey across the country and land there, below the bright lights.

The sign stood bright but under it stood a barren, golden wasteland. Every kid dreams of it, every adult dreams about dreaming about it, and those select few get to live it every day. All those people I'd seen on the screens—the beautiful people, the special, the seemingly immortal—could be found in the city, sipping iced coffees and scrolling through apps like everyone else. Maybe that's what it all boiled down to, the fantasy of it all, how unattainable it seemed to me. Maybe I couldn't enjoy the story of my Los Angeles getaway because I already knew the ending: a long flight back East and a few days of jet lag.

Maybe it was the water.

The next morning, I took it upon myself to spend the day taking in the Pacific. A beach trip hadn't been part of the packing plans, but thankfully overpriced hotel shops exist to solve any and all forgetful guest needs. I was able to supply myself with all the trimmings: obnoxiously large beach towel, cooler (with the ice and beers to go with it), and sunscreen. The trip to Santa Monica was a brutal one, and one that could have been avoided by heading to Long Beach instead, but I wanted to do it right and that required some suffering. After a few hours of growing very intimate with the voluptuous, sadistic curves of Interstate 405, I arrived at the pier, eager to embrace all the perfection I'd spent the entire last night researching on Google.

Santa Monica is the kind of place you can only imagine in your best mood, something pulled out of a picture book. The pier looked like Coney Island on dopamine, the fresh Pacific air a far cry from the aroma of the Atlantic. I swear the sand somehow looked cleaner, if such a thing is even scientifically verifiable. Hundreds of people, running around, enjoying the beachside bounty with family and friends and strangers. I set down my towel, cracked open my first beer from the cooler.

Falling in love with a day like that is easy, but love always fades away in the end. Somewhere between my fourth and fifth Corona the blue in the sky started to lose some of its sharpness. The playful cheers of fellow beachgoers sounded more like the standard racket of Times Square. The magic was lost, not likely to be regained. I packed my belongings up and decided to take a walk, see what sights and sounds I could absorb.

Maybe it was the people.

There's a remarkable difference between people watching in Los Angeles versus back home in NYC: the people. There's nothing new in that revelation of course, the differences between the New York rush and the LA stroll being a tried and true fact. People in New York have places to go, people to see, homeless people to walk by and fights to get into; people in Los Angeles seem to have more relaxing things on their mind, like which of their friend's improv shows to attend, what model of Prius they're getting for their next car, and whether or not that funny-looking guy in front of them at Starbucks was actually Steve Buscemi or not.

Everyone I saw looked happy, happy in a way that only really exists when it's sustained constantly and artificially. It bothered me for reasons that probably have a lot more to do with myself than them, but that didn't make them any less bothersome. Not all smiles are painted on or hiding something, sometimes people are genuinely in joyous awe at a beautiful day; I just don't understand how you can do that every single day. I'm not even saying they do, but just the idea that they could, that the place itself seemed to expect it, was enough to turn me off.

Fake smiles and faker noses, an Instagram wonderland. A bright and bold place, full of something resembling life, but not quite there. It's an ephemeral city, a sensation more than a location. It's a place that everyone wants to be but no one needs to be, empty but satisfying, like a fresh cigarette. Nicotine is far less addictive, but still more destructive; after all, there's nothing wrong with beauty, with escape. There's nothing wrong with superficiality, or the meaningless pursuit of beauty. There's nothing immoral about losing time to nothing, illogical as it might be.

Positive energy, good vibes; maybe that's what I couldn't stand. Maybe that's what it really all boils down to, that I'm just that much of a miserable sack of shit. It's certainly possible, but it's not the kind of thing anyone likes to think about, y'know? Pretty damn depressing.

I've been happy in New York. I've had great days, great weeks, even a few pretty great months sprinkled here and there. And New York can be a damn happy place, if you make it; for every overpriced, oversold experience that LA had to offer, the city surely offered something equal if not better. I'd wasted rent money to pop-up shops, influencer-approved restaurants, and every manner of niche bar I could be dragged to by Curtis' guiding hand. The petit-bourgeoisie lifestyle I'd spent my whole life chasing is just as evident and corrosive in the Big Apple, but it doesn't come with an all-expense pass to Disneyland.

Maybe I just hate everywhere, but the particular variety of bullshit one finds in New York just happens to suit me more.

My last day in the city of angels was spent on Rodeo Drive, sitting in a cute little café across the street from a yoga studio. It was a warm day, the sun soaking up all the energy from the pedestrians and transferring it into road rage. I was two iced lattes deep and determined to sit my way through the morning without a care or errand in the world, watching the people pass me by. I'd walked by a couple of trendy eateries, spotted what I could only assume to be one of the Kardashians looking at a watch, and been tempted to waste four-hundred on a tee shirt I couldn't possibly imagine wearing to a social function.

Again, any luxury offered there could be found back home, but what struck me was the lack of variety; everything looked the same. Everyone I saw wanted to be the same type of person. The celebrity. The dealmaker. The fashionable, the powerful, the exclusive. It's a race to the top that happened to mostly run through the bottom, a contest made by and for a special breed of nakedly ambitious. In New York people aspire; in Los Angeles they imitate. Even the creative spaces reek with the aroma of fashionability, seemingly focused entirely on the pursuit of Warhol-esque fame despite their lack of requisite genius. It wasn't a place where you discovered yourself, it was a place where you found the version of yourself you wanted to be in someone else, someone better than you, someone you needed to be as good if not better than.

This place was a bubble, wrapped tightly and resistant to all matters of external reality. There was a sense of unearned cultural exposure, a vapid insistence that everything the world had to offer could be found in the confines of this coastal enclave. They eat five-star authentic Southeast Asian cuisine and imagine themselves to have just come back from Shangri-La. They viewed their civilization as a refuge from the boredom of the outside world but in reality they're just content with their own blandness. It's one thing to not know any better, it's another thing to collectively agree to ignore the obvious. A grand lie.

New York's bullshit stands upon centuries of stories, the sweat and toil of an urban culture laying the foundations for a metropolis. Los Angeles was fabricated out of thin air, an ephemeral sensation perched against sunlit beaches; New York was built up from nothing, and rejects those who can't find their role to contribute. You need luck to make it anywhere but raw willpower is a baseline requirement to succeed in an environment designed to discourage settlement. People come to LA to chase dreams but they come to New York to make their own reality.

You know what it really might have boiled down to?

I think I was just lost. At some point, it occurred to me that this wasn't a place for me, somewhere I absolutely could not see myself. I knew it as soon as I stepped off the plane, but it took a few days to rationalize the sensation. It was the kind of place where a person can live the ideal version of a life, with all the inauthenticities of manufactured pleasure. It was a manufactured place, standing on top of nothing and rocketing upwards to new heights. It felt like the whole thing could float away at any moment. I needed two feet permanently on the ground. I didn't want to be in a place where everything's happening but nothing's going on. I needed to be somewhere with a pulse, a collective sense of mutually assured hassle, and an absolute, unyielding disinterest in who the fuck you are, what the fuck you want, and how the fuck you get it.

I wrote this on a rooftop. I looked down on this city, this strange land, and felt nothing but disregard. The stars were out in the sky.

A beautiful night in a beautiful place.

An Old Nightmare

Weights around my legs, chains on my neck. Bottom of a ship.

It's dark. Dark and wet and putrid with the smell of blood.

I'm going somewhere I don't belong and I can't move or yell or scream, the words won't break the seal of my lips.

Every time the boat rocks I crash against a mass of faceless bodies, all chained, all rotting away. We're stuck and stuck together and strangers and blood-related.

I don't know who they are but I know that they're my people and I know that we're not supposed to be here.

I take a deep breath, deep enough to reach every cell in my body, and collapse backward into a reclining seat.

Sanitized air and the low whirring of motion.

Blaring lights. A loosely buckled seatbelt around my waist.

A bag of peanuts.

I'm in a plane flying somewhere I can't remember for a reason I'm not sure ever existed.

Light turbulence has me make contact with the arms and legs to my left and right.

I don't know who the other people are and I don't know if I'm supposed to be here.

I feel like I'm falling before I realize the seat and the plane and the clouds and wind have all vanished into nothing.

Floating in the empty blue. Nowhere. No one.

Only two things seem to exist in the space.

On one side a bright, flashy tower, lit up with neon signs and images of fabulous parties, fine wines, and gold dust.

On the other, a beautiful home wrapped in palm trees and flowers and surrounded by the faint whiff of fried plantain.

I floated in place. The midpoint. Gravitationally locked between the only things on the horizon.

I see it all, all in front of me, but no paths opens. Nothing pulls me.

Floating in the emptiness of it all.

I closed my eyes. Opened my mind.

Looked for a sign.

I heard a voice.

Her voice.

The sweetest sound in all creation.

A Valentine

Valentine's Day was upon us and for the first time ever, all three of us had special people to take care of for the evening. Love was in the air and so was the sound of Hopper's excited barking. The poor guy must've thought we were going to take him somewhere special, or maybe he was just an unbearable loudmouth like his primary owner. Either way, I felt that he warranted a pet.

Ravi was planning to meet up with Xavier to go to a special Valentine's Day underground gallery exhibit put on by an up-and-coming abstract sculptor. Something about the artist "shattering the lines between vapid consumption of assembly-line romance and the genuine existential experience of love" (I threw up in my mouth after that too, don't worry). He said they would be going to a super-crazy-expensive steak restaurant afterwards, yet another one of Xavier's magical reservations.

As for Curtis, he was taking María to a Mediterranean place he'd heard about at work, and was planning to follow it up with a carriage ride through Central Park. In a moment of unbelievably competent listening skills, Curtis had gotten the idea after hearing María say how much she loved the carriage in *Cinderella* and how that was the only thing she asked for one Christmas. He was surprisingly decent at the whole relationship thing when he bothered to try.

I was taking Abi to a tapas joint that I had had on my list since forever, and I had booked the reservations weeks in advance just to make sure nothing got messed up. Not to be outdone by either Ravi's arts-travaganza or Curtis' midnight princess carriage ride, I'd gone and pulled off a guaranteed winner for afterwards: a full-sized private theater, good champagne, candlelight, flowers, and a viewing couch, all to enjoy the Great American Romantic Comedy, the single greatest musical of all time, 1952's *Singin' in the Rain*. The clincher? It was the same classic-film place from that very first night. I had to finesse the hell out of the theater owner, and it still cost me a small ransom, between the couch and the refreshments and whatnot, but it was worth every penny; I knew Abi would lose her mind over the surprise.

We were all in the kitchen, suits on and freshness engaged but stuck with precious minutes to spend bullshitting and discussing our plans for the evening. Ravi had gotten out the wine and we had all gotten out our phones, checking social media to see how much better our love lives were going than all our friends and family.

"When are you heading out for your thing with María?" Ravi asked.

"Well, it's six now, and reservations at seven, so probably right after this, get there early and mess around, double check with those clowns at the carriage place; I swear if they stick me with some limping horse or something, I'll lose my shit."

"I truly never thought I'd see the day when you would be worried about something like a carriage ride. Whole new guy over here."

"Hey, if I'm going to do this boyfriend schtick then I'm

going to do it right, you know I go all out. So, Kola, who's dick did you have to suck to book out a whole viewing room of a theater?"

"Neil Patrick Harris, but honestly I would have done it for nothing; and it wasn't that hard a sell, a lot of people go to see new movies on Valentine's Day, not the classic stuff, so it was good business for him."

"Speaking of blowing guys," Ravi added, braggingly but not braggingly enough to distract from how terrible his segue was, "Xavier's friend at the restaurant said that they were able to book us the special room in the wine cellar. I honestly can't believe my luck sometimes."

"You're paying extra money to sit in the basement?" Curtis asked, his genuine curiosity mitigating the biting effect of his sentiment.

"That's not how… God, you infuriate me. The wine cellar rooms have the best ambience. For someone who claims they're going to be a multimillionaire, you sure aren't very refined."

"If Donald Trump can learn how to be President, then I can learn how to be a gentleman. Besides, when I take my women out to eat I want to show them off, not hide them away in a cellar; paying money to be hidden away is, how would you put it, 'counterintuitive?'"

"Oh, I'm sure María would really appreciate being considered your eye candy, it's every woman's dream after all. In fact, you should tell her that in person, see how well it goes for you."

Curtis sucked his teeth in an attempt to dismiss Ravi's remarks but in truth he knew he was damn right; María would have slapped the smile off his face faster than a speeding bullet. It was funny to think how the man I was convinced would say anything to anyone (no, that is not a compliment) was now resigned to the shackles of common sense and civil decorum. It's amazing what a little feminine charm can do to a guy.

"So, Ravi, this is going to sound like a Curtis question, but how does the whole gift thing work when it's two guys? Curtis and I both got ours for the dynamic dame duo."

"Ask Curtis questions, get Curtis answers: it doesn't 'work' any particular way, we discussed if we were doing gifts or not and we both agreed not to buy each other anything. Now, that being said, if he decides to buy me something spectacular, then I'm certainly not going to complain, but still. Also, the notion that men need to buy women gifts, while benign, still embodies elements of heteronormativity and gender role conformity that contribute to the level of toxic mascul— "

BEEEEEEPPPPPP!!!

Curtis smirked satisfactorily as he took his finger off the screen on his phone. The asshole still had one of those airhorn sound apps that were funny one day in high school and then immediately lame on the day after. He saved it for special occasions or especially lengthy displays of didacticism, typically from his favorite target.

"You are an actual fucking child, minus the cute face. I'm shocked you even managed to remember to buy a gift."

"Yeah, I'm not gonna lie, man," I added, "I figured you'd blow it on that one too. The last time you had to buy someone a gift it was your little cousin for Christmas, and you ended up running around Toys "R" Us last minute like a madman."

"Hey, I wasn't the madman in that situation, OK? I saw a grown woman hit a man in the face with a child's bicycle just to get her hands on the last Optimus Prime toy; compared to that, running around the aisles looking for a My Little Pony plushie was absolutely sane."

"Jesus, it's like a Black Friday warm up," Ravi remarked, "at least you ended up getting the toy."

"I always deliver, as you damn well know, and tonight's no different. I didn't buy my girl a gift; what I bought was my secret weapon."

"Secret weapon?" I questioned, "What are you gonna do, get the horse to sing her a love song?"

"Nah, I tried that one, but the fucking thing can't hit a high note to save its life; after that failed, I figured this would work instead," he said before tossing me a long, wrapped box out of his suit jacket pocket, "Catch!"

"A necklace, huh?" I asked while inspecting his wares, "not bad, not bad; can't quite top mine, but it's a good attempt."

"'Not bad'? Hey, it may not be diamonds but Kay's makes a quality product. Besides, that's not the good part; she told me this long story once about how her abuela lost a gold locket necklace on the way over from Cuba, how it was given to her by her grandfather, etc."

"An exact copy?"

"Close as I could get without having to call her grandma myself. You gotta admit, fellas, I hit a home run here."

"Well, you did do well, Blondie, but you can't quite top me," I replied, bringing my ornate gift bag up to the table, "See, the best thing about nerdy women is that they tell you exactly what types of gifts they want without even trying to drop hints. If, for example, you happen to be dating a black theater nerd with an affinity for the classics, what do you do? You get her an original vintage photo set and playbill from the Broadway debut of *A Raisin In The Sun*, signed by the entire cast including Sir Sidney Poitier himself."

I pulled the playbill out from the ornate envelope to show Sidney's scribbled signature. You would think something like that would cost a few grand but it turned out to only be a couple hundred, leaving me enough to rent out the theater with amenities. Never thought I'd say this, but thank God the theater is past its cultural heyday.

"Huh… so, I know this isn't going to reflect well on me, but I'll just say it: who is this guy and why am I supposed to be impressed?"

Ancestors, give me the strength.

"He's a legendary actor, an ordained knight, the first black man to win the Academy Award for Best Actor, and so on and so forth. Read a damn book once in a while," Ravi quipped, doing my mental labor for me, "and Kola, I must say that is a damn good job. It's almost, almost, as good as my gift."

"Huh? Didn't you just say that you didn't get anything for him?"

"I said that I didn't buy anything for him; I got him something for free, and he's going to lose it."

"Well don't be a cock tease," Curtis demanded, "what'd you get him?"

Ravi opened the photos on his phone and slid it across to Curtis.

"This buddy of mine thinks he's going to be the next

Banksy and he's always looking for something to sink his teeth into; Xavier walks by that same wall every day to work."

The mural was a stunning sight, mostly in the sense that I didn't know what I was supposed to be looking at: two gold stars, the one on the right a little higher up, and a city skyline underneath, all in a starry night blue background against a red brick wall.

"Your gift to your boyfriend was to vandalize a wall with abstract art?"

"'Second to the right, and then straight on until morning', from the original *Peter Pan* by J.M. Barrie. It's his favorite quote from when he was on a kid, said it embodied the wonder of adventure."

I couldn't help but start chuckling.

"Oh? And what exactly is so funny about it?" Ravi asked, beyond irritated.

"No, no, it's not that, man… I just realized how different this all is from Valentine's Day from a few years ago. The one where we got high as shit and tried to watch all the worst rom-coms of the 2000s."

"Holy shit," Curtis boomed, "I remember that one, oh man, what was that really garbage one with Jimmy Fallon? The one where he's sexually attracted to the *Boston Red Sox* but it's all OK because in the end he learns to not be an absolute idiot?"

"*Fever Pitch*, him and that lady from the Adam Sandler movies."

"Ravi, referring to someone by their involvement with the exiled clown prince of comedy is insulting, and her name is Drew Barrymore. And that wasn't even close to the first one, which one's the one with like twenty different celebrities all giving one-twentieth of their effort?"

"*Valentine's Day?*"

"No, the other one."

"*Crazy, Stupid, Love?*"

"No, that one's the good one Curtis."

"Oh, it was *New Year's Eve!*"

"Ha! There we go, fuck that movie."

So on and so forth, all the way until the alarms on our phones beckoned us away to our evenings. Curtis used the best Spanish he could muster to give a little pre-gift speech, and while he sounded like a drunk who'd just watched Dora The Explorer, she really did appreciate the effort, making the necklace that much more beautiful to her. When Xavier and Ravi "happened" across the mural on the way back, it took him a little longer than Ravi would've liked to realize what he was witnessing. Having never been one for intentional subtlety, he had to drop the act and tell Xavier he was looking at his Valentine's Day gift, momentarily bringing down the mood until he suddenly felt himself picked up in the air and spun around.

As for me Abi and I, well... let's just say after an amazing meal, the thrill of her surprise and her fangirl meltdown from her gift—not to mention a good two or three glasses of champagne—that we ended up using the couch for a lot more than viewing.

There's definitely a joke to be made here vis-à-vis the female anatomy, sex, and "dancin' in the rain," but, quite frankly, I'm above that.

Mostly.

An Actor

"All right dear, now that we've done the herb blend, the saucepan, and the shrimp, the next step is the sautéing. This is critical; if you don't get the meats right in the beginning, the flavor doesn't come in for the final dish. I remember that I forgot to sauté the chorizos the first time I tried, and they were noticeably horrid compared to the rest. Oh, was Carlos furious ever furious…"

"Damn Ms. K, your man got angry over dull chorizos?"

"Oh, you know those Latin men, dear, all hopped up on passion. He couldn't help himself sometimes, but he was usually terribly sweet."

Not even having half the energy required to deal with the litany of problematic notions just uttered, Abi turned her focus to the rest of the ingredients and started separating them for convenience. She really wanted this dinner to go well; she loved going out to dinner with her man, and they always had a spot at Mr. Rahmani's for grub, but a nice homemade meal has its own importance. Under normal circumstances she would have rather died a thousand deaths than asked for help, but given how she had never made paella before, she deemed it necessary. She couldn't tell if she wanted to cook for her man out of some love-fueled kindness or out a subconscious strain of feminine domesticity, but what she did know is that anything less than one-hundred-percent praise of her efforts would result in a slow-but-conclusive breakdown.

"So aside from Carlos and his love of seasoned sausage, how was your time in Spain?"

"Oh, it was magnificent, you need to go! The weather is divine, every meal is better than the last, and the parties go on until the sun comes up. I'm starting to miss it already. Do you plan on going once you get big and famous?"

"If a bitch ever gets her Hollywood debut then yes, one of the first ones on the list. I gotta hit up Tokyo first, though, and then Dubai, but I'm definitely going to be hitting up Madrid before I know it. Hopefully it won't be too long now."

"Any day now, darling, any day now. You have more talent in your pinky than half of these girls out there could dream of. What parts are you up for right now anyway?"

"Well… not many, actually," she answered, her face giving off a little more than she might have intended, "it's been a little rocky. I ended up getting cut from the *Luke Cage* episode, and my last five auditions didn't pan out."

"Oh, dear, I'm so sorry to hear all that. Keep your chin up, though, it could be worse; at least you have enough funds to eat, when I was your age I didn't even know if that would be the case some weeks."

Abi wanted to tell her wistful companion about how, due to several totally unmissable online sales and a few too many bottomless brunches in the last month or so, she'd had to ask her father for money for the first time in years. It wasn't exactly the kindest conversation either; he'd acquiesced, but only after a solid half an hour of lecturing. Abi's big takeaway was that the next time she had to make this call, there might be some mention of the word "disappointment" involved, but she couldn't afford to dwell on that.

"Yeah, exactly, ain't like I'm out here starving," she responded, the confident bounce back in her words, "and that big break is right around the corner. Oh! I do have this thing for a new vitamin-water, super-food-drink thing, should be a big help for a while."

"Health water? I will never understand you young people and your corporately manufactured fads. The keys to a healthy, vibrant life are daily meditation, home-grown produce, and a never-ending pursuit of sexual gratification. Everything else is rubbish."

"The science is on the bottle, Ms. K, it's got all of the good ingredients. Antioxidants and shit."

"Bollocks, the whole lot of it. Enough about that, so tell me, how are things going with that gentleman of yours?"

"Oh, him? It's all fine, he's cool... he's getting excited about his new Lagos project, so that's keeping him occupied, but we still talk and get together all the time. Usually by this point I've already lost my patience, so the fact that the sound of his voice doesn't hurt my eardrums is a good sign."

"Dear, you know you're a terrible liar; you may as well be as pale as me if you can't hide when you're blushing. Come on, spill the truth."

"Ugh, I hate you. Fine; he may or may not have told me he maybe... loves me, and I may or may not have said it back... after I hit him. Y'know, the funny kind of hit, not the 'call an expert' kind."

"Oh, Abi, you're so sweet it's like you're made of cane sugar. To be young and in love, I miss those days. You should consider yourself lucky, boys today are hardly as interesting as they used to be, barely any use besides the one they keep in their boxers. That never changes, at least."

"Are you still seeing that one, Klaus?"

"No, I'm afraid Klaus and I had to go our separate ways, he's heading out to backpack across Cambodia. It's such a bother; I finally find a young man who isn't looking for another mommy in his life, and he has to go off and follow the call of adventure."

"So, the queen of the cougars is back on the prowl again? Poor guys aren't going to know what hit them; who knows, maybe all your old stories got to him, inspired him to follow his dreams."

"Perhaps… did I ever tell you about Deandre?"

"The boxer? Oh, no, this was the robotics guy."

"Neither, dear, Deandre was an actor, just like you. Never quite made it as far; he had a few off-Broadway roles but barely enough to get by. I met him in '74 one night in Max's Kansas City, used to be down on Park. He was something else, Abi, something else entirely; I'd never met a man so full of vigor. He had a lot of friends in the club scene and we'd always find a way to get free drinks. He had one of those smiles, too, the ones that twinkle in the mind's eye. A being of pure passion."

"Damn… so what happened to him?"

It didn't escape Abi's attention when Ms. Kenchington's eyes momentarily lost their glow, but she didn't feel the need to show a visible reaction.

"He moved back in with his parents, back to Mississippi… he wrote me a few years later, let me know how he was doing. Wife, three kids, a new job in Seattle; he said he'd finally gotten used to wearing a suit. I was… I was happy for him. I was. He seemed happy, too."

"A whole new life, huh?" Abi asked, sensing an unfamiliar strain in her friend's voice, "Well, I have to say, it's strange to see you talk so wistfully about some old fling. I figured they were all just notches in the belt at this point, a record of accomplishment. Few women can say they followed up a night of passion with a crown prince by having a gang bang with some mafia punks; you're in a league of your own."

"Hmm, I suppose… but I was young then, about your age. We had our fun, we both saw other people the whole time, and that was the way we wanted it. I knew that; I knew it, but part of me liked the idea that maybe, I don't know, maybe something could come out of it. I don't even mean marriage, just something… solid. Tangible. Something I could reflect upon now, not just remember in a flash of booze and bright lights and orgasms."

"Did you ever tell him? How you felt?"

"How could I, dear? Like I said, I was young; I had the world in front of me, and so did he. Who would throw that away over a few spurts of passionate bliss? No, no, I didn't tell him, and I'm happy I didn't; it would have been miserable, I know it. Me, a housewife, with children running around? I can barely handle you, and at best I've been more of a surrogate kooky aunt than a mother."

"Ha-ha-ha! You're about as domesticated as a tiger in the jungle, about as crazy too. I don't know about being my aunt though; I have about twenty of those, and you're not like any of them. It's good to hear though, that you don't have any regrets. It sounded like you'd lost your one true love or something."

"There are no 'one true loves' Abi, never think that," she mused somberly, going through the motions of the dish as her mind floated away to days long gone, "there's no fated soul who's going to come along and make all your life's problems, all the fear of loneliness, go away. Love isn't like that; it's not about whimsically going between the absolutes of joy and despair, fulfillment and desolation."

"So… so what then? What's it about?"

"Hope and pain. It's about hoping that out of all the people you decide to make a bond with, all the souls you encounter, that the few you choose to share those innermost parts of yourselves with are worth the pain that they're going to cause you, no matter how much they try not to."

Abi shifted nervously on the countertop as she sat. She knew that Ms. K was talking about something entirely different, she couldn't help but think about her own situation. Worth the pain? *Well, we'll wait and see I guess…*

"I do regret it, though; not that I let him go, or that I never told him. I regret having the questions linger, not deciding anything for myself. He told me that he was going home one night as we lay in bed, and then that was that; three days later, he was gone. I didn't know what to do what to do with myself for a few months after that… I almost ended up going back to England. Thankfully, someone I'd run across in Toronto phoned me up asking if I wanted to come up for a bit. It was just the push I needed to get back on with my life."

"So, it all worked out then? Well, if you want my expert opinion, you shouldn't feel any type of way about it. You lived a more amazing life than most people nowadays would even consider, and you didn't need any help or anything. Making your own way, having adventures, exploring the world; a life without fear is a life fulfilled."

"I suppose I am being silly, aren't I? Thinking about someone like this after all the lovers I've thrown away; it's downright hypocritical. I'm sure I've been quite a few people's unanswered question."

"Those are their lives, not yours; you're allowed to feel anything you want. The past is dead, Ms. K, that's why we mourn it every night in our sleep; the future is alive, and that's what we wait for in those same moments. Let the dead rest in peace."

Ms. Kenchington snapped out of her funk upon Abi's words: "Each night a tragedy, each night a joy; Abi, you may have to reconsider your career choice. You have the soul of a poet."

"HA! Me, a poet? Can you imagine me wearing a black turtleneck and beret, reflecting over every little second of my existence? Nah, fuck that, man, I have too much soul for poetry, not to mention a bitch ain't trying to stay broke either. Come on, Ms. K, let's get back to this cooking, you can tell me more about Carlos and his sausage."

They got back to their cooking, and a few minutes later, Abi received a phone call from a certain somebody asking permission to bail on dinner in favor of seeing the Cleveland Cavaliers play the Knicks at Madison Square Garden with his two best friends, courtside. Feeling a surge of rage take over but ultimately realizing its futility, she told him yes, in exchange for a LeBron James autograph (I did end up getting it, but I had to not-so-discreetly push a small child out of the way, so call it a win-lose).

Abi and Ms. K ate the fruit of their labors themselves, and as the stories flowed side by side with the wine, all their problems seemed to float away. They'd come back, of course, like they tend to do, but for that night, the picture of life was clear and vibrant, and their spirits followed suit. One last hooray for the dead.

A Crazy Train

The NYC subway system is the world's greatest involuntary social experiment, and if I didn't know any better, I would say it was created specifically for that purpose. First you develop one of the, if not the single, greatest cities in the world; then, you overpopulate it to the point where in order to do literally anything, civilized, normal people have to jet around in underground trains; finally, at least a hundred times a day, you toss in a complete fucking lunatic into one of these cars and observe their reactions. If you want to be a real dick about it, you make sure to delay the ever-living shit out of the train this car is attached with, just to provide your residents with that extra twenty minutes of mind-numbing aggravation. The sickest part of the whole thing? You make them fucking pay for the experience, safe in the knowledge that they have absolutely no choice and won't do a goddamn thing about it.

It's evil, but by God it's brilliant.

Among all the ridiculous clothing, antisocial behavior, and downright dangerous situations I've been privileged enough to witness under the streets of the Big Apple, it's hard to figure out what stands out. Fistfights aren't exactly common but the ones I've seen all resulted in knockouts, as the rules of the subway demand. Getting verbally assaulted in Mandarin by an old lady whose foot I stepped on was a bit annoying, but nothing compared to the dead-silent stare I received from a tall, gaunt man for half an hour after spilling a few drops of my coffee on him. Performance art seems to be a frequent occurrence on my underground travels, with pieces ranging from a man wearing an all-white body suit and dancing to Gymnopédie No. 1, all the way to what I still believe to be a faux-Satanic ritual, complete with fake animal heads, (hopefully) fake blood, chanting and horrifying yet tasteful black vestments.

Now, obviously when it comes to the issue of sexual violations, I get a bit of leeway seeing as how God decided to gift with me both a Y chromosome and a male-dominated social structure. There was one occasion where I had my ass grabbed by a very aggressive man at least twice on the same ride, but it doesn't quite compare to getting your skirt pulled down, your breasts squeezed, your thigh rubbed, or just having someone literally pull their dick out and masturbate to you while making eye contact… I don't really have a joke for this one, it's just kind of depressing.

The reason for this particular round of voluntary torture was one of our college pals coming to town for the weekend and inviting us to come out to Greenpoint in Brooklyn for a guys' night. The platform was empty, all the better for us and our loud talking, but we were a little annoyed by the few other passengers we did see; mainly this man in a brown jacket, with a disheveled afro, holding a book in his hand and a collection of pamphlets in his pocket. Years of living in the city had taught us exactly what was going to happen next.

"Five bucks says it's a reformed Christian preacher looking for converts."

"Nah no way, Kola, conspiracy theorist peddler for sure.

What do you think, Ravi?"

"Hmm…. I'm going with Kola but an alteration, this guy seems more like the damnation to Hell type."

"What makes you say that?"

"The nice subway preachers tend to be a little younger and more outwardly friendly, in my observation."

Just then the magic man who lives inside the roof of the subway station announced to us that our train was arriving, and in a few seconds, we felt the rumbles and saw the lights. I looked up and down the platform reflexively to make sure that no one was standing on the yellow line zone. It would be nice to say that I did this out of concern for my fellow New Yorkers, one city and all that other jazz, but the truth is that the only time I was late for a job interview in my life was because some guy, drunk off his ass at 2:00 in the afternoon, fell in front of the train and shut the whole thing down. Some people might call that the epitome of self-centeredness, but I prefer to think of it as radical utilitarianism – any person I look out for gets to live, and I get where I'm going on time. Symbiosis in action.

There wasn't any music that night, which was a real tragedy considering how trashed we'd all gotten; on a different occasion of equal intoxication, we'd performed a three man tango to the rhythmic stylings of a Spanish guitarist. Junior year at Ignatius, at the station nearest school, there was this one reggae band who was particularly talented, and I always made sure to leave some patronage. The rappers were by far the most annoying, mostly because half of them were absolute garbage and the other half were somehow even worse than that, the occasional hot-fire wordsmith aside. On some fortunate occasions, I was blessed with some sweet, sweet jazz, the luscious sound of saxophones and trumpets matching with perfect percussion; I once contemplated skipping out on a date just to watch a band play at Astor Place. The strangest music I ever heard on the subway? The medieval-style bard troupe that I was given the pleasure of accompanying on the 4:00 AM E Train; that was something special, and still the only time to this day that I've seen both a lute and a four-foot tall man in purple tights. I will give them this though: they really nailed the harmony.

We hopped on board the train and picked one of the good seats in front of the map. It was a decent-sized crowd: a lot of young adults ready to party the night away; a lot of older people ready to get home after being away until this ungodly hour; two very young high-school girls who were clearly about to make a lifetime's worth of mistakes (one of them indiscreetly uttered the phrase "some random dick tonight," which could have been a part of some funny story about her day, but I somewhat doubt it); a few too-old-to-be-this-drunk guys, who, of course, were vigorously eyeing said high school girls; and what appeared to be two thirds of a basketball team, judging by the matching clothes, height and racial resemblance to me. Oh, and our friend from earlier, of course, who was just about to make his introduction.

"Brothers and sisters!"

The three of us were as giddy as schoolchildren, ready for some classic, cringe-worthy goodness.

"My name is Reverend Lucas Foxwood, of His Holy Name Presbyterian Church in The Bronx, New York," he yelled, with the dignified air of a man who had the most important thing in the world to say and no one in the world to hear him, "and I'm here to talk to you tonight about a subject of the utmost importance."

It was like waiting for the twist in one of M. Night Shyamalan's three good movies, I couldn't handle it.

"That, my dear children of God, is the safety of our own children, who are being plagued by drugs!"

"UGH!"

The groan was simultaneous and heartfelt; of all the crazy people we could have gotten for our subway trip, we had ended up with a damn wannabe D.A.R.E. officer. It was the subway ride equivalent of going to your girl's house while her parents were out and only getting a half-hearted hand job. It seemed that all hope was lost and that we would now have to derive the entertainment we'd been craving from actual human interaction, but then, like all of God's mysterious works, something beautiful revealed itself.

"See now the reason I'm talking to you fine people tonight is that a lot of you don't even know where your kids are getting these drugs from," he said, apparently having never listened to a speech by a Republican politician, "but the truth is going to shock you, and here it is."

He reached into his pocket and pulled a small green plastic bag with an image and writing that I couldn't quite make out.

"Do y'all see what this is? What this shit says?" he queried, refusing to wait for an answer, "THAT, my dear brothers and sisters, is Scooby the goddamn, motherfuckin' mystery solvin' dog, and this right here reads 'S-C-O-O-B-Y S-N-A-X,' 'Scooby Snax!' They're selling our damn kids Eastern European street drugs and calling them Scooby Snax!' 'Ruh-

Roh!' indeed!"

Out of the billions of human lives lived and the near-infinite number of words and ideas expressed by those souls, how many of us can truly say that we've been blessed to have heard one of the greatest combinations of words to come out of the English language? This man, nay, this gift, had just uttered by far the most absurd thing that I had ever heard in my life, and there I was, half-tipsy and without any way of recording the moment for posterity. Even thinking about it now fills me with so many questions: where had he learned to do such a terrible impression of a beloved cartoon icon? Why was he walking around with a bag of drugs in public transportation that police officers use all the time? What exactly did he expect a train car full of mostly young people to do with this information, besides ask where they could get some? And, most importantly, how amazing would it have been if the drug was just part of a guerilla marketing campaign for a new movie, *Scooby Doo: Inner City Scarefest?* The answer to those questions, of course, is that he definitely just heard it one time as a kid, he was batshit crazy, he clearly didn't think his plan through, and only if Ronald Reagan's ghost made a cameo at the climax and saved the day, finishing The War on Drugs once and for all.

He reared up to keep going, causing the three of us to cease our barely-restrained laughter to hear better.

"Now, I myself am no stranger to drug use. I used to love that shit. Love it. Back in the 80's man, crack cocaine was my love and joy, the apple of my eye, the ray of sunshine after the long, black night."

Shakespeare had nothing on this crazy motherfucker.

"Man, I swear I was about this close to sucking dick for a hit a few times, but thankfully my momma raised me better than that."

Everything else that I'm about to quote from him comes indirectly via Ravi, the reason being that at this point I had started to laugh so violently and loudly that I could no longer hear my lecturer speak. It's a good thing I was too, because if I had heard this next part I would've probably pissed myself.

"That's right, brothers and sisters, my life was all about drugs and I'm not proud to admit that I simply didn't want to get help for it, but eventually, through the help of God and a lot of prayers from my momma, I finally got clean, and turned my life around. Y'know, I promised my momma one day, I said to her, momma, I ain't never, never, never, NEVER, gonna get high again, but you know what? I lied to her that day, because not even one week later, there I was getting high again, but not on crack, no, on something better, something stronger, the most powerful, addictive drug in the world: the love of our Lord, Jesus Christ. Thank you all very much, enjoy your evenings." He hopped off the train, waving goodbye to an audience that hadn't paid him a second of their time, Scooby Snax in tow and heart aflame with the power of faith.

You want to know the actual funniest part of all of that, the cherry on top of the crazy sundae? He never even handed out his fucking pamphlets.

A Lack of Words

"Kola, you know you can't beat me when I'm in the zone like this, I'm basically superhuman. It's a noble effort, but you will end up fruitless."

"I remember you said that the last time too, before I came back and banged in three goals in the last twenty minutes, and this time you don't even have a lead. You've somehow found a way to get even more arrogant."

Hopper had been watching the screen intently but got bored and decided he wanted to nuzzle up next to me on the couch instead. He wasn't shedding at that point, so I let him get in there, even taking my eyes off the screen to give him a quick pet. I swear that little guy had a spell on me or something, I couldn't help myself around him.

"I believe the term you're looking for is 'hitting my stride,'" he offered, "and besides, that was bullshit - the ref fucked me with that red card. FIFA always has these glitchy fucking refs."

"What exactly did you think was going to happen when you slide-tackled me from behind and didn't even touch the ball in the process?"

"Fuck you, that's what. Enough yapping, it's time for the takeover."

Ravi hadn't been around a whole lot for a long while at that point, and while the reason was understandable, it didn't make it less noticeable. Xavier had his own apartment, a spacious one-bedroom, appointed in a refined manner, with a great view to top it all off. I know Ravi still loved us and our place, but the appeal was hard to pass up, and I can't blame him; I knew even then that if I ever ended up moving in with Abi, I'd have a hard time leaving my own place too. Sharing may be caring but caring is fucking overrated, especially when your man is stock-rich and not parent-rich; money that makes itself.

"YES! Ha-ha-ha, get some bitch! Oh man, Kola, you're about to get smoked worse than those rednecks in Django."

"Shouldn't this situation be in reverse, blondie? I'm Django, you're Monsieur Candy, even though the comparison to Mr. DiCaprio is in and of itself a compliment."

"Why can't I be the German guy instead? I'm not an impeccably-dressed, smooth-talking racist."

"You're right, you're not any of those things, not in the slightest," I chided, "and besides, you're the one who grew up in a literal all-white town. Not even a damn token just to make y'all feel better, just a sea of paleness as far as the eye could see. I'm honestly surprised you turned out like this."

"I told you already, my folks are pretty good with all that stuff, my mom liked you way more than any of the other kids in the neighborhood. It took my dad some time, but he got there."

"Right, like the time the cops picked us and those two other white boys up for drinking in public, but my ass was the only one that got a ticket, and then your dad wanted to ban me from seeing you until you explained that you were actually the one drinking the alcohol. My dumb ass just read the bottle and handed back it to y'all; I learned my fucking lesson that day, that's for sure."

"OK, OK, that was fucked up, I get it, but you know he loves you now, says you're the brother he wished he could've given me. But the other old people in town? It's like they think Black Lives Matter is a rebel army or something, fucking absurd."

"Wasn't it your ass the other day talking about how you didn't 'understand' why those protests have been going on?"

"Whoa now, that's an entirely different thing; it's not like I don't think the cop got away with murder, I saw the same fucking video you did. What I didn't get was how burning down your own shit and robbing stores is supposed to do something? Who does that help?"

"It's not about… We tried to get something done in the courts, they robbed us, like they tend to do, so the anger needs an outlet. Have you ever heard 'Riots are the language of the unheard?' It's from the non-whitewashed version of Martin Luther King, the communist sympathizer/public menace, not the 'I Have A Dream' guy."

"Cut the shit man, I'm not even going into that. The piece-of-shit cop killed Hakeem, I know it, you know it, we all know it; I just don't get why stealing a TV from a local electronics store, owned by another black person, is the immediate and logical response to that situation. I mean, it would make more sense if they went after the city government buildings, the precinct, the places that are fucking them over; they're hurting the same people they claim to care about."

"If thousands of angry black people tried to march on city hall right now we'd get Bloody Sunday 2.0, especially when they have cops out there pretending that they're soldiers. You should know though, it's not like my godfather's golf buddy is the one who signs for the weapons acquisitions."

"Don't! Don't start that with me, I fucking mean it. You know the only reason my mom got to keep our house after the divorce was because he got her a job in the DA's office, I'm not about to listen to you say anything about him. You're acting like something that happened in fucking Orlando has anything to do with the guy."

"The fact that you think this shit is isolated like that… I can't fucking even. And I don't give a shit if he was the one hugging you at graduation, it doesn't change the fact that my ass has to look over my shoulder every time I see flashing red lights. If you love the guy so much, maybe give him some advice on his hiring practices."

We could both tell that the argument was reaching that place, that place where venom starts floating in the air and words form on the tongue that normally wouldn't make it past the conscience. It had happened a few times before, always about race; for all the love we had for each other, this twinge of animosity always lay dormant, waiting to be unleashed, spurred on by life experiences that varied to the point of dissonance. The All-American boy and the African immigrant; we were a match made in diversity-quota heaven. It was something we kept quiet with effort, something big enough to damage the bond but not nearly big enough to justify doing so. A few seconds of silence passed, and the air went back to normal.

"'Language of the unheard?' Crazy anger isn't worth hearing."

"Curtis, when people who look like you, who could be you, or your family, get murdered on tape, on national TV, and the system still finds a way to take away justice, logic stops mattering; it's all pain and righteous anger."

"You can say whatever you want, white privilege and all that, but you can't convince me that burning down your own neighborhood is justifiable."

Part of me wanted to say something like, white privilege is thinking that you're entitled to a justification for shit you don't experience and can't understand; or maybe, The fact that you're not boiling in anger over injustice is a reflection of your apathy, not their lack of emotional intelligence; or maybe just start giving him a basic history lesson on the American justice system, but another part of me just wanted to drop the axe before the conversation became my whole night. That part tends to win out in the end.

"Whatever, let's just drop it. One more?"

"Fuck it."

"Alright, after I score two more and get the win we'll restart."

"In your dreams, pal."

While I didn't end up getting the win (fucking ref and his late penalty), we did restart and continue with our standard inane banter, Hopper asleep with his head on my lap. A few minutes in, the dog suddenly shot up and ran to the door, barking joyfully in expectancy, and then bounded back into the room.

"Fuck, Ravi, what's wrong?" Curtis asked, "You see a ghost, or was the art that bad?"

Without even taking a second to do a quick-shot response,

he went to the kitchen and poured himself a tall glass of the red stuff. He grabbed a deli bowl of mozzarella out of the fridge, took the bottle, and sat himself between the two of us, without a word.

Ravi had a look on his face that I'd never seen before: absolute, mind-numbing shock. He was one of the most stone-faced, expressionless people that I'd ever known in my life, so you can imagine my surprise to see him nearly quaking in his Hugo Bosses. At one point, I really think his eyes started fucking twitching.

"So…," he began, barely able to comprehend his own words, "Xavier asked me to marry him."

My eighth-grade history teacher once told us in class that he witnessed the Challenger explosion, and he described the reaction as "the most soul-piercing, mind-numbing silence that the mind can imagine." At the time, I thought of his reflection as little more than hyperbolic showmanship meant to pique our interest in the 80's; but at that exact moment, in that apartment, I realized exactly how wrong I was. If it wasn't for Hopper grumbling and playing with his chew toy, I swear you would have been able to hear a fly on the other side of the window.

There always has to be someone ready to break the ice, and that's why God made people like Curtis: "Well, that's certainly one way to make all your Indian aunties like you more."

"Um, Ravi, let's… let's back up a few steps. What exactly do you mean, he asked you to marry him?"

He took a long swig from the bottle.

"What I mean," he said, "is that on the way back from the

art show, he got on his knees, took out a ring… and asked me to marry him."

"…And then?"

"And then… well, and then, I sort of, kind of, didn't say anything, and then I remember running… and now I'm here."

It was like talking to a brick wall at that point. The silence came back.

With Curtis and I both able to do nothing more than stare in awkward panic, Ravi got up out of his seat, walked into the bathroom, closed the door, and proceeded to scream obscenities at the top of his lungs for ten minutes. I don't know if he thought that we couldn't hear him or if he assumed we wouldn't immediately bring it up upon his return, but regardless he just came out and sat back down on the couch.

Ravi then proceeded to provide us with the missing information; on the way back from the art show, during a conversation about Les Misérables and Jean Valjean's moral failure in turning himself in to the police, they had both been taken in by the sight of two sparrows chirping together on an empty tree branch. Xavier pointed out how happy they must have been, two souls in a moment of harmony, and Ravi said that if man was able to speak with the beasts, the joys of the universe would no longer remain a mystery (I can't stand it either, just bear with me).

The two poet laureates continued to observe their new friends, all the way until Xavier decided to ditch his previous plans he had made for a restaurant proposal and just go for it right there, in the middle of the street. Ravi, usually as unfazed as humanly possible, did not react well, at all, opting to go for the running away and turning off his phone strategy. It was very effective, but temporary at best.

"Ravi… you know that you have to answer him, eventually, right? Like, sometime soon."

"Huh? Oh, yeah, yeah, no, like, I know that, yeah. I just… don't, really want to, so I think that I'm just going to… not. Yeah, that's it," he continued, at this point far more spaced out than he was scared, "I'm going to not do that. It's perfect! I'm just, not going to do it. Perfect!" He had that forced, overly-relaxed smile on, the one typically reserved for only the most enthusiastic of breakdowns.

"I don't think that's really the best id— "

"You know what, I feel better already! Thanks guys, you two were a big help." He tried getting up, but Curtis put his arm across his chest.

"Hold it right there, pal, this shit's not ending like that. You can't just pretend all your problems don't exist like some middle-aged, drunk housewife. It ain't like you to take the irrational route, and that's coming from me."

"For once I agree with Blondie, you're not acting like yourself."

"Huh, OK… well tell me something, how the fuck exactly am I supposed to act? Hmm, got any bright ideas, either of you?" he asked, a mad look brewing in his eyes, "well, look at that, two people who didn't get a surprise proposal have absolutely no useful input in a conversation that they're forcing me to have. I'm shocked, shocked I say. It's almost like you have no idea how utterly absurd the last hour of my life has been."

Knowing that his descent into dramatics was going to be the death of the discussion, I took my foot off the gas and decided to go with a different approach.

"Fuck OK, we get it," I said, resigning myself to abandon any attempts at some big emotional spiel, "look, you can do whatever you want, but you can't leave the poor guy like that, it's a dick move at best. Right, Curtis?"

"Huh? Oh, sorry, María was sending me something dirty…" he said, continuing to look down and text while talking at us, "look man, I don't get the big deal. He's clearly lost his mind, so just dump his ass and move on, end of story."

"Don't you think that would be a bit much? They should at least talk about it first."

"Kola, there's nothing to fucking talk about! Xavier's like, what, thirty-eight? It makes sense for him to be worried about dying alone. Ravi, we're still in our twenties, don't be an idiot, there's nothing to consider. You can either dump him now, or tell him you're 'not sure yet' and wait until it becomes the only fucking thing he talks about all day."

"Ravi," I replied, avoiding taking the side of the romantics but still erring towards sentimentalism, "look, you two have had a lot of good times, you like him, I just don't see any point in getting rid of all of it. Pick up the phone, talk to him, have an actual discussion before making a decision, that's all I'm saying."

"Bull. Shit. Ravi, the guy wants to get married. Think about that for a few seconds, really think about it: better or worse, in sickness and in health, until death itself comes for one of you, or both, if you're lucky. Do you know what happens when two people who barely know each other get married? No one ends up happy except for some greasy divorce lawyer and the kids, but only on Christmas when they get double the gifts. Speaking of which, you said Xavier has an ex-husband right? As in he's already done this once and failed at it? If that's not a bad sign, then I don't know what it is."

"That's totally different!" Ravi replied, snapping violently out of his fog, "Xavier and his ex were never right for each other, it's not the same with us. It just isn't."

"So, let me get this shit straight, you're honestly getting married to a divorcee, who you've only been dating for months, because you like him and because you're convinced that you two are 'different' from his previous failed arrangement?"

This would usually have been the point where a smartass reply got thrown in the mix, but neither of us had the right ammo, especially not the one under questioning.

"Whatever," Curtis announced curtly, standing up and getting his jacket on, "I officially don't have time for this anymore, I gotta get to the gym for my boxing class. Ravi, you're my brother, and I love you, but I guarantee that if you trick yourself into this, you're going to regret it, if not immediately then eventually. My parents did, and so have billions of other people, but hey, what do I know? You're the smart one after all. Later, dipshits!" He made sure to slam the door on his way, a victory lap of sorts.

"I really, really hate to say it aloud, but he can't hear me anymore, so I might as well: Curtis has a point. I still don't think that you can ignore talking with Xavier about it, but you can't get married, man. It's just too much, too soon."

"I'm not stupid, Kola, I know that already," he answered, finally back to his calm verbosity, "I knew it the second he asked me. I wanted to say no immediately, but my body just shut down and the brain went with it. It's... I don't know, it's strange. Everyone says you need to have this plan, you know, this fixed, unalterable image of your future life that has everything in it, somewhere down the line, in some distant space and time. The right job, marriage, kids, a house… you have this chain of events, with everything in its proper place, and then just one individual segment shifts out of position and the whole universe starts unraveling at the seams. After he got down on his knees it was like I couldn't tell which way was up; complete disorientation, a world-shaking sensation.

"As for now, well, now I either say yes, throw the entire path of my life to the wayside, and take the Kierkegaardian leap into the unknown, or I say no and move five steps backs, with some new person, new experiences, new emotions, new, most likely equally-fucked-up baggage. Even then, I could start over and just… stay there. Not find anyone else, not make that same connection, just floating by until everything in my image starts to fade. I could end up with no one and nothing but myself, and in my last days I'll be able to look back and pin it all to this exact moment, in this exact place, to one single choice I made in my youth.

"When you think of it like that, our entire concept of time… it's cruel. Cruel and dishonest. An amalgamation of poorly-made choices, regrettable actions, permanent memories, and people, making their own plans and living for themselves, only keeping you around to the extent of convenience. We get dumped into all of that and then have carpe diem shoved down our throats, promises of better things to come and limitless ways to change the past, but it's bullshit, all of it. How the hell is someone supposed to live for today when yesterday already ruined everything and tomorrow may only make it worse?"

I didn't know what to say, and I didn't even know if he wanted me to say anything. In that moment, I almost wished that he was still going mental or snapping at us like before; he was back to himself, but it was a much more depressed version. I must admit, I was scared; with him being how he was, I wasn't entirely sure that there would be a return to normalcy. For all my bad moments, all my worst days, all my conversations with the nothingness in my head, I knew that I had a floor, a point I could hit and bounce back up from, something to prevent me from sinking. It was how I had learned to live with the ramblings masquerading themselves as coherent thoughts. Ravi never had that floor; he tended to slip and drop farther and farther down, only coming back up after days spent in the depths. His mind was always sharp enough to cut through the noise, but it took a while to temper the blade.

My work there was done. I got up and left. He lay down and pulled out his phone, hit the contact, and waited for the ring.

For better or worse.

A Chance Encounter

There was this 50s style diner on Broadway she always loved, Big Daddy's. Never being one to turn down a cheeseburger-fries-milkshake combo, I would often find myself down there with Abi and some assortment of her theater world buddies. Now, don't get me wrong, I enjoyed their company, but it was often difficult to keep from observing the more peculiar ones, and even more difficult to keep from feeling lost in conversation. Some new show this, some big recasting that, and always scandalous gossip about rising stars and fading names. If I could remember half of what they said I'm sure I could write a truly salacious novel about the theater scene but unfortunately, the wonderfully bright color scheme, 50s jams, and my cellphone were more than enough to keep the noise out.

It was after one of these get-togethers, following a mesmerizing viewing of *The Band's Visit*, that we found ourselves standing ourselves waiting for our Uber. We had planned to head off to our favorite movie theater for a late night showing of *Persepolis*, a personal all-time favorite in the adult animation category, when all of a sudden Abi noticed someone she knew coming up the block. She asked me to give her a second and went up to the sophisticated-looking older gentleman, hugged him, exchanged cheek kisses, and began to engage in lively conversation. As you might imagine I wasn't particularly amused by the sight but I decided to keep my cool and wait for her to bring him over and perform introductions.

"Kola, this is Bernard van Straaten, my director from *Sins of The Sea* and the most debonair fellow this side of the Atlantic Ocean."

"Oh, darling, you're too much, stop it! Pleasure to meet you, Kola, you must be quite the lucky man to have this delightful creature on your arm."

"Well it certainly wasn't the charm that did it," I replied, self-signaling a shift into small-talk mode, "Pleasure to meet you. You're the man who made my girl a star, I hear?"

"Oh, you silly thing, I do nothing but paint the landscape, it's the colors who create the wonder and capture the imagination. One is essential to the other, irreplaceable, and you, my dear Abi, shone brighter than the rest."

Between two men singing her praises, she couldn't help but have her face light up. "Yes, yes, I'm amazing, we all get it; Bernard, what are you doing here? I thought you were back in Cape Town until the summer."

"I'm only in the city for the evening, off to my cousin's place in the Hamptons in the morning for a few days before I head back home. You happened to catch me on the way to an engagement, actually; would you want to come along? It's a fabulous little soirée in Gramercy, supposed to be a small thing but he never minds a good guest."

I briefly contemplated rejecting the offer, but between Abi giving me her patented "Nigga, don't even" face and the sheer exclusivity of the invite, I had no choice but to accept.

"Wonderful! Come on then, I'll grab us a car, and, Abi darling I have the absolute juiciest bit of news about that little row in the Shubert Organization, I've been dying to tell someone since I arrived." It was an extraordinarily long ride.

We arrived about forty minutes later and were led up to the penthouse apartment by our sponsoring guest. The host of the get together, a Mr. Hans Vogel, was just as polite and cheerful as Bernard, albeit only after a brief explanation for our—mainly Abi's, to be honest—presence. Crashing a party wasn't normally something I would consider a worthwhile activity, but insofar as my curiosity on Gramercy wealth, I was satisfied: in short, I was astounded. It was the kind of opulent setting you'd imagine your favorite celebrity in while playing you in your B-movie biopic; miles of perfectly situated space, polished Carrara marble finishing in the kitchen, a collection of original Kandinsky paintings, a heavy postmodern theme and decadently exposed brick for the walls. I may have been missing the movie but I was certainly getting a show.

Quickly realizing that the fellow guests of the evening were likely to be even more aggressively niche in their conversation topics than the usual theater socialites, I strapped myself in for an evening of silence. After sampling some very foreign hors d'oeuvres and grabbing myself a Crown Ambassador Lager, I found my way outside to the balcony and took a seat on what I have to assume was a chair worth my yearly salary. The view was equally as magnificent as the interior, if not more; the whole city was sprawled about before my eyes, the nighttime pulse glowing so brilliantly that it truly resembled a living organism. It was the kind of sight that forces you to take time for reflection, and as I looked down on this beautiful scene, this place that I had come to see as part of myself in the latter half of my short life, my mind naturally turned to thoughts of my possible departure.

Once the job offer was actually in my hand, once an entire pathway opened up in front of me, my mind went ahead and opened up a special section just for existential contemplation.

What did I remember of Lagos? Plenty, I have to say, but they were memories of a childhood laced with nostalgic euphoria, a notion of home and ancestral longing detached from the person I'd managed to make myself. I remembered grandma's fufu and the sickly sweet satisfaction of my daily malt drinks; the traffic on the roads to school that even the wealthy kids had to endure, albeit accompanied with the comfort and reliability of a family driver; the dryness of the heat and the cool relief of the rain, the sting of the mosquitoes and the nuns' rulers, the spirit of the church celebrations and the brightness of traditional festive attire.

I remembered so much that I wondered what I was forgetting... and then I remembered.

Her.

The fact that I still hadn't told her about all of this had been weighing on me, no matter how hard I tried to convince myself otherwise. I wanted to believe that since I hadn't made a decision, there wasn't actually any lie being told, but that was a loophole at best and dishonesty at worst; the fact that I was considering made it real enough to warrant discussion. It was simply a matter of time before my indecisiveness brought forward unwanted consequences.

I love her, I love her and I want to stay with her but this is what I've been dreaming of my entire life. The boy with the flowers? Isn't that what you want, to do something about it, something important.

If you really loved her, you wouldn't be trying to guilt

trip yourself into leaving her; you didn't ruin your homeland, and you're delusional if you think you're gonna save it. Stay in New York and keep your girl, don't screw this up.

So that's it? I get a chance at something I've dreamt of and I'm supposed to drop it because I've found a person I'm happy with… isn't that just fear wrapped in romance?

It's reality, something I thought you already understood. Think of the last time you were ever this happy in your life, and then think of how and why you messed it up. Once you're done doing that, think about this: you're young, but you ain't that young, and time isn't getting slower. You got Ravi to say no to Xavier but what about you? Don't you think it's time you start making choices based on the clock and not just your clichéd, melancholic overthinking.

Oh, OK, perfect then, so forget love and all of that, you just think I should turn it down so that I don't come back lonely and desperate to settle down. You call me clichéd but you're plucking shit out of bad movies? Fuck off with that; I love her, OK, I know that for a fact, but it doesn't change the fact that I want to do this, and what I do not want is to wonder what life could have been if I had done it. I love Abi but she is not the be-all and end-all of my brief existence, and no amount of paranoia is going to change that… I have to take the job. I have to take the job and I have to tell her… God help me, how am I supposed to do th -"

"KOKO!"

She practically tackled me as she leaped into a bear hug and proceeded to engage in some aggressively affectionate PDA. Not knowing what was happening but certainly not wanting it to stop, I only moved out from under her because I was worried we'd break the chair.

"What's the occasion, short stuff? Figured we could at least wait until we got back to me."

She proceeded to (very drunkenly, making me realize exactly how long I'd been outside for) explain the cause of her joy: Bernard, after pulling her away from a riveting discourse with a *New Yorker* writer on Wallace Shawn's *Evening at the Talk House*, had informed her that he'd been on the phone with the cousin of the fiancée of the accountant of the personal casting director of esteemed Italian filmmaker Federico Biagini. It just so happened that Mr. Biagini was starting work on his next project, his latest in a recent line of passion projects, and was searching all four corners of the globe (New York, LA and London) for his ensemble of talent. Bernard, being an expert judge of talent, took it upon himself to throw a few names into the hat, and one of them just so happened to be…

"Can you believe it?!?! Babe, oh my God, this is so crazy! Federico is a genius, I've watched all his films, even the early stuff from when he was in Rome, and I've seen all his interviews and oh my God did you see *A Storm's Last Song?* It was the best film ever and now I'm going to be in his movie, and it's going to be the best film ever and I'm going to be in it and oh my God wait what if I don't get the part, what if I fuck it up, shit, wait, why am I even trying this, what if this is my last shot and I mess it up and I never act again and then I—"

As I listened to her attempt to be the first person in history to fast talk their way through intoxication, I came to a revelation. It was one of the very few times in my life where I can say that; my thoughts tend to be manufactured rather than inspired, but, in that one instant, there was no thinking involved. A moment came and I knew, knew with the entirety of my being, exactly what I had to do.

One kiss was all it took.

"You've got this, baby, trust me; I can't wait to be there every step of the way. I'm here for you, always."

She returned the gesture.

It was a beautiful night.

A Ruling

The wind howled all around me. I took out a cigarette, my first of the evening.

"That's just stupid."

"What do you mean?"

"It's not a great way to make a case for yourself, pal, that's all. Essentially, you're saying that you can't be crazy because you know exactly what's happening and because you pick and choose when it occurs."

"How is that not a legitimate argument? If I'm in control of the situation, then I'm not crazy; I decide when it begins and ends, and therefore I maintain my grip on full sanity."

"Right, that makes sense, but you're not getting our point; it's not the amount of time or frequency of the occurrences that determines whether or not you have the mental imbalance. The issue is that you have the impulse at all; you can't argue against the scale of the problem without addressing the root causes."

"No, the impulse is just that, an impulse, an unconscious, involuntary desire to engage in some behavior or another. Impulses aren't abnormal in and of themselves, the willingness or tendency to act upon them can be."

"So, do you not have a willingness or tendency, then?"

"I have neither; I have impulses, I usually ignore them because I have the control to do so, but sometimes I choose not to. Is a guy who gets hammered at parties but won't even drink wine at a restaurant an alcoholic? No, of course not. This is my version of binge drinking; well, I do the real kind as well, but I digress."

"Don't you think you're comparing apples and oranges there? Binge drinking at least has a payoff, a desired result from the self-harm. What exactly is the benefit of this?"

"With all due respect, I don't quite feel inclined to tell you that. It has nothing to do with the argument anyway; whether my reason subjectively fits into your paradigm of benefit, it exists to me, otherwise I wouldn't do it. Ergo, there is no objective difference between this and getting drunk."

"With no due respect, the idea that all people only do things that have a benefit for themselves is horseshit. A rare display of faith in rationality from you."

"You're all still operating on the idea of objective benefit, a premise that I'm disregarding. A benefit can be anything you want it to be, however insane it may seem to the rest of the world. The ability to rationalize poor decision-making is the cornerstone of our humanity, after all."

"Do you always become a preening pseudo-intellectual at this late hour?"

"Not always, but it is the only time I smoke cigarettes anymore... *ahh*, there we go. And that wasn't Intro to Philosophy nonsense, I mean it; that ability is the single most radical departure from the rest of the beasts in God's Kingdom. The fact that we're able to think at this level is a radical departure in and of itself, yes, but we still use that higher brain function primarily to optimize our survival and livelihood. Power love, money, fulfillment, all the things we spend all our days thinking about, using these brains we were given. We want to be happy the same way a dog wants to be fed; once you take the conceptual complexity away, the desires are no different."

"You said it yourself, dogs can't think of concepts like harm and benefit, all they understand is that they like certain things and dislike others. If they want to be fed, they do actions that get their owner to feed them; if they want a treat, they sit or beg."

"Would a dog skip a meal?"

"Pardon?"

"Would a dog skip a meal? Would a dog choose to make itself hungry?"

"No, a dog would not choose to make itself hungry."

"If you could talk to dogs, and you got to ask one if it wanted to skip a meal, what do you think it would say?"

"…It would ask why it would want to skip a meal."

"*Wrong!* Dogs don't have meals, they have food; they can't skip food because they don't understand the idea of schedules or skipping things, only their biological clock. The dog would ask what you meant, and when you had to explain that you're asking if the dog would ever make itself hungry, it would just think you're stupid. Compare that to girls who starve themselves to get a thigh gap, and see if the difference isn't clear."

"It seems like we're getting really off track with this animal metaphor; fine, so irrationality is what makes us human, whatever. What does that have to do with the fact that the person you seem to enjoy talking to the most about your problems is yourself? Isn't this shit what friends and family are for? Or that little girlfriend of yours, for that matter."

"Nothing, you just threw me for a loop and I had to create a nonsensical trap. My original point still stands; I actively choose when I do this and for how long, I take some strange benefit from doing this, and, most importantly, I don't let doing this affect any other aspect of my life. Friends and family? If I told them I talked to imaginary voices they'd put me in an institution, or at the very least go and see a therapist. And if I told Abi, well, she'd probably get scared."

"So, everyone else would think you're crazy, and you're saying that they'd be wrong?"

"Everyone's crazy to somebody, man, that's what makes it all so interesting. What's perfectly rational is idiotic babble to another."

"Alright, you know what, we're tired of this; this is the two-hundred-thirteenth time that we've had this conversation and we always end up here, caught in a never-ending series of pointless diatribes completely unrelated to the topic at hand."

"Well, yes, obviously; how else did you think this would go down?"

"Something constructive, maybe, something that might get to the depths of the issue and actually put us on the path to figuring you out."

"OK, I'm down, let's see if we can achieve constructiveness this time; what do you want to try?"

"All right, I got one for you: why are you so afraid of the silence?"

The wind howled all around us, blowing the cigarette out of my hand. I lit another. It waited.

It wanted to hear my answer.

"Why am I so afraid of the silence… why wouldn't I be? Who isn't? Silence is serene terror, it's cruel; I hate being trapped with my own thoughts. They're either boring, inane, or downright evil. Even the sound of the rats scurrying along the alleyways is music compared to that. I mean, fear of silence is a fundamental part of the human condition, isn't it? Since the dawn of man, danger and death emerge from the silent, dark night; all the demons and monsters of legend, they all come out at night. We had to conquer nature itself to get over it as a species, but we're still trapped by it as people, no question about it.

"Why am I scared of the silence? Why do I talk to you guys? Why am I like this? Well, the truth is simple: I don't know. I don't know, and I don't believe the pursuit of that knowledge is going to do anything but cause me stress in my life. Maybe that's just cowardice, but honestly, I don't care: this isn't something worth derailing a functional life over.

"I think that's enough for tonight, guys; I have to take Hopper to the vet tomorrow morning. I'll see y'all next time."

The wind howled all around me, blowing the smoke into my face. I stood and left. They were gone. They had heard my answer.

The voices were done talking.

A Heartbreaker

The following text excerpt was transcribed from a recording of Ms. Abiodun Olatunji, produced by Aaron Shapiro Casting Inc., featuring adapted material from Ephemeral Films' Dandelion Bonfire

"There was this lovely little pond by all the old hickory trees. Daddy said those trees had been there since the beginning of time immortal, but I never much believed him. He was always telling tales about things like that; said the songbirds were children's angels and that when you talk to the fire you can get visions from the beyond. He even said once that you could find the Lord himself in the forest, in those silent moments when even the creek stops babbling. God never seemed like the type to be hanging around in no forest, but I liked the way Daddy told the stories.

"After he passed that winter, I didn't have no more stories, except the old ones, I thought about them down at the pond. It was lonely, quiet, peaceful, but in that painful manner. It was somewhere I could go and let the moments roll over me like the morning air, fresh and free. Momma needed lots of help taking care of Isaac and Betsey, and even though Uncle Darryl was helping on the farm… well, let's just say the bank man was coming 'round more and more them days. Chores, chores, and more chores, and that was just in the morning before school time; most of the other girls weren't even going no more, but Momma wouldn't hear none of that, said learning was the best thing I could do with myself. I admit, in my youthful foolishness, I thought she was utterly wrong on the matter, but I praise good fortune that she never gave me the choice to screw it up. Wouldn't be where I am now without her.

"There were some nights, down there at the pond, some nights I just wanted to escape. Run away, run far to some town, some place far away… maybe Nashville, or Knoxville, hell, one night I even tried to figure out how long it would take to get to big ol' New York City, all those pretty lights and tall buildings. I wanted to escape, truly wanted to, but one night I realized something: escape isn't a solution to your problems, and it's not the answer to any question you have about yourself or life or love or the universe. Escape is a drug, a quick fix; we take it, use it, abuse it, and try to be done with it when the habit becomes too much of a problem. Wanderlust sustains itself on our saddest delusions; if we don't keep believing that out there, past everything the eye can see, beyond what we imagine, there's something or somewhere that can make us feel like the world itself is worth all the suffering, then what's the point of seeing the world? Why see more of it when the part you have can't fill the hole in you? It would be absurd.

"I guess that's all I ever was back then: absurd. Absurd and alone, waiting for my next adventure… it was an interesting time, James, I'll tell you that, but I'll also tell you something else: I revel in the memories of those summer nights. The water and the hickory trees… what a wonderful time it was."

A Bowl of Rice

It was never a question of faith.

I knew she would get the part, knew that she was a great actress, knew that the weeks she spent between that night at the party and her audition practicing and rehearsing every day would pay off. I believed in her talent and trusted her resolve; I did all that, and yet, I couldn't believe it when she gave me the news.

Federico Biagini, in all his artistic wisdom, had decided that rather than simply bringing Abi on for the side character role and a few months of filming out in L.A., she was going to be the lead actress. Furthermore, she was going to be the lead actress on a shooting schedule spanning five continents, thirty countries, a surprisingly tight budget, and, most importantly for our purposes, two whole years.

Two years.

The words hit me like a slap in the jaw, the impact no softer accompanied by her ecstatic retelling of the phone call. She had gone in full of nerves and pre-failure regret, but, as she told it, something switched on the inside and she simply succumbed to the power of her moment. Her paraphrased scene reading had already sold the casting director into giving her the original role, but once Mr. Biagini had gotten a look at the tape, the choice was clear. Unfortunately, my choice was less so.

I know I lost the right to feel slighted the moment that I decided not to tell her about the job. I knew it when I went in for the interview, I knew it when I got the offer, I even knew it after I decided not to take it. My dishonesty had combined with her opportunity to put me in a position of aimless despair. She had called me immediately after getting the news, far too excited to have considered the ramifications of a two year commitment. I'm sure her immediate thoughts were that I would be excited to enter the tried and tested ease of a long term relationship, but after her comedown from euphoria, reality must have set in. She asked me to meet her for a cup of coffee, and I prepared myself for two difficult conversations: the one being thrust upon me, and the one I'd brought upon by my own poor decision making.

Neither turned out very well.

She reacted poorly, as one might imagine, after I explained that I'd been keeping my potential three year move to Lagos a secret, even though I was planning to turn it down; she reacted even more poorly when I told her I was having second doubts about that last part. I didn't react all so well either when she revealed that she'd been offered the choice of accepting the side role and rejecting the two years abroad, but thankfully my acute awareness of hypocrisy kept me from excusing myself. In a wave of emotion she said that she'd turn down the role if I turned down the offer, but the wave subsided and she realized the foolishness of ultimatums at a time like this. There was a silence after this, not the empty kind ready to be explored but the heavy, grey fog that keeps words in the mouth and thoughts murky. I dared to wade my way through it by saying that we both needed time to think, really think, and that we'd meet up in a few days, equipped with final answers and resolute wills. She agreed, we shared a sullen hug and a longing kiss goodbye, and then went our separate ways, both of us praying it wouldn't prove the penultimate time.

I don't know where she went, but I could only think of one voice to seek out.

...

"And that's pretty much it, Mr. Rahmani... I'm stuck. Trapped. Screwed."

His brow furrowed and his eyes rested somberly, the troubles of his young friend weighing upon his mind. He'd even gone out of his way to prepare me a plate of my favorite order: lamb and rice, extra tahini, side of chickpeas. I wasn't in the mood for tea but he made us a pot anyway, of which I dutifully partook.

"A man on an island is trapped, my boy, you are merely lost on a beach. When do you think you two will meet?"

"Friday, probably, so I have a little while. Not that it will help much."

He took three puffs of his pipe and watched the smoke bloom from his lips, deep in thought. "Let me see if I understand: you and Ms. Abi have both been handed the chances you've been seeking, but at the expense of the love you've found. She has spent her whole life chasing a dream, and you have spent yours haunted by a nightmare. These lives of yours, separate and divergent, have become entwined, my boy, for that is what true love pertains of, and now there is contemplation of separation. Am I correct in this?"

Showoff.

"Couldn't have said it better myself."

"Before I begin, I need you to understand," he replied, ready to dig into the meat of his wisdom, "this decision will not be made based on my words. I am merely seeking to provide you with illumination, by which you must find your own path out of the darkness. Neither I, nor your two companions, now anyone else you know or trust can do anything more for you; if you make a choice you do not own, then you have made nothing and lost more than can be gained. Am I clear?"

"Crystal. Please, Mr. Rahmani, illuminate away."

"First, a question: if I told you that you could go back to your homeland, do your work with these people, and help a million children, would you be happy?"

I looked into his eyes for a moment, subconsciously desperate for an answer, but I quickly remembered his warning and pulled my focus back inwards.

"Yes, I would be happy. Very happy."

"A thousand. Would you be happy if you helped a thousand?"

"A thou—yes, yes I would be happy."

'Five hundred? One hundred? Ninety-nine? Fifty? Ten? One?"

"One? No, I would not be happy if I spent three years working to only help one child. It would be a waste. What would have been the point?"

"Are you saying one child's life mean nothing? Is this not all driven by your memory of one child? If you could only have helped him, would you not be happy?"

"OK, wait, that's different, you're talking about a person

that was in my life versus the idea of a single child. Time is a finite resource, and it's natural to want to use it as effectively as possible. If I spent three years working specifically to help people and I only help one, then yes, I would be upset. What does that have to do with any of this?"

"You want to help people, as many as possible, and in order to achieve this, you will have to sacrifice. If there is a minimum amount of people required to validate your sacrifice, it's important to know, is it not?"

"I mean, yeah, I guess, but I don't see the point of that, it's not like I'll come running back just because things don't go well. Even if I help less people than I wanted, it's the work that matters."

"Which is more important: the work or the outcome?"

"That's a ridiculous question."

"Answer it."

His eyes didn't betray intent in the slightest, while I'm sure mine screamed with confusion.

"The work, the work is what matters. Failure and success are uncontrollable outcomes but effort is purely in our hands. Trying is better than nothing."

"Hmm… alright, new question: how does this girl make you feel?"

Afraid. Afraid that I've lost the ability to think straight, afraid that I've handed over control of my life to emotions, fleeting fits of passion. Hate. I hate how much I miss her already. I hate how afraid I am. I hate how much I love her. Love. I love her.

"I don't know, man, I just don't know. It's crazy. I mean, I like her, don't get me wrong, and if this hadn't happened I don't think I'd have a single thing about her worth complaining over. I know that I would rather be with her than not be with her, but I also know that those emotions have as much to do with fear of loneliness as it does with her herself."

"How do you mean?"

"I mean that… no one wants to be lonely, no one wants to jump back into that pit of the unknown, not after they've had a taste of connection, even just a little one. The idea of giving it up for everything and nothing, it's terrifying. I can't tell if I'm more afraid of being alone than I am actually in love with Abi, and even if I could tell that, it still doesn't help me figure out the practicality of pursuing a life of love over something that I've wanted for as long as I can dream."

"I am having some trouble, young Kola, with your motivations, and please excuse me if I cause offense, but I must have answers. You witnessed this atrocity in your youth, and you have remembered it since that day, never forgetting, yet also never acting upon it. Why did you not devote your life to helping others sooner?"

"Wait, wait, you're questioning my motivation?" I responded, faint pangs of rage flaring up, "What, just because I decided to take up an office job that means my motivations are misplaced? Give me a break, man, I did what I was supposed to do, made it to where I needed to be, and now I have the chance to do something for myself. This isn't some, 'finding myself' self-discovery bullshit, all right, I know who I am and I know why I want to do this. I want to do this because… I need to… I just need to, OK? I need to."

The words had emerged strongly but quickly grew weak with doubt. The feeling of losing to myself was starting to weigh on me.

"You have heard yourself, have you not, Kola?" he asked calmly, writing off my outburst with fatherly dismissal, "You just said you need to do this, and that you are doing it for yourself, after doing what you had to do. You have said that the effort matters more than the outcome, and you have admitted that your love for Abi may not be stronger than your fear of loneliness. These are the foundational components of your truth, your personal truth, and your truth is as follows: I see in you a selfish man aware of his selfishness, a thinker afraid of action, and a believer in the betterment of self. I think you're waiting for a moment of inspiration to strike you and guide your hand. Lastly, I believe that there is a separate reason for all of this besides that night; it may have been born from it, but it has become something wholly unique. I also believe you know what it is, and I believe you should take some time now to reflect upon it."

The puff of his pipe and the ticks of the clock; those were the only sounds in the room.

I sat there, stunned into introspection, forced into silent thought; his words, like many times before, had seized me. The time passed and left me behind, and as I continued to struggle for an answer, a true answer, minutes moved without a care in the world. By my best estimates it took me five, but it could have been as few as one and as many as ten. They didn't seem worth counting.

The silence ended on its own time.

"I'm tired, Mr. Rahmani, I think that's the ultimate truth of it all. I'm tired of giving up. I'm tired of the cynicism and the sarcasm, the long-winded musings about how awful everything is and how the only solution is to get with the program. I'm tired of pretending I'm as smart as I think I am, and I'm tired of trying to act like these aren't the things I think about every day, in-between everything else yet constantly present. I mean… there's got to be something more than this, right? Beyond my own self-fascination. Something tangible, real, something that I can hold onto and light my path with. Something good and noble, honorable. A purpose.

"That's what I'm looking for, man, that's all I've ever wanted. It's the most meaningless word in the English language but I can't escape my desire to realize it. When I think about everything I've done up until now, and then I think about what I have the chance to do over there… it's incomparable. Maybe that means I'm really only doing this to make myself feel better, and maybe it will never be anything more than that, but I have a chance to do something good and worthy and I want to take it. The only thing keeping me back from it, really, is her. What does it say about me that I'd choose one person over potentially hundreds? What does it say that I'd choose the pursuit of purpose over love? I don't know, man, I just don't know. I need answers."

He laid his pipe down and took a long sip of his tea, sipping as if the liquid was nourishing the words he was about to impart.

"OK, Kola, one last question: if you died, right now, right this second, in the middle of grappling with this choice you haven't made yet, what would your number one regret be? What would be the one thing you would want to return to Earth to do?"

I thought. I thought. I thought. I experienced a few moments of crippling existential terror, and then I thought some more. I found an answer. I got depressed, mostly with myself.

"I don't know."

Mr. Rahmani smiled his damn smile.

"Exactly, my boy, exactly. You know nothing, just like everyone else. There's no shame in it. I want you to ask me a question: why is the heart like a bowl of rice?"

"A what?"

"A bowl of rice. Ask me the question."

"Huh, OK… why is the heart like a bowl of rice?"

"There are times where the harvest is bountiful, and feasts are held across the land; there are times when the earth rejects man's toil and laughs as we waste away. Whether the village has abundant stores, or each man must starve so his family can eat, there is always a bowl of rice. It is the one thing we can rely on, the one thing that will always be there, through good times and bad. It is undeniable, unalterable, and underappreciated, but most importantly, it can sustain you day by day, for all your days to come.

"I do not know what choice you should make, Kola, and neither will you nor anyone else until you make it. But do not discard your rice; you may see yourself starving soon enough."

A Bright Blue Sky

There's something about nature that liberates us, I've always believed that. Fresh air, sunlight, birds and bees, flowers and trees; the mind becomes entranced and thoughts flow with ease. Living in the city doesn't offer many chances for transcendentalist escape but what few respites were available I always took: gardens, parks, conservatories, you name it. Hell, I even took Curtis up once on a weekend in his dad's cabin; I had a terrible time, but the forest was the only saving grace.

That afternoon in Central Park was no different, and as I sat waiting on Cedar Hill—my favorite relaxing spot—even the impending tension couldn't stifle the natural calm. The dogs were running wild and their owners resting in the sunshine, performing activities ranging from scrolling through their phones to scrolling through books on their phones. Kids were laughing, music was playing somewhere, hell, even the grass looked particularly green. I felt relaxed, too relaxed actually, to the point where I found myself falling asleep; thankfully, my wakeup call arrived right on time (twenty minutes late).

"You know this isn't bedtime right?"

I opened my eyes to find a smiling face, dark curls raining down toward my head.

"It's so nice out I just decided to sleep my way through it. And I believe that you're the one who's late, pal."

"It was so nice out, I took the scenic route."

"Uber took a wrong turn?"

"Bingo. Enough room down there for the two of us?"

I patted the grass and she laid at my side, no more than three inches of space between us but more than enough anxiety to fill the air. We let the sun work its magic for a few glorious minutes, rejuvenating us, replenishing our strength after our long tribulation. A breeze rolled by; it felt like heaven.

"You mind if I start?"

"Um… no, no not at all, go ahead."

She took a deep breath, deep enough to take in all the anxiety of the moment, almost as if she could exhale her way to a calm mind.

"I don't know the best way to start this, and it's not because I haven't been trying to think of one; it's just harder than I imagined. These have probably been the longest few days of my life and I guess the reason why is because I never thought I'd find myself here, stuck making some big decision. I always thought that the day, no, the moment my big break came, everything in my life would suddenly become clear, some great, existence-defining moment. Instead I've been sitting at home trying to sleep my way through seventy-two hours. Isn't that just inspiring: 'Follow your dreams, achieve them, and still end up drowning your sorrows in trash TV!'"

Normally I would've cooked up some line like, "You make it sound so picturesque," cock a half-smile and then make a point, but the mood didn't strike me.

"Shit, Abi, I'm sorry about that; I know we said we shouldn't text but I wish I could've helped a bit."

"No, not texting was the right call, that would've only made it worse. And you? You've been OK?"

"Relatively, yeah; work doesn't exactly stop, and I didn't tell Curtis or Ravi about this, the only person I've talked to is Mr. Rahmani. Well, him and God, but Mr. R has a better response time."

"Well that sounds blasphemous but whatever," she replied, a faint smile returning only to get dashed away in preparation for the next clause, "so… what did he say?"

"He said… he said a lot of things. That I needed to make a choice that was truly my own, not some reason that I'm either using or that I invented; that I'm selfish by nature; that I don't know what I want. The fact that I knew he was right on all counts didn't make it me any less gnawing to hear, but the honest truth is rarely a pleasantry."

"He sounds like my kind of guy, straight shooter. Just like my grandma."

I briefly imagined the light scolding I'd received in the shop coming from the mouth of a Nigerian matriarch, and couldn't help but chuckle at my own hypothetical terror.

"Maybe they can meet up someday. Anyway, besides when I was with him, and before right now, I guess I haven't been doing too much else besides thinking about this and thinking about everything else. Still though, sorry you were having a rough time."

She couldn't tell, but I saw her smile out of the corner of my eye. That same damn smile.

"You always say sorry too much."

A hand reached longingly at mine across the narrow sea of grass and found its target, nestling tightly and softly against it. We let the sun rejuvenate us, bringing back our strength after our long tribulation.

"Look, Abi, I -"

"Please… please, Kola, please… I want *this*, I want this so much it's killing me. You're the only person I've ever felt this happy to know. Since that very first night, from the second we went to the movies… I just knew something. I can't even begin to describe what it was, but it was clear as the blue sky above us. I know I wasn't wrong then, and I'm still not wrong now."

I reluctantly released the wandering hand, sitting up to ensure proper comprehension.

"What are you trying to say? You want us to stay together?"

"Don't you?" she responded, pleading with pride, "Isn't that what you want, too?"

"Of course that's what I want, Abi, you know that, but it's not that simple. I want to go to Lagos too, and it doesn't matter what you're saying right now, you know you want to take this role. Think of how insane this all is, how lucky we've been. You're going to get your big break, and, well, I get to try and be the person I've always imagined. Maybe I'm just delusional, and maybe you're in over your head, but isn't it worth finding out? Even if it means losing something that feels so right."

She sighed, the weight of my questions bearing down on her, and sat up as well.

"I don't know. I wish I was as smart as I like to pretend I am, as deep or intuitive, but I have no idea what I'm feeling or how to feel about not knowing what I'm feeling. I spent three days trying to come up with an answer and the best I could manage was indecision. You sound like you already made up your mind…"

"Hey, I haven't said anything yet, OK? I'm just trying to… to understand myself, actually understand what I want and why I want it. To avoid regrets."

"You can't avoid regrets, Kola, they're part of life; we just have to learn to accept them."

"Oh, so what, just make any decision and learn to live with regrets? That's crazy, things need to be thought through."

"Why? Why do things need to be thought through? Why does everything have to come down to some long, drawn out internal debate for you?"

"As opposed to what, surrendering to inertia? What am I supposed to do? How am I supposed to choose something when the only thing I know for sure is that part of me will regret that choice forever? How is that possible? How is that *fair*? How is that… how?"

The words crawled out of my mouth, lacking the conviction to emerge fully. I retreated into the silent pause, eyes cast aside, as she looked up at the sky, searching for a response. The light shone down on her, adding bright shine to her rich ebony. For a moment, I was transfixed.

"What if… what if we don't choose anything?"

"Huh?" I replied, the confusion snapping me out of the trance, "What do you mean?"

"I mean, what if we don't choose anything?" she answered, standing and suddenly full of that same vibrant energy that had hooked me from our first moments, "We, as in you and I; we, the singular plural, us two in this moment. We choose nothing. I choose what I want, you choose what you want, and then, if we both decide to stay, we can keep being together."

Something was wrong but I was unable to comprehend it. Her eyes had a bright, desperate eagerness, begging me to come and inhabit whatever fantasy she was constructing by the second. Her mind must have been racing behind all that newly done hair, but all I could see was a beautifully chaotic creature who was starting to make just a little too much sense.

"Wait, wait… Abi you're not making any sense. You want to break up? And you only want to break up so that we can feel less pressure to choose staying together, all with the idea that maybe we stay together anyway?"

"Don't you get it? I want us, each other, to be free, to be free and live for ourselves, because if we don't then we're only going to hate whatever choice we make. People trap themselves in their own heads, just like you, because there are always too many different reasons to do too many different things. Kola, I love you, I love you more than I knew it was possible for me, but life isn't just about love; we glorify this single experience so much more than all the others because it provides the greatest joy and pleasure, but it's not the end-all, be-all. I love you today, and I will love you for the rest of my life, because love doesn't vanish; true love is eternal, and it's limitless. Even if we stay together and end up apart for some other, unimaginable reason, that part of me would still exist. Would it still exist in you?"

I was dazed. She had grabbed with her speech but lost me with her words, and as I tried to make sense of what was happening, it dawned on me that the only thing I could think of was her question.

"Yes," I replied, sure but confused as to why, "yes, I would still love you. I love you now."

"Then why are we doing this to each other? Why are we making each other suffer? Why are we letting this day, this beautiful, God-given treasure, be a day of pain?"

Because that's how it has to be, Abi, because we have to talk about this until we know what we want to do, what actions we want to take. You're living in a fantasy right now, a magical world where things can just end on a high note without painful resolutions. You think I don't want to escape too, that I don't want to just move past the hard part and pretend that everything's fine? It's not about being happy, it's about being real, it's about realizing that this thing we hold so precious, this love, this relationship, is in our hands and we have to make an agonizing decision, that we have to sacrifice something that we want for something else we want. THAT is what life is, that's how it works. That's what we have to do.

We. We. We.

We?

Why?

"I don't know."

The wind blew past us and shook the grass in its wake. We were locked in a stalemate. Every thought in my head was screaming to get out and break the silence, but there was no escape. I said nothing, and she followed suit, our eyes doing more than enough. She looked at me as if seeing someone in a dream, as if I was already beginning to fade away yet more real than anything she'd ever known. I wonder if I looked the same.

She laid down next to me, wrapped her arm around me in our preferred resting position, and nuzzled her head onto my chest. I followed suit and wrapped around her shoulder, rubbing up and down her back. Her hair had that same, familiar aroma: cocoa butter and shea oil, the scents of earth and the heavens. Every inch of her, the divine canvas to which I'd been granted access, I could feel as part of myself. It was pure connection, somber and serene. I felt at peace. I felt restful. I rested.

. . .

A field of flowers. There were more colors than my mind could conceive of, every point on the rainbow. It was an endless terrain, stretching past the horizon and doubtless beyond that. The sky was blue, but, well, a brighter blue, as if only a thin inch of atmosphere was separating me from the blackness of space. I looked down and saw a path forming itself, so I began to walk. The path kept forming and I kept walking, marching mindlessly, eyes forward, focused solely on movement. Time passed, although I can't say how much.

I arrived at a golden-white door. Tall as a mountain, wide enough to block my vision of what lay beyond. I rested my hand upon it, and found it near weightless, only insurmountable to the eye but not to touch. I began to open but hesitation struck me, fear gripped me, my fingers began to tremble. I didn't know what to do.

I froze.

. . .

She wasn't there when I awoke, and neither was the sun. The streetlights did their best to illuminate, but the beauty of the day was gone, and only night remained. I checked my phone. She'd sent me a text.

<3

What's that old cliché again?

"An emoji's worth a thousand words?"

A Goal

There were three minutes left on the clock. Three goals apiece. 113 degrees Fahrenheit of God given, all-natural solar rays beating down on the pitch.

One step back. Two steps back. Three. Then two to the side.

My breathing was calm, deep, focused. A moment of calm before the fury.

One step, two steps, slow jog, sprint, foot back and—

"SHIT!"

All right, so, in my defense… well shit, what can I say, Dapo got me. The son of a bitch was already 6'6" with a crazy wingspan, all he had to do was learn to watch the ball right. Besides, I'd already scored one, and for a guy my size, playing midfield was already impressive, didn't need the penalty to feel accomplished; not saying I wasn't furious, just that it wasn't necessary.

After an intense extra time punctuated by a last minute score from the other team, the whole crew retired to the picnic tables for some post-match beer. The weekly matches had grown from boasting-fueled messing around to full scale competitions, complete with makeshift uniforms and optional training sessions. The teams changed but there were some consistencies: Ikemba and Emuobosa were brothers and fellow goal-snatchers so competition was natural; Dapo always got picked third overall, and always to play in the net; as the only former American football player, I was a lock for midfield enforcer, albeit a frequently exhausted one; and Temi, well, Temi was easily the best player, but easily the worst teammate, earning him a far lower pick than deserved but for very good reason. Just because you can score after dribbling for a whole sixty seconds doesn't mean that you should. It wasn't quite as much fun as my high school football days, but still, it made the transition far easier than lounging about trying to figure out what the strange sound in the apartment was (still no clue, really pisses me off).

Returning somewhere that you'd largely forgotten is a strange experience; you can't really tell if your experiences are new or relived. The last time I'd set foot in the country had been my last step out of the airport, and it was the first place my feet touched on my return; when I visited my grandmother in Ikeja, it was like stepping into a time machine. The dishes she showered upon me were the same as I'd grown up with but they tasted different, new and fresh. The street side merchants sounded the same but I found a certain excitement in their wares, almost as if they were exotic to me. For the first few days of training at headquarters I tried public transportation, but I soon came to my senses and hired a temporary driver, which, of course, brought back a whole new wave of déjà vu, the streets of the city passing me by from a rear window.

For the first few weeks of my new life, I have to admit, part of me thought I'd make an enormous mistake. In New York I'd left behind a beautiful three bedroom apartment, my two best friends in the entire world, a dog who I had started to love most likely more than my own children, and, of course... a cushy office job with great benefits.

Oh, and Abi. Left that bitch behind too.

Relax, I'm kidding.

It had actually gone a lot better than I'd imagined. After she parted in the middle of my rest, I took some time to think about her proposal. On the one hand, it was nonsense, fanciful nothings that had come bursting from a moment of mind-numbing panic; on the other hand, it made all the sense in the world. Making decisions based on the desires of others is a recipe for insanity. It was a lesson that she was teaching without even knowing what she was saying, but I had received it nonetheless. Selfishness isn't a debilitating condition, it's a fact of reality; we have to be selfish in order to find the happiness required to share with others. We have to forge the paths we seek in order to arrive at a place where those special individuals can find the space they need. If we don't, if our lives become entwined too early or stay unshaped for too long, that point never comes, and we're left with nothing worth sharing at all.

I decided to go to Lagos, but not for the reasons I wanted to believe. That fantasy I'd imagined of some noble pursuit was just that, a fantasy, and one I abandoned well before I made my choice. The boy with the plastic flowers—whose name I never even bothered to ask—wasn't a figment of my mind, but he might have well as been, just a figure that I projected my own self-discontent on. That night represented a lesson, but I'd learned many more since then, and none of them were enough by themselves to define me. The noble image of me someday avenging a dead child was a great coping mechanism as I continued to work my way through a laundry list of middle-class opportunities, but it was a false, shameful charade, one I couldn't bring myself to continue.

In the end, I chose to go because I couldn't tell myself not to, and Abi chose to follow her dream. We met up one last time, with much less dramatics, both fairly sure we knew what the other would say. After confirming the truth for each other, we shared one last embrace as a couple, and our first conversation as exes, mostly concerning when she would need to come by and get her things. It was somber, but still, through all the hurt and the questions, she was smiling.

That same damned smile.

Curtis and Ravi, having to deal with the shock of both my breakup and departure in one justification-laden explanation, managed to take things fairly well, after a while anyway. It was mostly just confusion on their end, especially from Curtis, considering that any hints of emotional complications usually sailed right past his field of vision; after all, this is the guy who didn't notice that his mom's cat died until she came into the house with a parrot one day. I answered all their question and assuaged all their concerns, knowing that I owed them whatever they wanted to know. We ended the friendly interrogation with a brief silence, a silence that was immediately broken by Curtis announcing my farewell party, that very same night. I'll give the man this, he keeps the good times going.

There were still two months between my official acceptance and my departure, and there was plenty to be done before then. Curtis and Ravi were more than capable of finding a third roommate by themselves, but once I actually thought that sentence through, I realized I would need to be heavily involved. Eventually they settled on one of our old college buddies, Álvaro, who had just returned to the states after three years back home in Madrid working for Facebook. He was an ideal third piece to replace me in this puzzle of a friend group; enough unbridled energy to keep up with Curtis' nature, with just the right amount of wit to keep up with Ravi's musings. He lacked a certain je ne sais quoi that I imagine myself to embody, but he was a friend, and someone I knew I'd be down to hang with on my visits back to the US.

Originally I had been under the assumption that while Ravi, who was single and only slightly lonely following his proposal rejection, would want to stay in the apartment, Curtis would start thinking about moving in with María. It turned out that he'd actually been trying to break up with her for a while, but was waiting for the perfect excuse; apparently, both of your best friends breaking up seems to be a good one. At first I was disappointed, thinking that all the growth he'd showed in trying to abandon his playboy ways was for naught, but when I confronted him on it, he left me with something I found rather inspiring: "I loved being with María, but I didn't love her, y'know? I just loved the idea of being a different kind of guy for a while. Now I know that I like being in a relationship as much as I like being single, so I think I'll just wait for a girl who makes me not give a fuck about the latter. That, my friend, will be the woman I marry, but until then... yep, three Tinder matches in a row! HA! Ten bucks, dickhead, pay up."

So close... so close, yet so far.

It turns out that Ms. Nkrumah had been—to the displeasure of pretty much everyone, not that she noticed or particularly cared—holding the role open for me, somehow knowing I wouldn't (or couldn't) turn her down. My passport was up to date so all we had to was figure out my housing, which she was more than happy to help out with. She knew a local landlord and got me a nice, clean condo on Victoria Island, Lagos' very own combination of Midtown East and Gramercy (sans white people), about thirty minutes from the office and two hours from the village sites barring nigh-inevitable traffic. I could already picture the tasteful decorations adorning the walls and sweet, sweet Fela playing off a vinyl, an idyllic picture only slightly marred by having to deal with a new roommate, Thibaut. Nice enough fellow, clean and quiet, but certainly no Ravi and definitely no Curtis… that last one isn't the worst thing in the world, but still.

While she was happy to play the helpful mother figure, she sure didn't let me forget that I'd signed up for a job, not a vacation; between studying the organizational literature, reading up on education development, reviewing old notes from classes, and running through draft SWOTs and PESTELs (it would take too long, trust me), I still didn't quite get over the learning curve in time, but I had just enough to start. She had to give me a few scoldings now and then when I made an error, but she was always constructive in her critique, and my supervisor, M. Dumas, was always helpful. He had that goofy uncle vibe, complete with the comical mustache, impeccable taste in sweatervests, and a bottomless treasure trove of dad jokes. Fun fact: awful jokes, when told in perfect French, are still awful.

Normally the hardest goodbye would be to my parents, soon to find their little boy 52,70 miles away from them, but since it was the place they'd call home for far longer than the one I announced my choice in, the impact was softened. There were questions and crying and a little bit of doubt, but overall they couldn't help but be happy that their child seemed like he'd found a way to make himself happy. The actual hard part of the conversation was when I realized that I'd almost left without telling them about the breakup, which I then informed them of rather unceremoniously outside the house. As any African child can tell, any time the promise of grandchildren (and, let's be real, especially when they're from a spouse of the same people) is compromised, reactions are not fantastic. After making a vow that I would at least talk to my matchmaker auntie once I got settled, they finally agreed to let the subject rest.

Mr. Rahmani didn't allow me the chance to say my farewells; the second I told him what I'd decided he ordered me to get out of the door. I was absolutely shocked, completely taken aback by what I assumed to be random hostility, but, sensing no sign of humor in his eyes, I turned and starting to leave. It was only after my back was to him that he made himself clear: "I do not like farewells, friend, but not out of spite or anger; it's the faces. Faces haunt the mind and hang like thick smoke from the fire. Forgive my weakness, but I would rather wait to see your face in joyful embrace than remember it as a sight of pain. Return in time, my boy, and we will share our tales once again. Now go."

I wanted to say something, but I knew better; a perfect moment only comes around every so often. I waved my hand, walked out the door, and turned the corner, not a look back to be taken.

My door was waiting to be opened.

A Memory

"So, the whole movie's just two guys talking? For two fucking hours? That's the dumbest thing I've ever heard, Ravi, and I've heard a lot."

"If you would actually watch it, Curtis, you would realize you're not grasping the core beauty of the simplicity. And it's more than a talk, it's a true discourse on the modern condition, on theater, on existence and religion and the soul. Kola, you would probably like it."

The sound of my name pulled my eyes up from the Politico article and demanded my re-engagement with the room. The movie menu remained unmoved, as it tended to do, as they had been debating the merits of several films not even available to watch in painstaking detail. Hopper was on my lap, eyes lovingly fixed to the TV, waiting for sounds and lights to appear. I pet his fur, embracing the softness.

"I've always heard of My Dinner With Andre," I noted, "but I just never got around to it, it's still on the list."

"The list?"

"'Movies I Should Have Watched By Now But Haven't So I'll Just Keep Pretending,' that list. It's a little less extensive than my book one, but still quite hefty."

"Well, make sure to get it crossed off your list before you're off to Lagos again. They gave you until next Sunday, right?"

"Correct my friend, then it's back to the motherland. You know, by this point I figured I'd get used to the fourteen hour flights but honestly I think they're just getting worse. On the way here from there I had to do six hours with this goddamn two-year-old bitching about not getting a toy he wanted for his birthday, swear to God I was this close to stuffing him in the overhead storage."

"Pretty damn sure that's a felony, pal," replied Ravi, "besides, all you'd have to do to get some quiet is slip a sleeping pill into the kid's drink. Objectively creepier, but far more labor-efficient."

"You're a terrifying man, you know that? That reminds me, where's Álvaro at?"

"He usually gets up around 3 PM on Saturdays, he'll emerge at some point," Curtis responded. "Not gonna lie, the first few weeks when he was operating that startup of his out of the apartment, I was about ready to crack him with a baseball bat. They finally got that office space on West 30th near the Garden and it's been a lot better since then."

"What do they do, his startup?"

"Something, something, 'blockchain risk management,' something, 'disruption,' something, something, 'redefining the crypto space;' honestly I couldn't tell you if I tried, but he and his two Eurotrash bros are getting a shit ton of funding so God bless them."

"God bless capitalism."

Hopper jumped off of me and strolled over to his bowl, having exhausted his excitement to see his dear old buddy. I was a little hurt, but I respected the effort.

We started watching the movie, Shawn Wallace and his tall

friend managing to keep me entertained with nothing more than dialogue, when all of a sudden it dawned on me that -

"Hey, Kola," Ravi said, waking me up once again, "check your Messenger, I sent you something."

"What is it?"

He didn't respond. I opened up the link and in a few seconds, I understood why: the hair in the picture was radically new, but there was the name, plain as day. I'd almost forgotten how to say the long form.

She talked about it one night, what she would do the day she got her own IMDB page. She talked about all the people she would send it to for bragging purposes, all the teachers and directors and mentors she would present it to as the smallest token of her appreciation. Her parents, of course, would need to see it, hopefully with teary eyes swelling from their love and pride.

Then me.

I guess we both just thought I'd be around when it happened.

I guess we thought a lot of things.

They say we're not supposed to have regrets in life, especially after we come to terms with our decisions, but whoever the hell those people are, must be far stronger souls than me. All those weeks that had gone by since that last moment with her, weeks that had grown into months, I couldn't get the inevitable questions out of my head, even as they were accompanied by equally inevitable answers. Why'd I leave a woman I loved? Because I had to. Didn't I miss her? Of course. Did I make a mistake? No. Really? No… I hope.

It was a long few months.

I had done some thinking on the ride to JFK, that fateful day a few months prior to my departure. It was about Abi, a bit, but it was a lot more than that; it occurred to me that it had been a year since that night, that strange first night. A year to the day. Three hundred and sixty-five. All those days and weeks and hours and months and minutes, all those experiences and lessons, all those conversations and internal monologues and long nights spent talking to fucking lights, and you know what the funny thing is, the goddamn cherry on top? I still have no idea what the fuck any of it was good for.

Had I improved as a person? Had I grown into a more mature adult? Had gaining love and losing it transformed me into some better, more in-tune version of myself? No, no, I honestly can say that none of those things happened, but before you say that that's just me confusing being edgy for having a point, hear me and believe me when I say that I don't think anything bad happened either. I hadn't become jaded about relationships, I wasn't questioning my worth, and I wasn't even doing my classic, quintessential overthinking about life and love and the universe— well, maybe a little, but no more than usual.

But I mean, that's bullshit though, right? Right? How can I honestly sit here and write about how much I didn't change, how little everything affected me, when I just spent an entire fucking book detailing everything and showing my life. Of course I changed! I took the chance and started my dream job in Lagos, I met a woman who I thought I could marry, I felt that love explode like a burning star and emerge as new matter, I watched my friends' lives and their twists and turns; of course I changed! I was a new man! It was a new day! I was… I was…

I was trying too hard, wasn't I?

I must have looked fucking ridiculous going through an existential freakout in front of the cab driver. That's the thing though; this idea we have of changing and growing as a person, we cling to it, all our lives, because it makes everything make sense. All the joy and pain and love and loss, it's all adding up to something. We all want it to be a happy ending, naturally, but we don't need it to be; we just need to know that it ends with something, anything. We need to know that there's some other ending for us besides the ultimate, and when we don't get that, when it seems like the sum of all those parts can somehow equal an undefined value…

I still don't have the words for it. I could have spent hours on that couch pondering my cab ride reflections, but thankfully Curtis had a better idea.

"Yo, Kola, clean the dust out of your fucking ears. Want to get dinner now?"

"Dinner… yeah, dinner. Good idea. Mr. Rahmani's?"

"Cool. Ravi?"

"Let's go."

They got up and grabbed their things. I went to go pick up my wallet on the kitchen countertop.

I looked out the window.

Buildings. Rooftops. Wires. Windows. Sky. People.

I don't think I'll ever stop missing that view.

I hope it never changes.

Itua Uduebo was born in Lagos, Nigeria, graduated from Georgetown University with a degree in International Politics, and resides in New York, NY. He is currently working in the financial technology industry. His writing journey began in his college years and to date he has several essays, articles, freeform poems, and short stories published online and in print. His focuses are new adult fiction, urban literature, science fiction, thrillers, politics, racial justice, culture, and global affairs. He is currently working on his second novel manuscript and always looking to take on new creative challenges.

A Note to our Furious Readers

From all of us at Read Furiously, we hope you enjoyed our latest title, *Parade of Streetlights*.

There are countless narratives in this world and we would like to share as many of them as possible with our Furious Readers.

It is with this in mind that we pledge to donate a portion of these book sales to causes that are special to Read Furiously. These causes are chosen with the intent to better the lives of others who are struggling to tell their own stories.

Reading is more than a passive activity – it is the opportunity to play an active role within our world. At Read Furiously, we wish to add an active voice to the world we all share because we believe any growth within the company is aimless if we can't also nurture positive change in our local and global communities. The causes we support are culturally and socially conscious to encourage a sense of civic responsibility associated with the act of reading. Each cause has been researched thoroughly, discussed openly, and voted upon carefully by our team of Read Furiously editors.

To find out more about who, what, why, and where Read Furiously lends its support, please visit our website at readfuriously.com/charity

Happy reading and giving, Furious Readers!

**Read Often, Read Well,
Read Furiously!**